VENGEANCE IS MINE

Rules of Vengeance, Book IV

GIACOMO GIAMMATTEO

Inferno Publishing Company

Chapter One

INTRODUCTION

I sit and wait for death's onset, though I shall sit no longer
I long to hear that sweetest voice. I know She grows much stronger.
And if I die a sacrifice, a martyr for Death's cause,
Then let no soul come question me. I have breached no laws.
If in my death Her glory shines even one iota brighter,
Then in my death I now can rest, no more a need to fight Her.

Found in a priest's grave in the northern Sethian Desert

SAFE IN ENTIRIA

Mikkellana fidgeted on the edge of her seat near the fireplace while Melissara paced and Wisp trimmed his nails with one of his many daggers. All of them showed signs of nervousness.

"We've waited long enough," Mikkellana said. "Rhaven, see if you can find Tobias and Mollie, and when you do, bring them back quickly. And remember not to let anyone see you."

Rhaven stared. "Considering we'll be returning to Talanvar's manor—the most powerful noble house in Sykor—remaining unseen may present a problem."

Mikkellana brushed her hand in the air. "I know. I know. Just do what you can, but get them here. We can't leave without Tobias."

Wisp stopped what he was doing and put his dagger away. "You want company, Rhaven?"

"As long as you keep your hands to yourself, your company would be welcome. I doubt many know the streets of Sykor like you."

Wisp followed Rhaven out the front door and through the gate, then they walked down the steep hill leading them out of High Town. "Any ideas on where to start?" Rhaven asked.

"Knowing Tobias and his penchant for eating sweets, I'd say we look where he might satisfy those urges."

"And where might that be?"

"There are a lot of possibilities," Wisp said. "But let's start with the Hungry Crow. It's known to have a good morning trade, not to mention it's not far from Mollie's house. That combination might lure Tobias to eat there."

"Lead the way, then," Rhaven said. "But do it quickly. I haven't seen Mikkellana this upset since before Aentarra died."

As Wisp predicted, they found Tobias and Mollie at the Hungry Crow, eating pie, drinking khaffe, and, of course, chatting with anyone foolish enough to listen.

Wisp approached them nonchalantly, leaned on the edge of the table, and whispered. "Tobias, Mikkellana said we need to go but don't say a word to anyone. You and Mollie only."

"Go? What for? Where?"

"We're leaving now, and we need to hurry. She said don't even pack anything. New clothes and supplies will be gotten later."

"Well, that's not—"

Rhaven moved alongside Tobias. "Now," he said. "Mikkellana said it was of the utmost importance. Something about Anciara— the goddess who escaped." He took hold of Tobias's sleeve and tugged. "I think it's best if we go."

Tobias shrugged. "All right. Didn't even finish my pie." He took another bite of pie, then said, "Mollie, girl, you better come with me."

"Where are we going?" Mollie asked.

"I'm sure it's someplace you've never been, so count yourself blessed on that." Tobias reached out. "Just grab my hand and follow me. It seems like Mikkellana is in a hurry, so we won't be long."

· · ·

R haven returned to Talanvar's manor with Tobias and Mollie, making it back with no trouble, at least no obvious trouble. Once he returned—and once everyone gathered in Talanvar's library—they prepared to Shift.

Mikkellana looked to Aenaila and Darstan. "Do you have the steps in front of the temple fixed as a Shift point?"

Aenailla nodded. "Top step in front of the far column on the right."

"I've got it pictured," Darstan said. "I can almost feel the stone."

Even with confirmation, Mikkellana pressed her point. "Make sure you do; if not, we could end up in the middle of the sea."

"I'm set," Darstan said.

"I am too," Aenaila said.

"I don't know if I like this," Mollie whispered to Tobias.

"You'd like it a lot less if you stayed here until Anciara came. And Melissara said she *will* come. There's no doubt about that."

Wisp turned to face Talanvar. "Are you sure you won't come? There's not going to be anything for you here. I doubt people will even be able to ply their trade."

Talanvar shook his head. "My deepest gratitude, but my place is here. There are people who need me. I offered to let Dirk and Birol go, but they elected to stay. We'll be safe, though. At least I hope so."

Wisp nodded. "Maybe I can return from time to time and check on you. If anything happens, try to make your way to Pomanda or Genda. And don't forget to keep a low profile. Anciara is the worst I've seen."

Talanvar patted Wisp on the back. "I'll heed your good advice. Now go."

"Hold on tight," Mikkellana said, then looked to Aenaila and Darstan. "When I say *go.* Grab hold of one another's hands."

They nodded, and Mikkellana said, "Go."

A moment later, they appeared in front of the temple in Sunnara, the main city of Entiria.

Mollie looked down as if to check she was all there, then quickly looked for Tobias. "Don't worry, lass. We're here, and now we're safe."

Adju rubbed Mollie's arms. "It's all right to be afraid, Miss Mollie. The first few times they did it to me, I was scared too."

~

Anciara stormed through Sethia, leaving a path of destruction in her wake. She killed numerous Sethian Guards, just in case they had confused loyalties, then she razed the palace with a few strikes of BlackLightning. She smiled as people ran to hide, seeking shelter in their homes or places of worship.

She waited for one of the houses of worship to fill up, then she sent a wall of BlackFire to burn it down, along with the people inside. "Fools! You'll soon learn that the only one owed worship is *me*, and you'll learn the punishment for idolizing others."

Anciara looked down to a mother running with a child in arms. She wrapped her in a shield and approached at a slow, steady pace. "Where do the other humans live?" she asked.

With fear in her eyes, and tears rolling down her cheek, the woman pointed toward the west. "Many of them live that way, in Sykor." She trembled, teeth chattering. "But many also live that way," she said, and pointed east.

"Please don't hurt my baby," she asked.

Anciara frowned. "I would never hurt a child," she said, and undid the shield, allowing the woman to go on her way.

Anciara looked to the west, then thought about it and decided to try the east first. "Accompany me," she said to Tirzinitzia. She then Shifted by sight, going a mile or two at a time, depending on the terrain. Before long, the city of Khatara was in view, causing Anciara to smile. *At last.*

She Shifted to the entrance, found a contingent of guards, and demanded to know where the mortals with powers were.

"We know of no one with powers," the lead guard said.

Anciara struck him with Fire, eliciting a scream. "Does anyone else *not* know where they are?"

The second-in-command stepped forward. "I don't . . . they were here, but it was long ago. They fought several battles, and many people died, then they left."

"Where did they go?"

The guard shrugged. "I don't know where, My Lady, and that is the truth. I don't even know which direction; they just vanished."

"Vanished?"

The guard nodded. "Yes, My Lady. They were here fighting one minute, then they just vanished."

Tirzinitzia whispered to Anciara. "They must have Shifted somewhere. I'd guess Sykor."

Anciara turned to her. "Do you have a Shift point?"

"Not to the city, but we could Shift back to Sethia, then Sight Shift to Sykor. I know the roads to take."

Anciara turned back to the guard. "Be thankful, soldier. You have earned a reprieve. But spread the word among your citizens. Tell them Anciara is free, and I *will* return."

The guard bowed. "Yes, My Lady. It will be done."

Anciara spun around and took hold of Tirzinitzia's arm. "Let's go. I'll get us to Sethia, then you take command. And waste no time. I want to find them."

Anciara Shifted to the spot where the palace was, then she instructed Tirzinitzia to take the lead, and she wasted no time, moving along the road to Sykor at a blistering pace. Sight Shifting proved easy as the land of the Nyaurans was somewhat hilly, but often stretched for leagues with almost no elevation, allowing a person to see a long way. Before long, they stood in front of the gates to Sykor.

T he guards atop the wall fired bands of arrows at her, but she laughed as they struck, then yanked the arrows out one-by-one. "I now show you the futility of your valiant but foolish actions."

Anciara attacked the guards with numerous bolts of BlackLightning until all atop the wall lay dead. She then used a ForceBolt to burst through the front gate and strolled along the streets as people scattered out of her way.

Anciara continued her walk through Sykor. She turned a corner to find a merchant selling goods. "Which way is it to the guards' barracks?"

The man pointed south, so she headed in that direction.

She approached the two guards at the gate, smiling all the time. "Who is in charge?"

The guard on the left smirked. "Who wants to know?"

The other guard stepped close to Anciara. "Force Commander Takar doesn't see just anybody. Tell us what you need, and we'll pass it along."

Anciara placed her hand on his neck and squeezed. The guard gasped, then signaled to the other guard that he needed help. When the guard on the left moved toward Anciara, she placed a shield between them and continued torturing the first guard.

He choked a few times, then passed out, his body slumping to the ground. Anciara absorbed his life, and once he was gone, she turned to the other guard. "Your turn," she said, and reached out to him. He turned to run, but she held him in place with a shield, then absorbed his energy as well. When he was gone, Anciara walked inside and made her way to Takar, who was inspecting the troops before the morning posts.

Several of the guards stepped forward, swords drawn. Anciara looked to Takar, and said, "If I were you, I would tell your men to stand down before I am forced to do something they won't like."

Takar sensed her powers. He'd been around enough people with powers to recognize it; besides, this one bristled with energy. "Stand down, men," he said.

"But, sir—" one of his men said.

Takar held up his hand to stop him. "No argument. I said to stand down, and I mean it. "He got closer to Anciara. "You want to see me?"

"I see I'm dealing with a sensible man," she said. "Now listen closely to what I need."

"I'm listening," Takar said.

"Then listen well. I will give you one week to find the ones with power. And don't tell me you don't know who I'm talking about. I know they were here, and I'm sure someone knows their whereabouts."

"They're not here," Takar said.

"I know they're not here now," Anciara said. "If they were, I'm sure I'd Sense them. Or at least sense them when they used their power. What I want to know is *where* they went."

"I'll try," Takar said.

Anciara turned to leave. "I strongly suggest you do more than try. I won't be so pleasant next time."

After Anciara walked out the door, one of the guards approached Takar. "What do we do, Force Commander?"

Takar glared at the man. "Do you know where they are?"

"No, sir. No idea."

"Neither do I, so that's what we tell her."

"I beg your pardon, sir, but she didn't seem like the type to accept that kind of answer. And I've seen what people like her can do."

Takar nodded. "I've seen it too, and I'm aware of the impatience. We'll have to deal with that when the time comes."

The soldier shook his head. "I don't know, sir. If I were you, I might consider leaving the city."

"I'm not leaving my own city," Takar said. "Now go to your assigned post and do your job. And there's no reason to talk about this with anyone. Keep it to yourself."

"Yes, sir. I'm leaving now," the guard said and walked out the same door Anciara had.

Chapter Three

EVERY PLAN HAS A FLAW

R ahg wore a worried look as he paced from one end of the room to the other. "This is getting to be too much to handle, Dar. I can't even sleep at night."

Darstan leaned against the wall and chewed on a twig. "Rahg, nobody promised you a good night's sleep. Assume every night will be bad so that when you get a good sleep, you'll be doing better than expected. Besides, you need to quit worrying. Anciara won't find us here."

A nod from Rahg acknowledged he heard. "I'm not worried about her finding us. I think we have to do something about her. We need to try to kill her."

Darstan laughed. "Killing her isn't going to be easy, Rahg. You know how powerful she is."

"I know, but I also know that *anyone* can be killed. Remember what we thought about Lukaan? Before we fought him, we didn't know if *he* could be killed, but we did it. He's dead."

"I understand, but Lukaan wasn't a god, and, according to those in the know, *she* is."

Rahg picked up his pacing. "I know what's said about her, but it's worth a try. Maybe if we attack her all at once? How strong can she be?"

"She can be really strong. And who did you mean when you said 'We'? We meaning who?"

"You, Mikkellana, Melissara, Aenaila, Wisp, Camissa, and me. Everybody we've got. Ask Rhaven, Takar, and anyone else to join the attack as well. And I'm sure Takar could get some guards to help."

"Have you got a plan?" Darstan asked.

"Not an organized plan, but I'm sure one of the du Savarra sisters can come up with something," Rahg said. "They've had a lot of experience fighting battles."

"Let's hope it's something that works." Darstan stood, stretching while he did. "Time to go, brother," he said, and walked out the door, then turned left down the hall.

Rahg rushed to catch up. "Time to go where?"

"Kill a god. That's what you said, right? Besides, it's almost time for supper, and if we get to the table early enough, we might get extra food. I know that interests you."

Darstan led the way down the corridor with Rahg at his side. "Darstan, how do you stay so calm? We're talking about doing battle with a god, and you're not even breathing hard."

"It was *your* idea, brother; besides, there was a time when I'd have been scared to death. You remember the battle at Twin Forks, and when we first went to Sykor. Back then I was plenty afraid, but something changed when I lost my hand. I don't know if it changed because I lost my hand or because I gained the powers, but I'm guessing it's one of those two."

"If you're not afraid, what do you think about during times like these?"

Darstan glanced at Rahg. "The job to be done. If the job is to kill a god, that's all I think about. Nothing else."

Rahg shook his head. "I hope I get like that someday. I'm sure not that way now."

"I don't know if you want to be, Rahg. It's great to not be afraid, but it does something else to you. Makes you . . . numb to other feelings."

"Numb how?"

"Numb as in it's difficult to feel other things. Difficult to get excited, or be happy, or be in love. It reminds me of when I lost Mirana. Come to think of it, that may have contributed more to these feelings than the other things I mentioned."

Rahg shrugged. "Let's hope we can do something about Anciara, and then we can finally get back to normal."

Darstan reached for the door handle.

"Where are you going, Darstan? This isn't the room."

"I'm getting Wisp and Aenaila. We'll walk to supper together."

"Are you going to tell them before we get there?" Rahg asked.

"I think we should. Then all we'd have to do is persuade the others they should risk their lives and probably die, and all for the slim chance of killing Anciara."

"I know it sounds bad, but if it works, we win."

Darstan looked back at Rahg. "And if it doesn't, we die."

Rahg and Darstan entered, then he sat in an empty chair next to Camissa. He leaned in and kissed her. "I missed you today."

"I miss you too," she said. "I saw you come in with Darstan, but he left quickly. Where is he going?"

"I'm sure he's going to sit with Aenaila and Wisp. He became close to both of them when they went to Cergala."

"I know that, and I understand, especially considering what happened with his wife, but he seems aloof, almost as if he doesn't want to talk to me. Or anyone else, for that matter. I keep wondering if it was something I did or said."

Rahg squeezed her hand. "It's nothing you did. I talked to him about it today. He thinks it's partly due to losing his hand and getting powers, and he also said some of it may be the result of losing his wife."

Camissa nodded. "I can see that," she said, then sipped wine from Rahg's goblet and gave a sigh. "This wine is the best I've had. I wouldn't mind staying here and making a home."

"I don't know," Rahg said. "Sooner or later, Anciara is bound to find us."

"I know it's a possibility, but if she does, we could go to Arangar or Cergala. I'm sure she doesn't know those places any more than she does Entiria, so we'd be safe—at least for a while."

Rahg nodded. "I know the world seems big, Camissa, but there are only a few places Anciara doesn't know about, and you can bet she'll find out about them quickly."

"Rahg, it sounds as if you're thinking of options. What are they?"

Rahg took a few bites of some snack food, took a sip of the wine, then placed both of Camissa's hands in his. "Darstan and I talked about it. We think a planned attack on Anciara would be in our best interest."

Camissa almost spit out her food. "What! Attack her? Are you crazy? She'd kill us all."

"Not necessarily," Rahg said. "*Anyone* can be killed."

"I don't know who told you that, but they obviously didn't know Anciara."

"We'll see," Rahg said. "We're going to bring it up at supper. Put it to a vote."

"And you think you'll get support for this . . . this crazy idea?"

"I think we'll have to see," Rahg said, and he gestured to Aenaila and Wisp, who were leaving the room with Darstan trailing behind them. "And it looks like it's time to find out." He took Camissa by the hand and stood. "Time to go, Camissa."

Rahg and Camissa walked slowly through the long corridors, but they didn't say much.

"The room's ahead on the left," Camissa said. "Everyone should be there by now."

Rahg entered ahead of Camissa. He embraced Aenaila, smacked

Wisp on the shoulder, and hugged his brother, then nodded to Melissara and Mikkellana. "Good to see everyone," he said.

Melissara stood and addressed the others who were seated at the table. "Rahg has something to say. If I'm not mistaken, Rahg has a proposal to make, an interesting one."

Rahg seemed stunned until Darstan laughed. "I told them, Rahg. But don't worry, I told them it was both our ideas, so they didn't think you were the only one that was nuts."

"Let's hear your plan," Rhaven said. "It's long past time we did something."

Rahg shifted on his feet, cleared his throat, then said, "Darstan and I were talking, and we figured it was time to do something about Anciara instead of sitting around waiting for her to find a way to come after us."

Melissara scoffed. "You have no idea who you'd be dealing with."

"And she has no idea who she's dealing with," Rahg said. "Besides, there are more than a few of us. We could attack her from all sides at once. With all our powers, *some* of it has to do something."

Mikkellana shook her head. "A brave and valiant thought, Rahg, but I doubt it would do any good. She would likely absorb our attacks like you do a lighted candle."

Darstan spoke for the first time. "But that's a guess. You don't know that. If all of us attack at once, maybe she *will* suffer damage."

Mikkellana's back had healed to some extent, but she still had difficulty walking. She stood and walked around the table, using the backs of the chairs for stability. "You're right, Darstan, we don't know that an attack won't harm her. The other side of that coin is that you don't know if an attack *will* harm her." Mikkellana pointed her finger at Darstan in a jabbing-like manner. "And you don't know if she'd kill us all for trying either."

"Maybe if we hit her with Slicers just before we attack, it would help," Darstan said.

Melissara laughed in a derisive manner. "Don't forget, young man, my other sister is no longer with us, and no one here can command Slicers."

Darstan turned and stared. "I can. And we have Aentarra's Slicers to use."

Melissara almost fell down. "You can use Slicers?"

Mikkellana nodded "I saw him do it several times." She stopped short of telling Melissara that the Slicers from Aentarra's pouch refused to enter Darstan's mind. Some secrets were better kept.

Her sister picked up her goblet of wine and drank from it. "Knowing that, I'm almost tempted to try. I don't like the idea of hiding from that witch all my life."

Darstan smiled and looked around the table. "Anyone else in for a challenge?"

A long steel blade stabbed into the table, and Rhaven stood. "I'm always up for fun."

"Rhaven!"

He faced Mikkellana, a dour look on his face. "It's time, Mikkellana. You don't have to go; in fact, I'd rather you didn't, but we need to stop her."

"I'm with Rhaven," Wisp said.

Tobias, Camissa, and Aenaila were the last to raise their hands. "It better be a good plan," Aenaila said. "I promised my parents I'd bring home a husband."

Mikkellana stood behind Rhaven and rubbed his shoulders. "Before I say yes, I want to make sure Darstan has control of the Slicers; they'll be an important part of any strategy we come up with."

"Where are they?" Darstan asked.

Mikkellana reached inside her robe and held up Aentarra's pouch. "In here." She started to make her way around the table, but Darstan stopped her.

"No need to bring them here." He closed his eyes and focused. After a moment, a dozen or more Slicers emerged from the pouch and raced to Darstan, stopping just shy of entering his body. A moment later, almost a hundred more followed, then another hundred.

"Satisfied?" Darstan asked.

Mikkellana made her way back to her chair. "I'm impressed." She looked to Melissara. "Convinced, sister?"

"I think we can do something with this, but I insist on a quick and foolproof escape route being an integral part of any plan."

"I'm in if the escape plan is good," Aenaila said.

Within ten minutes, everyone agreed, then Rhaven spoke. "Let's eat a good meal. We can think of possible plans, and we'll discuss them afterward."

"Sounds good," Rahg said. "I'm starved."

After supper, everyone retired to Mikkellana's room so she could rest. "Anyone come up with good ideas?"

"I think it should be done in Sykor," Rhaven said. "Most of us know the city well. Those who don't," he said, gesturing toward Melissara, "will be positioned in easy-to-escape locations."

"I was going to suggest Genda, but I like Rhaven's idea better," Aenaila said.

Tobias lit his pipe and shifted in the chair. "Tell us more. Give me specifics. I've been doin' this long enough to know every plan has a flaw."

"I know we'll have to refine it, but here are the details."

Chapter Four

ATTACK UPON A GOD

For two days they strategized, refined the plan, and simulated attacks.

As Mikkellana got into bed on the second night, Rhaven said, "I think we're ready. Are you?"

Mikkellana kissed him, then hugged. "We have fought many a foe, but Anciara should be the last. I'm as prepared now as I ever will be, and as long as we stick to our plans, we should all be fine."

"I know we have a plan to follow, but just make sure to follow *my* plan if things go wrong. And stay out of the line of fire; besides, with your skills, you're going to be better off in the rear position using your Shielding power."

"Tell me again who's going to be in the front?"

"The thief and others. But enough questions; we'll go over plans in the morning. And make sure you get some sleep because we'll be leaving early."

. . .

After breakfast, everyone gathered in the middle of the room. "Ready?" Melissara asked. They nodded and joined hands.

"Don't forget to focus on the spot outside the gate," Aenaila said. "If we Shift too close, she'll be able to Sense us." Aenailla looked to Melissara. "Don't worry about not knowing the Shift point; we have plenty of power to enable the Shift."

"We're ready," Darstan said.

Aenaila squeezed Wisp's hand. "Everyone focus. We'll go on three. One, two, three."

~

Aenaila appeared on the road outside the gates to Sykor. They began walking, and in short order entered the city, then made their way to High Town, where before long, they stood in front of Talanvar's house, causing Dirk to gasp and take a step back.

"Kender! Where have you been? And where is Adju?"

Wisp pulled him close and hugged him. He leaned down and whispered. "Good to see you, Dirk. I've missed you."

"I've missed you too, Kender. Is Adju with you?"

Wisp stood up straight but kept his hand resting on Dirk's shoulder. "Adju stayed behind, Dirk. I didn't want to risk his life by bringing him. What's been going on here? How have things been since Anciara arrived?"

Dirk shook his head. "Not good, Kender. Lord Talanvar will tell you, but things aren't good; in fact, they're worse than when Ludar was in charge." He held up his hands, showing his missing thumbs. "And you know how bad that was."

The door opened, and Talanvar came out and hurried down the walk. "Kender! I hadn't expected to see you so soon; in fact, I didn't know if I'd *ever* see you."

Wisp grabbed him by the shoulders and hugged. "You should know better than to count me out, Lord Talanvar. I'm not going to let some old witch take me from this world."

"From what I've seen of the things this 'old witch' can do, it wouldn't take much for her to do it."

"Tell me what it's been like. What's she done?"

Talanvar took Wisp by the elbow. "Come inside in case someone is watching."

"You think that may be a possibility?" Wisp asked.

Talanvar nodded. "I *know* it is. She continually questions people to try to find you and your friends. Some people survive the interrogation; others don't. And she handsomely rewards people who provide her any tidbit of information."

"Do you have people you can trust?"

Talanvar opened the front door and held it open while everyone entered. Once seated in the library, he leaned his elbows on his knees and spoke with a lowered voice to those around him. "To answer Kender's question, yes, I have a few people we can trust, but *only* a few. People are so afraid of her, you can't pay them enough to be loyal. There are still a few who are deeply indebted to me, and I feel I can rely on them, but the rest of the city is suspect at best."

"Does she have any routines?" Melissara asked. "Any place she goes on a regular basis? Or anything she does that can be relied on to place her at a particular spot at a particular time?"

"Definitely," Talanvar said. "Once a week, everyone—and I mean *everyone* is required to attend her announcements in the plaza."

"What are the announcements for?" Mikkellana asked.

"She asks the same questions all the time, and all the questions are about finding you."

A servant entered carrying a tray with refreshments, and the room grew quiet. He handed the drinks to the guests, then exited the room, closing the door behind him. Talanvar checked to make sure he was gone before speaking. "These meetings—or announcements—are where she gets the people she interrogates."

"What does she hope to get from them?" Wisp asked.

"The talk in the streets is that she has the ability to reach into a person's mind and take information from them. Some people say this process leaves a person as much as dead. Whispers from others say some people *do* die."

"Why do people agree to be questioned?" Melissara asked.

"They don't," Talanvar said. "She scans the plaza using her probes or whatever it is she does, then she selects those she suspects may know something of your whereabouts—even a hint of it."

Darstan stood and looked around. "Then it's up to us to do something. We came here to kill her, so let's make sure we do."

"We don't even have to switch the plan," Tobias said. "The plaza is where we planned the attack, and it sounds like it's still the place to trap her."

"Or be trapped?" Wisp said.

Tobias laughed. "That's why I like you, boy. Always thinkin', you are." He faced Talanvar and asked, "When does she have her gatherings?"

Talanvar smiled. "You're in luck—or not—her announcement will be tomorrow morning. Once you hear the bells ring, you'll only have minutes to get there."

Mikkellana stood with Rhaven's help. "With that information, I say we get lots of rest. Tomorrow will be an important day. One last warning—*no one* use powers of any kind before it's time to start. Any hint of powers, and she'll know, and that will foil all our plans."

Another servant entered and put a plate of food in front of everyone, then brought khaffe and te to accompany the food. Rahg sipped on the khaffe, then looked to Mikkellana. "Are we ready for this? How will we know when to start?"

Mikkellana fixed her glare on Rahg and held it. "I am going to assume that was a nonsensical question. We have been over this more than a few times, and everyone claimed to know their roles."

Rahg swallowed the last bite of a piece of bread. "I *do* know. I was just double-checking. I have no plans to be the one to ruin this."

"No need to check. I'm confident you won't forget, Rahg. And if anyone else is confused about what to do, I'm sure they'll say something." She looked at each person and stared. "Isn't that right?"

Darstan cleaned his plate and sipped the last of his khaffe. "I'm sure everybody knows what to do and when to do it. Let's just finish eating and go."

"Eager to go to the Chugaran Path?" Aenaila asked.

"I don't intend to go to the Chugaran Path or any path like it," Darstan said. "I intend on finishing our plan to kill Anciara. And anyone else who gets in our way."

Wisp pushed back his chair and stood. "No sense in waiting any longer. The bell should be ringing soon. At least it will seem like soon."

"I suggest we rest as much as we can before the morning," Mikkellana said. "We're going to need to wake early so we can be prepared."

After a good night's sleep and a hearty breakfast, Wisp and Aenaila left the house first and made their way down the hill through High Town. Darstan waited until Wisp reached the bottom of the hill, then he followed, closing the door behind him as he left Talanvar's manor.

When they arrived at the plaza, Wisp positioned himself on the east side next to a tavern boasting a hearty and tasty breakfast. He sat at an outside table and ordered khaffe to drink.

Aenaila crossed the plaza and browsed a few racks of clothes sitting outside a merchant's shop. She looked like any other Sykoran out shopping for the day.

Darstan entered the square from the north and made his way to the far west side where he mingled with a few early arrivers, chatting casually while making sure to hide his missing hand.

The bell rang as Melissara and Mikkellana, accompanied by Rhaven and Tobias, made their way from Talanvar's house toward the plaza.

Rahg, who followed closely, increased his pace when he heard the peal.

Melissara found a seat ten feet away from Wisp, and Mikkellana took respite in a comfortable chair situated between Aenaila and Darstan.

Rahg joined a growing crowd of people in the middle of the plaza, close to where Anciara would likely be, and Rhaven and Tobias stood on each side of him.

A few moments later, the bell rang again to announce Anciara's arrival. A wall of mist descended from the rooftops, then Anciara appeared in the middle of the plaza. She stood at the center of the plaza, brimming with confidence. She was a formidable sight.

Camissa arrived just as Anciara spoke. She got as close to Anciara as she could, filling out the front line of the crowd.

Rahg shifted weight from foot to foot and watched Anciara's every move. She looked left to right, and her gaze caught him and held him fixed. As he stood, brushing shoulders with others, words sounded in his head—her words—but she wasn't speaking.

Every person here knows what I want. I want the whereabouts of the ones with powers, the ones who were here before I was.

Rhaven and Tobias mingled with the guard patrols—the ones with a death wish—screaming for Anciara's death and demanding freedom for the people. As soon as they began the chants, Camissa used her powers of Persuasion on both patrols, urging them to attack Anciara. After a moment's pause, they charged her from both sides, spears and swords flailing.

Aenaila took her cue and joined the attack, using Illusion to confuse Anciara, while Melissara aimed Lightning at Anciara's head and struck one blow after another. Aenaila continued using Illusion to make it seem as if hundreds of guards were attacking. It proved good enough to provide a distraction.

Now it was Darstan's turn. He sent a concentrated wall of Cold-Fire at her, and at the same time, he ordered the Slicers to attack.

The Slicers erupted from the pouch at his side and raced toward Anciara, entering her head and torso just as the ColdFire struck.

Mikkellana smiled as she added strength to her shield. *It's working. We're winning.*

Rahg looked to his left, then behind him. People trembled. A few women cried. And small children clung tightly to their mothers' dresses. No smiles or grins were in sight other than smirks on the faces of a few guard patrols protecting Anciara's back.

Rahg's shield buckled some, but he held it, even though it proved to be a strain. He tried not to show his discomfort, but the force was too much, so he placed his hands on his head as if to squeeze it, thinking it might somehow reduce the pressure. It didn't work, and his shield collapsed. When it did, he fell to the ground.

Fearing the worst, he scrambled to his feet and moved through the crowd toward Darstan. If they had to abandon the cause, he needed to be near someone who could Shift.

Tobias and Rhaven must have had the same idea because they moved toward Darstan and Mikkellana respectively just as Anciara struck out against the guards attacking her with a narrow wall of BlackFire.

The guards fell like toy soldiers, and each death stung Camissa like a bite from a shont'zu—a wasp that lived in the deserts of Khatara. She reeled, falling against the building behind her.

Aenaila grabbed her arm at the elbow and helped her up. "Stay here. I need to get Wisp so we can get out of here. Our plan's not working."

Fully cloaked with Stealth, Wisp sneaked behind Anciara undetected. He drew a knife from a sheath at his side and plunged it into her calf, then he did it again on the other leg.

Fortunately, he moved to strike the first leg again, just as a bolt of BlackLightning hit where he'd been heartbeats earlier. Assuming the plan wasn't working, he abandoned his idea and rushed toward Aenaila.

More Lightning struck by Anciara's other leg, then in spots surrounding her. Wisp made a sweeping arc back to Aenaila, who met him halfway with Camissa in tow. "We need to leave now," she said. "It's not working."

With that, she took hold of Wisp's hand, and they Shifted to a predetermined spot in Genda, one they had all known.

Darstan fell backward when Anciara blocked his ColdFire, and though he felt nothing when she ejected his Slicers, he was aware of it. Rahg found him first and Tobias a moment later. "Let's get out of here," he said, and Shifted.

Melissara fired three more blasts of BlackLightning, then she too Shifted, but she went straight to Entiria since she didn't have the image of the location in Genda.

Mikkellana was the last to admit defeat, but once she did, she acted swiftly, holding Rhaven's hand and taking him with her.

Once gathered in the room of a small house in Genda, they all joined hands and Shifted to Entiria. Melissara waited on a sofa, sipping a drink.

"Well, that didn't go well, did it?" she said.

Chapter Five

THE NEXT PLAN

Rhaven helped Mikkellana to the sofa where she sat next to her sister and stared at the rest of them. "So much for overpowering her," Mikkellana said. "I won't go so far as to say it was a bad idea, Rahg, but it wasn't the best one, although I'll take an equal share of the blame for going along with it."

"I didn't expect it to work," Melissara said, "but it was worth a try. At least none of us died."

Sobbing from the side of the room, turned Mikkellana's head. "What's wrong with you, Camissa?"

"All those men died because of me. *All* of them. There were dozens, maybe more."

Rahg patted her back and held her. "No one died because of you. It was Anciara who killed them; besides, they had their mind made up to go against her. You heard them. Anciara would have killed them no matter what you did."

"But they would have never attacked her without my suggestion implanted in their minds."

Melissara stood and walked to her, showing an unusual amount of compassion. "Persuasion doesn't work like that, girl. At least not that I know of. Persuasion only strengthens a person's resolve. It won't make them do something they wouldn't ordinarily do. Either way, I don't think those men were long for this world. You heard them chanting against her. You don't think Anciara would allow that, do you? Persuasion may have brought them to an earlier death, but it was an inevitable one."

Camissa looked up at Melissara and sniffled. "What do you mean by it can't make them do something they don't want?"

"I mean, if those soldiers hadn't thought about—and wanted to —attack Anciara, they wouldn't have done so, even with your suggestion. The only thing your power did was strengthen their courage to act on what they already thought. And from the way they were chanting, they had thought long and hard on what they were doing. They must have known the consequences."

Camissa accepted a cloth from Rahg and used it to wipe her tears. "Are you sure?"

"As sure as one can be," Mikkellana said from the sofa. "I haven't known a lot of people with Persuasion in my lifetime, but my life has been long. The ones I did know who had the power said it worked like my sister explained. You can't *force* someone to do something."

"Whether you can or not makes no difference. If a few people have to die so we can defeat her, so be it." Darstan took a seat in a chair against the side wall. "We are all willing to die to defeat her. Others must be too."

"I'm wondering where Tirzinitzia was," Melissara said. "I expected her to be there."

"Don't discount the fact that Anciara may have done away with her already," Mikkellana said. "It wouldn't surprise me."

Melissara returned to her seat on the sofa. "You're right, sister. I hadn't thought of that."

Rahg got a seat for Camissa, then asked what everyone must have been thinking. "What now? We attacked with everything we had, and it did nothing."

Mikkellana laughed. "Now we come up with a new plan. We can't quit trying or we're dooming ourselves to a life of hiding."

"And she'll eventually find us," Melissara said. "It's not a question of *if* she'll find us, only *when.*"

"How are we going to beat her?" Camissa asked. "You saw what happened. Nothing hurt her. Not the BlackLightning, not the soldiers, not Darstan's ColdFire or even his Slicers."

"That worries me more than anything," Melissara said. "I've never seen anyone capable of rejecting Slicers."

Mikkellana stood. "Darstan did something similar in Pomanda. Whether it was more or less I don't know, but if I had to, I'd say it was more; the Slicers refused to enter him. They wouldn't even go in."

Melissara looked to the side, a suspicious glance at Darstan. "What did you do?"

"No idea," Darstan said.

"We've got time to figure it out," Mikkellana said. "There has to be a reason."

"I don't know why you'd waste time on that," Darstan said. "I blasted her with a hundred Slicers, and she spit them out as if they were nothing. And she absorbed my ColdFire as if it were a match."

Melissara nodded. "I know, Darstan, but there's a difference between spewing out the Slicers and being able to reject them. I don't yet know what that difference is, but there *is* a difference."

"But will that difference mean anything?" Darstan asked.

"We don't know that yet either," Melissara said. "But you can bet we'll find out."

Melissara turned to Camissa. "The same goes for you. That display of Persuasion was impressive even though it didn't help with anything."

"It got a lot of people killed," Camissa said.

"Like I said, Camissa, you got no one killed. They did that themselves."

Rhaven walked across the room to get some water. "With all

this talk about how good we did, the fact remains, we did nothing. It was as if we were never there. And if we stayed a moment longer, we'd have all been dead."

"I hate to say it, but I agree with Rhaven," Tobias said. "It was like jumpin' into a swamp full of sangras. We didn't stand a chance. I think the only reason we didn't die is because we took her by surprise."

"I think we acted in haste," Mikkellana said. "The next attack will have to be thought out better."

Melissara walked across the floor and stopped to get a mug of water. "I'm sure she can be hurt. Ages ago, the legends told of the gods fighting, and in those stories, they *were* able to be hurt. Tales told of their suffering."

"Then perhaps we aren't strong enough to hurt her," Rhaven said. "Or she's gotten stronger."

Melissara shook her head. "I don't know, Rhaven. I might agree with you, but according to everything I know, Darstan's ColdFire power is near the maximum, so it should have had an effect on her."

"Unless she was Shielded, and we didn't know it," Mikkellana said.

Melissara spun around, her eyes lit with excitement. "That has to be it! Just like your shields wouldn't be affected by someone with the normal power of Fire, her shields must be so strong that even Darstan's ColdFire doesn't affect her."

"But the Slicers went in her," Rahg said.

"Slicers go through anything," Melissara said. "Even her shields couldn't stop a Slicer."

"All that is good," Aenaila said. "But knowing she has shields and doing something about it are two different things."

"Exactly," Melissara said, and faced Mikkellana. "So let's figure out what would make you vulnerable to a lesser attack, sister."

Mikkellana thought for a moment or two. "If I got tired, the shield would weaken."

"What else? What makes a shield strong?"

Mikkellana shook her head, then stopped and stared. "Focus," she said. "I have to focus for it to remain strong; otherwise, it loses its resistance."

Mikkellana sat up straight. "And having the shield attached to something makes it even stronger."

"What do you mean?" Melissara asked.

Mikkellana hesitated.

"Well?" Melissara asked. "What?"

"It was how I made the Sethian Shield. I attached it to the ground. It became one with the world."

Melissara smiled. "Assuming that's what she does, all we have to do is figure out a way to sever her ties."

"I said that's how *I* did it, sister. I have no idea how she does it."

"I'd bet it's the same," Darstan said. "My ColdFire goes underground, at least a little. I know that. It did it in Khatara when I fought Lukaan."

"You fought him yourself?" Melissara asked.

Darstan nodded. "For a while, then I had to quit and join Aentarra. Even then, we couldn't hold him back."

Melissara pursed her lips. "I'm impressed. Not many would have survived even a moment against him."

Mikkellana laughed. "Don't be surprised, sister. He's the one who killed Sendra. And he did it by himself."

"By *himself*? What about Ghruehne?"

Mikkellana shook her head. "Aentarra killed Ghruehne, but Darstan killed Sendra. I have no doubt that he would have killed them both though, and as much as I don't like it, he saved my life. Ghruehne had crippled me with a Lightning strike, and he would have killed me if Aentarra hadn't intervened, and then Darstan arrived."

"I don't know about anyone else," Darstan said. "But I think we need to try again. Maybe not today or even tomorrow, but soon. We can't give up."

"I'm with Darstan on that," Rahg said. "I know I can't contribute as much as he does, but every bit helps. If Mikkellana comes up with a plan, I can definitely help with the shields."

"I think we're settled then," Rhaven said. "Let's think separately on ways to defeat her. Afterward, we can get back together and compare ideas."

Chapter Six

MIKKELLANA'S RESPONSE

For two days, no one mentioned anything about Anciara; instead, they wandered around Entiria and enjoyed the luxuries and tranquility the remote island offered. The Entirians smiled and spoke politely, but as time passed, it became obvious the people didn't want them as guests.

Mikkellana stopped the shulan in the hall just before supper on the second day. "Shulan, I sense a bit of hostility from your people. Is there a reason?"

The shulan bowed low, and his face flushed. "My apologies, My Lady, but my people have surmised from conversations they've overheard that you are hiding from someone, and that makes them afraid. They've seen what your kind can do, and they wonder who it is that you have to hide from."

"It makes them afraid?"

The shulan nodded. "As I said, they are afraid because they watched you defeat Iazzo, so they wonder who is so powerful as to force you to hide. Even the priests have not been immune to this talk."

"And what do you think?" Mikkellana asked.

"It is not my place to do so," he said. "I serve the people."

Mikkellana nodded. "I understand it's not your place, but that is not what I asked. I asked what you think?"

The shulan paused for a moment, then spoke. "I think, My Lady, that whoever it is you seek shelter from must be very powerful. Nonetheless, you and yours may stay as long as need be. We remain in your debt."

Mikkellana bowed. "You have given the type of answer I expected, and I thank you. Rest assured, we will not abuse your graciousness."

The shulan bowed. "Of course, My Lady."

As the shulan walked away, Mikkellana said, "Shulan, know that I will do everything to ensure your people are protected. We only need the safety of your isle for a short time."

The shulan bowed again. "Many thanks, My Lady. You are welcome as long as you need."

~

Darstan fidgeted with a dagger while Rahg sat on the edge of the bed staring out the window. "I know something's up when you get like this, Rahg. What's bothering you? And don't tell me it's because you're hungry. You're always hungry."

"Nothing's wrong. I'm just thinking."

Darstan grinned. "Rahg, you might—*might*—fool Wisp with that lie, but you can't fool your brother. Spit it out."

Rahg walked across the room, the sound of his boots against the wooden floors thumping loudly. "I've got to go to Nelstar. I need to kill those Lights."

"I know that, and I already said I'd go with you. Besides, what's the hurry? Is it the oath you recited? Is that what's doing it?"

Rahg shook his head. "I don't know, Darstan. How can an oath make you want to do something? I can't believe it's that, and yet . . . I don't know. I just don't know."

Darstan gave thought to what his brother said. "I'm not eager to fight the Lights—not after hearing what Mikkellana and Melissara have said about them—but I'm not going to let you go by yourself either. I said I'd help, and I will."

Rahg spun to face Darstan. "Do you think we can do it? Kill the Lights, I mean?"

"I don't intend on going all the way to Nelstar just to die." Darstan laughed. "And if we ask nicely, I'm betting Wisp will go too. Aenaila might not like it, but he'll go."

Rahg went from excited to depressed in a heartbeat. He sat in the chair against the wall. "It all sounds good, Dar, but there's no way to get there. It's not like you can use that Shifting power to take us. We'd have to go through the Paaren, and that's a horrible place; besides, I have no idea how to get to Nelstar."

"No, but Melissara might. She was in stuck in the Paaren with Aenaila and Mikkellana."

"She's probably no different than her sister, and you know what Mikkellana says—that no one should ever go there again."

"Mikkellana might *say* that," Darstan said, "but she entered Sethia when it meant getting Lukaan, didn't she? Maybe her sister feels the same way about the Lights."

"Where should we start?" Rahg asked.

"I'll be back in a few minutes," Darstan said. "I need to talk to Wisp. He's our first challenge."

"No, wait," Rahg said. "Maybe we should talk to Melissara first. She may have some other ideas."

"Then let's do that," Darstan said.

A few moments later, Darstan and Rahg knocked on Melissara's door and waited for her to answer, which she did within seconds. She appeared surprised to see them. "Yes? What can I do for you?"

Darstan spoke, but hesitantly. "We, uh. We—"

Rahg stepped forward. "We want to talk about going to Nelstar. I need to kill the Lights."

Melissara smiled and swung the door open as she stepped aside. "Perhaps you boys should come inside. This is a conversation better had alone."

Melissara sat and encouraged them to sit as well. "Perhaps you should have some wine," she said. "Then you can tell me what you want again."

"I need to kill the Lights," Rahg said.

Laughter erupted from Melissara as she rose to get more cheese and wine. "Go to Nelstar? To kill the Lights, no less? And what, may I ask brought this on?"

"They need to die," Rahg said.

"There will be three of us," Darstan said. "Wisp is coming too. At least I think he will."

Melissara sat and sipped her wine, then nodded. "If you take anyone with you, he may be the most useful considering his Stealth ability."

"I was thinking the same thing," Darstan said, "But Aenaila may be a problem. I doubt if she'll want him risking his life, and we'd definitely be doing that."

Melissara said, "We could get Camissa to use Persuasion."

Darstan shook his head. "Two things wrong with that. You said it doesn't work unless the people *want* to do something anyway, and besides, I wouldn't trick Wisp that way."

Melissara smiled. "I'm not talking about tricking Wisp. Ask him if he'll go, and unless I am dead wrong, he'll want to help, but insist on asking Aenaila for permission. Have Camissa use the Persuasion on Aenaila to reinforce her decision to let him go. If she's dead set against it, she won't anyway, but if she's only partially convinced, it may help her decide. Either way, the Persuasion isn't changing Wisp's mind."

Darstan sat quietly for a moment, then said, "I understand what you're saying, but Wisp and Aenaila are friends—dear friends. I won't do this to them. I'll ask him if he'll go with us, but if he and Aenaila decide not to, so be it. We'll have to do it ourselves."

After staring at Darstan and Rahg, Melissara spoke again. "Do you realize what you're in for? Do you know who you want to kill?"

"It doesn't matter," Rahg said. "I swore I'd kill them when Aentarra died. From what I understand, I'm now committed."

Melissara nodded. "I know. I was there when you did it. Foolish lad." She nodded a few times, then said, "All right, I'll go with you. First, we'll have to persuade Mikkellana. For now, finish your wine, and we'll map out a strategy. We'll tell Mikkellana tomorrow after breakfast. It seems as good a time as any."

Darstan smiled, then Melissara said. "And you better talk to that thief tonight. Make sure you persuade him to join us. He may be the key to success.

After a night of strategy, Rahg and Darstan returned to their respective rooms, ready for the long day ahead.

As Darstan lay in bed trying to fall asleep, he remembered he hadn't talked to Wisp. *He'll definitely still be up,* Darstan thought.

He got up, dressed again, and walked down the hall to see Wisp. He knocked lightly on the door, then waited until Wisp opened it.

"Darstan, what are you doing here?"

"We need to talk, Wisp. Let's take a walk."

Wisp walked alongside Darstan as he meandered the halls of the temple. "Are you going to tell me why you dragged me from the room at what is often considered a late hour? Or do I have to guess?"

Darstan laughed, then he stopped and faced Wisp. "Rahg and I are planning a trip and we'd like you to join us."

"A trip? That sounds ominous. Where are you going?"

Darstan sighed. "Nelstar. We're going to kill the Lights."

Wisp narrowed his eyes and stared. "The Lights? Aren't those the ones who killed Mikkellana's father? The ones who are supposed to be so powerful?"

Darstan hesitated, then nodded. "Yes, Wisp. I can see your mind working, so I'll say it now. I'm asking you to go on what many would consider a sure journey to death, but I don't think it has to be. In fact, if you accompany Rahg and me, I think we have a good chance, especially with your Cloaking."

Wisp smiled. "You know I'll have to talk to Aenaila."

"I understand," Darstan said. "Let me know in the morning, after breakfast."

Wisp turned around. "If I need to know that quickly, I had better get back to the room."

While everyone ate breakfast, Rahg put down his utensils and stood. "I have an announcement. I know some of you may not agree with this, but I am going to Nelstar."

Mikkellana laughed and shook her head. "Just like that—'I'm going to Nelstar.' It's not so easy and not so bright, boy. Even if you could find your way there, and that might take a hundred years or so, the Lights would kill you as soon as they found out who you were. And that would only take them a day or two."

Melissara stared at her sister, not laughing. "He took the oath," she said. "He swore the same oath Aentarra did—to kill the Lights."

Mikkellana jumped up. "You idiot! I had forgotten you did that. You blithering idiot. How could you possibly swear to something that you knew nothing about?" Her face turned red with rage. "These are the Lights who killed my father? That's how strong they are." Her head shook like a fish on a hook. "Might as well dig your grave now, boy. If you ever make it to Nelstar, you won't be coming back."

Darstan stepped forward and stood alongside Rahg. He placed his hand on Rahg's shoulder. "I'm going with my brother, and I'll help him kill the Lights."

Mikkellana shook her head again, but she shook it harder. "Then you'll both be dead."

Melissara finished the wine at the bottom of her mug, then stood. "I'll join you as well, Rahg. You'll need someone who knows the worlds, and though it's been a while since I've been there, I still remember a lot."

Mikkellana gawked at her sister. "Have you gone mad as well? Was there something in the wine? You can't go there. You might remember Nelstar, but you have obviously forgotten the centuries we spent trapped in the Forsaken Lands. And the ease with which the Lights killed father." Mikkellana turned to Rhaven. "There goes any chance of killing Anciara. Without the three of them to help, it will be impossible."

Melissara shook her head. "I didn't forget, sister, but I also didn't forget that it was the Lights who killed father. Aentarra may have been the one who swore the oath, but it doesn't mean she was the only one who sought vengeance. I have du Savarra blood as well."

Mikkellana almost stumbled but caught herself on Rhaven's shoulder. "Am I the only one with sense? The Lights will kill the three of you. If there were only three of them, they'd kill all three of you, but there are *seven*." Mikkellana stared at each of them, holding her gaze for more than a moment. "Think of that—*seven*. How will you fight them? How will you kill them?"

"The same way they killed father," Melissara said. "By making use of the Book."

Mikkellana laughed, a scornful laugh meant to sting. "The Book? And how will you get hold of it. Do you remember where it's kept? In case you forgot, I'll remind you. It's in the center of the Council Table where the seven Lights sit, and at least five of them occupy chairs every day. Furthermore, when they aren't there, hundreds of the strongest guards protect it. More than enough to stop the three of you."

Mikkellana sat back down. "Have you thought of that, sister?"

The door opened and Wisp, Aenaila, and Adju walked in. "I'm sure she has, Mikkellana. And that's why I'm going to help them. If I Cloak us, we can steal whatever it is you're talking about."

"By all that's holy!" Mikkellana said, and then she sat back down. "I guess it's just you and me, Rhaven. We'll have to try to kill Anciara ourselves."

"I'll be here to help," Camissa said.

Aenaila took a seat next to Wisp at the table. "As will I. I'm not going with them."

Mikkellana shook her head and leaned back. "Sister, you better have a good plan. One mistake fighting the Lights and you'll die—all of you."

Melissara nodded, a somber look on her face. "I know, dear sister. I know. Any advice you have will be appreciated."

"I have advice all right. Don't go."

Chapter Seven

IT'S TIME TO ENTER THE PAAREN

Melissara reminded her sister to let her know if she thought of anything, then she got up and left the room, though she waited in the hall while Darstan and Rahg finished breakfast. When they came out, she went to them and whispered. "I think it's time we prepared to leave," she said. "I see no reason to remain any longer; besides, my sister was right about one thing. It may take us a while to get there."

"I'm ready," Darstan said. "How about you, Rahg?"

"Ready for what?" Rahg asked.

"To go to Nelstar," Darstan said. "We'll figure out how to kill the Lights on the way, and from what Mikkellana and Melissara are saying, we'll have plenty of time."

The door opened and Mikkellana entered the hallway. "You can't really be considering this, Melissara. You can't go to Nelstar." Mikkellana scoffed. "The only way there is through the Forsaken Lands, and if that doesn't kill you, the Lights will."

Mikkellana stared at Melissara. "Remember what the Lights did to father. Don't go mad on me like your sister did."

"I'm far from mad," Melissara said. "I'm just thinking that if we go back and steal the Book, we might be strong enough to do something to Anciara."

"Not mad! Do you *really* remember what the Lights did to father?—they cut his head off. And you're a far cry from father's strength. Even if Lukaan was still with you, you couldn't do it. Not against all of them."

"I remember what they did," Melissara said. "How could I forget? It's what put us in the Forsaken Lands to begin with. And not only did I not forget, I have not forgiven. As I already mentioned, Aentarra wasn't the only one who carried du Savarra blood."

"I see. Who knew?" Mikkellana said, then she faltered, losing her balance, but Rhaven helped her stand. "Then you better tell me what you've got in mind, dear sister."

Melissara gestured to the boys. "It's as Darstan said—we'll go back to Nelstar, kill the Lights, then we'll bring the Book back and use it to help defeat Anciara"

Mikkellana shook her head. "The Lights will kill all of you."

"I'm sure if the Lights *can* kill us, they will," Melissara said. "The question is *if* they can."

Mikkellana stood straight with Rhaven's help. "Let's say you *do* go back and you're fortunate enough to find your way to Nelstar in a reasonable amount of time. Even if that happens, how do you plan to get the Book away from them so they don't do the same to you that they did to father?"

Melissara gestured to her other side, where Wisp stood. "Like we've already mentioned, we will preclude them from killing us by taking *that* one with us. He already said he would go, and his Cloaking will be invaluable."

"Who *are* the Lights, anyway?" Darstan asked. "Aren't they just people?"

Mikkellana laughed, again with scorn. "They are people, it's true, but calling the Lights 'just people' is like saying a lion is just a house cat. They quit being 'just people' long ago, thousands of years ago. Think about that for a minute, Darstan. They've been alive for thousands of years. Do you consider that 'just people'?"

Rahg interrupted. I think Darstan was—"

"They *rule* Nelstar," Mikkellana said. "Nelstar consists of seven worlds. And the moment you step foot on any of those worlds, they'll know. A moment after that, you'll be dead."

"What makes you think so?" Darstan asked.

"They killed my father, and they exiled us, including Lukaan. If they can do that, you'll present no problem."

"That was more than a thousand years ago," Darstan said. "We don't even know if they're still alive."

"And why wouldn't they be?" Mikkellana asked. "*We're* still alive. Or at least some of us are."

"My point exactly," Darstan said. "*Some* of you. But how many—maybe two out of a hundred? Three, if we count Tirzinitzia. If the majority of *you* can die, then so can the majority of them."

Melissara walked to the front. "I find myself agreeing with Darstan. We should at least explore the possibility. If we go there and the Lights are firmly in control, we leave. It's as simple as that."

"Melissara, we've had our differences, but I can't let you go back to Nelstar. You'd be killed, and you'd kill Rahg, Darstan, and Wisp too. When dealing with the Lights, nothing is simple."

"I disagree," Melissara said. "It might be dangerous, but that doesn't rule out *simple*."

"I say we go," Darstan said.

"I'm going regardless of who goes with me," Rahg said.

Melissara stepped forward. "Don't worry, boys. I said I'd take you, and I will take you. I've already cheated death, and though I swore to kill my sister for one thousand years, I wanted it to be me, not someone else. Now I want vengeance on the Lights. I don't *have* to have vengeance, like Rahg, but I want it."

"You mean because of what happened to father?" Mikkellana asked.

"Not just him," Melissara said," But I may as well get it for him while I'm at it."

"And how will you find Nelstar?" Mikkellana asked.

"The Forsaken Lands, of course," Melissara said.

"The Forsaken Lands? You say that as if it will be a walk in the park. In case you've forgotten, we were lost for hundreds of years, not knowing where to go and fighting more than our share of formidable foes. And that was *with* Lukaan and many others, all of whom are dead now."

"Get me into the Paaren—or the Forsaken Lands, as you call it —and I'll get us there," Darstan said.

Mikkellana laughed. "And just how will you do that? You've never been to Nelstar."

"Don't ask me how, but I *know* I can do it."

Mikkellana was about to say something, but then she remembered how Darstan healed her back, and how he used FearMist, and how the Slicers acted around him. "All right. So be it. I can take you to the entrance after resting."

"I can do it," Darstan said. "I remember the spot well, and I'm ready."

Rahg stood. "I'm ready, too. Don't forget I have an oath to keep, and, as Mikkellana is so fond of reminding me, oaths must be kept."

"Don't forget me," Wisp said. "I'm going with you."

"I've changed my mind," Camissa said. "Rahg isn't going without me."

Rahg stepped in front of her and hugged. "Yes, I *am* going without you. I won't endanger you because I swore an oath; besides, as you so rightly presumed earlier, Mikkellana needs your help. You need to stay."

Aenaila walked to Wisp and hugged him, then she kissed him. "As much as I want to go, I can't. I need to help Mikkellana, and I must get back to Cartena and warn them of what might be coming. Although Anciara can't get there yet, I have no doubt she eventually will."

"I agree," Wisp said. "Besides, if you went with us, I'd be worrying about you all the time. It might make me careless."

Aenaila laughed. "Careless? *You?* Imagine that." She kissed his lips again. "Take care, my love. Don't dare get hurt. And don't worry over that beggar boy. I'll take care of him."

Wisp smiled and tousled Adju's hair. He knelt, took hold of Adju's shoulders, and whispered. "Be good for Aenaila. Don't give her any trouble."

Adju wiped tears from his cheeks. "Don't worry, Master Kender. I'll be good."

Mikkellana shook her head, frustrated. "I guess it's settled then. You four are going off to die, and you're leaving us *here* to die. I imagine it would be too simple to try to do this as a unified group."

"You sound like an old crow," Melissara said. "We tried defeating Anciara already and got nowhere. We're going to need help, and Nelstar is the only place I know to get that help."

"Help?" Mikkellana almost choked. "What kind of help are you going to get from Nelstar?"

"The Book," Melissara said. "Remember? After we kill the Lights, we'll take the Book."

Mikkellana leaned on Rhaven, then she nodded. "If you get the Book, it *could* make a difference." She stared at Melissara. "Get the Book, sister, and you may change my mind."

"In that case, I'll take my leave. I have a lot to do, and I plan on leaving early." She walked past the boys as she moved down the hall toward her room. "I know the day is young, but remember we leave at dawn tomorrow. Be ready."

Rhaven rushed to Rahg before he left. He handed him two pouches bulging at the seams. "Can you take these to Kyra? I told her I'd leave her these every so often. Just dangle them from a rope near the entrance. She'll find them."

Rahg smiled. "Rhaven, you're in danger of being considered a nice man." Rahg took the pouches and attached them to the sash at his waist. "I'll make sure it's done."

. . .

That night Rahg lay in bed against the wall, Darstan occupied a bed on the other side, and Wisp used a cot on the north wall. "Darstan, are you scared? You know we'll probably die."

"Everybody dies," Wisp said, interrupting. "Besides, it's not like we haven't risked our lives already. Fighting Lukaan was no picnic."

"It doesn't make much difference to me," Rahg said. "I have to go to Nelstar anyway—if I plan to fulfill this oath, that is."

"And according to what Melissara said, getting this Book may be our best chance of defeating Anciara." Darstan breathed in deeply and slowly. "Besides, I wouldn't mind testing my strength against one of the Lights."

"All right," Rahg said. "I'm going to sleep now. I think we all better try to get *some* sleep."

Just before dawn, Melissara knocked on the door. "Time to go, boys. No sense waiting."

Wisp opened the door and invited her in. "We're ready," he said. "Everything's packed, and we've already eaten."

"I need to get a Shift point from my sister, then we can leave," Melissara said.

"No need," Darstan said as he came to the door. "I told you yesterday; I have the point."

"Can you get us there yourself?" Melissara asked. "I've heard it's a long way."

"Don't listen so much to your sister. I can Shift there with no problem."

"My sister had no input on my assumption. I heard how far it was and made my own assessment based on your age."

Darstan laughed. "It looks as if you'll have to adjust your basis for assessing people."

Melissara nodded. "If we don't end up in the middle of the sea or inside a mountain, perhaps I will."

"Then take hold of Rahg, grab my hand, and we'll go."

"You're not waiting for me?" Wisp asked.

Darstan smiled for the first time that day. "How could I forget you, Wisp? Grab hold."

"You can't fool me with that, Darstan. I know you didn't forget me. If for no other reason than you wouldn't try this without me."

Darstan clasped his arm, then hugged him. "You're right. I wouldn't."

"I'm betting you thought Aenaila would convince me to stay."

"I wondered about Aenaila, but I was more concerned the little thief would keep you here."

Wisp lost his smile. "He almost did, Darstan. He begged me to let him come, and when I wouldn't, he turned it into begging me to stay. It was difficult."

"I understand. I'm just glad you decided to come with us. You're welcome company, not to mention I'm sure we'll need your special skills."

"Stealth is always handy," Melissara said.

Darstan nodded. "I agree, and his powers have been getting stronger."

"Then you will indeed be a welcome companion," Melissara said. "I suspect we'll need you as much on the way there as we will once we get there."

"Can the Lights detect people with Stealth?" Rahg asked.

"I don't know, but I'm sure we'll find out. Regardless, we may as well be on the way," Melissara said, then she joined hands with Rahg and Wisp and finally Darstan, who instantly Shifted to the portal on the side of the mountain in Arangar.

After they appeared at the foot of the path leading to the portal, Melissara looked around. "Is this it? Where's the portal?"

Rahg pointed toward the middle of the narrow trail. "You can't see it, but it's right there, in the middle of the path."

Melissara stepped forward, heading toward the path. "No sense in waiting. Let's go."

Rahg pulled her back. "I'll go first," he said. "We've been here before."

He moved in front of Melissara and stepped carefully along the path toward the portal. "Stay close. It's not far."

The four of them inched along the path, and somewhere near the middle, Rahg announced they'd reached their goal. "This is it. Be careful because it may be a fall."

"Take hold of my arm," Darstan said. "You're right that it may be a fall, and I can Shift; you can't."

"Thanks," Rahg said.

Darstan laughed. "After all this time, I'm still having to take care of you, little brother."

Rahg and Darstan disappeared through the portal, followed quickly by Melissara and Wisp. They stepped through into a field lush with green grass and fruit trees. "It's a lot different than the last time," Rahg said.

Melissara nodded. "It's been forever since I've been here, but I remember that aspect well; everything changes on a moment's notice."

"How long were you here?" Rahg asked.

Melissara continued looking around. "If I told you one hundred years, I'd be underestimating by many, many years. Let's just say it was a long, long time."

"Did you run into the beasts that are in—"

"If you mean the dorgans, yes. We did more than run into them; they killed most of us. We entered the Paaren one hundred strong, and by the time we got out, we only had twenty-one."

"Even with Lukaan?"

She nodded. "With Lukaan and many others almost as strong. The dorgans attacked in droves. Countless numbers of them."

"How did you kill them?" Darstan asked.

"We didn't. We risked Sight Shifting and were lucky enough to get away with only a few deaths."

"From the Shifting?" Rahg asked. "Why can't you Shift in here?"

"Because this place is in a constant state of flux. What you see one minute may not be there when you Shift. If that happens, you're lost. When we first came here, Lukaan's brother tried Shifting, and he disappeared. He was never seen again. Perhaps he was taken somewhere else, but if he was, we never saw him again. It's not worth the risk."

"What about—"

"Enough for now," Melissara said. "Perhaps another time. We're likely going to be together for a while, so we'll have plenty of opportunity to chat."

"Which way?" Rahg asked.

"Your guess is as good as mine," Melissara said. "I'm the one who was lost in here for years on end."

"Since that's the case, I say we head east," Darstan said. "Don't ask me why. I'm just following my gut."

Wisp headed east. "In light of another plan, I'll trust your gut."

When no one offered objections, Darstan followed Wisp, and Rahg and Melissara joined in.

"Wait," Rahg hollered. "I forgot to leave the pouches for Kyra. I'll only be a moment."

Rahg tied the pouches to a rock and left them dangling near the portal. He then rejoined the others.

"Remember to listen for the dorgans," Melissara said. "It's been a very long time, but I remember the rumbling that preceded an attack."

"I still wake with nightmares of those sounds," Rahg said. "Not much was more frightening."

· · ·

The day began with a comfortable temperature and a pleasant breeze, but by early evening, it had turned cold enough to make all of them think of a fire to keep warm.

"I'll get some wood," Darstan said.

"No, we better not," Rahg said. "When we were here, Rhaven made us go without fires because of the dorgans."

"I've heard what you said about the creatures," Darstan said. "but are they *that* bad? Can't we risk a fire?"

Melissara shook her head. "Rahg is right. I wouldn't do it. It's difficult to explain how dangerous they are and how futile fighting them with such a small force would be."

Chapter Eight

A JOURNEY THROUGH THE PAAREN

Melissara sat with her knees tucked under her chest, and her hands wrapped around them. She continually glanced all about, although she stood now and then to scan the landscape.

"What are you looking for?" Wisp asked.

"Dorgans," she said. "If you had fought them, you'd be looking too."

"They're that bad? Even for someone with your powers?"

Melissara took a moment, then spoke. "I don't know if you heard me tell Darstan, but at one time there were one hundred of us lost in here, including Lukaan. Before we got out, they killed almost eighty of us."

"With such a frightening prospect facing us, what do we do if we run into them?" Wisp asked.

"Run," Melissara said. "It's all we can do."

"That's not encouraging," Wisp said. "I'd be willing to wager these things can outrun us."

Melissara almost chuckled; instead, she frowned. "The discouraging part is you're right. We *can't* outrun them; they're fast, and they possess an excellent sense of smell."

"What can we do?"

"Keep watch. Listen. Position probes."

"Probes?"

"I've been placing them around us at night, for all the good it will do. It won't do much more than give us a short warning. The sound of the dorgans approaching is usually more warning than that, and during the day, they can be spotted coming from farther away unless the view is obstructed by something."

"I'm sorry I asked," Wisp said. "I think you've ruined my sleep at night."

"I'd rather ruin your sleep than our lives," she said. "The more people we have on alert, the better."

"I'll be happy to get to wherever it is we're going," Wisp said.

Melissara laughed. "Don't be in such a hurry. The Lights make the dorgans seem like pets. At least with the Book, they do."

After eating a cold breakfast of gathered fruits along with the bread they'd brought with them, they set off again.

They traveled for about half a day when Melissara said, "Remember to keep watch and look for any change of color on the horizon. Also listen for any rumbling, like a herd of horses running."

"It's nice that you care so much," Darstan said, "but somehow I suspect it's yourself you're worried about."

"Of course I'm worried about myself," Melissara said, "but we're all family. I'm concerned about all of us."

"All family? What do you mean by that?" Rahg asked.

Melissara laughed. "I guess you don't listen to idle gossip. My sisters and I discussed it before—most recently when Aentarra died."

"Discussed what?"

"We may as well stop for lunch," Melissara said. "I'll enlighten you once more."

They found an enclave of rocks offering good protection, not to mention a nearby valley lush with fruit trees and a stream of fresh water. "This looks like a good place," Melissara said, and plopped down on a large rock offering a good seat.

Rahg and Darstan returned from gathering fruit, and Wisp carried the water. Rahg handed her some fruit and sat at her side. "What were you going to tell us?"

Melissara sighed. "I said we were all family, because we are."

"And how is that?" Darstan asked.

She pointed to Rahg. "He is my sister's son—Aentarra, of course, not Mikkellana. And Wisp is as well."

Wisp sipped on his water, but he kept an eye on the horizon. "I heard Mikkellana say that, but there's no way, Melissara. I'd never seen Aentarra before a couple of years ago."

"That means nothing. My sister never was one to dote on someone, and it didn't matter who. But for better or worse, there is no question about you. No one else could have given you the powers of Stealth. Only her."

"And that leaves me," Darstan said. "Whose loins am I supposed to have come from?"

"Mine," Melissara said.

Darstan almost fell over. "What? That can't be. I was told Lukaan was my father. Your sisters told me."

Melissara nodded. "He was, Darstan. He raped me. I didn't want you growing up with him, so I made plans to sneak you out of Sethia; I didn't want you to be influenced by his ways, and I knew if I waited, you'd be too strong to get out through the shield."

"How did you do it?"

"I had a nice, caring couple take you out when you were a baby. I never saw you again until we met in Sethia, and despite the strength of Camissa's Persuasion—effective as it may have been— the reason I joined the fight against Lukaan was because of you."

Rahg gawked. "By all the . . . No wonder you're so strong, Dar. Lukaan *and* Melissara."

"It doesn't always work that way," Melissara said. "But sometimes it does. In this case, it obviously did."

Darstan got up and stood in front of Melissara. "You're saying I'm your child?"

Melissara lowered her head and spoke. "I'm both proud and sad to acknowledge it, but yes, you are my son. After carrying you for all that time, the only thing I wanted more than raising you was *not* raising you in Sethia."

"No matter what you say, I don't believe it," Darstan said.

Melissara pulled down her top, exposing a birthmark resembling a lightning bolt. "You have one of these behind your right knee," she said. "It's a du Savarra birthmark."

Darstan seemed shocked. He gritted his teeth. "And all that time, you couldn't have gotten me a message to let me know?"

She squared her jaw and stood face to face with Darstan. "And let you know you were the child of the most hated man in the known world? What would you have felt like then?"

Rahg placed his hand on Darstan's shoulder. "You wouldn't have wanted that, Dar. Remember how much we hated him. I wouldn't have wanted to know my mother was Aentarra, and she wasn't even that bad. She even helped us."

Wisp nodded. "I'll second what Rahg said, and not because he's my half brother, but because it's true."

Darstan paced while shaking his head. "I don't know. I just don't know."

"Now's the time to think about it," Melissara said. "There's no sense in going on if we can't leave the past in the past." She looked to Darstan. "Can you do that?"

Darstan paced more and stopped in front of her. "Don't expect me to call you my mother."

She smiled. "If this weren't such a serious topic, I'd laugh. As it is, I'll just say good decision, young man."

Melissara stood, concern on her face. "And now, I think we better be going. Quickly."

"Why so soon?" Rahg asked. "I'm still eating."

She pointed to the west. "Because dorgans are coming. I feel the rumbling"

Wisp raced to the top of the enclave and peered out. "And I see them," he said. "Let's go."

"Which way?" Rahg asked.

"North," Melissara said. "Toward those mountains. They'll offer better protection."

They started north at a fast pace. "Can you use your Stealth?" Melissara asked.

"For a while," Wisp said. "Everybody grab hold."

When everyone was touching, he used Stealth, and they disappeared. "I'm increasing speed so I don't run out of power. If we go fast enough, maybe it will last."

"Let's hope so," Rahg said. "I don't want to fight those things again."

They reached the mountains and found good cover behind several large boulders. Wisp let go of his Stealth and breathed deeply. "I didn't think we'd make it," Wisp said. "Keeping cover for four people is a lot tougher than protecting just me."

"For all our sakes, get better," Rahg said.

The dorgans advanced to where the others had stopped for lunch, looked around, then split into two groups. One group went due east, away from where they were, but the second group headed north, straight for them.

Wisp leaned close to Melissara and whispered. "What do we do now? Should we make a break for it?"

Melissara looked behind her, then to the west, then glanced at the dorgans. "There doesn't seem to be any place to hide, and if they see us, we're dead. There are far too many to fight, and they are too fast to outrun."

Wisp looked all around. "I don't see anywhere to hide."

"If they come in here, hiding won't do any good. Their sense of smell is too good. We'll have to stay here until they are almost on top of us, then risk using Stealth again."

"I'm afraid it won't last long enough."

"Then let's pray your fear gives you extra strength," Melissara said.

Ten or twelve dorgans approached at a quick pace, and all the while, they scoured the area around them. "Be ready," Melissara said.

Within moments they got to within thirty paces. "Now," she whispered, and all of them grabbed hold of Wisp.

"Hang on," he said, and used Stealth, turning them invisible.

The dorgans entered a moment later and came behind the rocks. One of them stopped and sniffed numerous times, then it went all around the small clearing as if searching. After several more moments, the dorgans left and continued on their northward path. When they were out of earshot, Melissara tapped Wisp's shoulder and said, "You can release it now."

Wisp let go of Stealth, and they all appeared. "That shouldn't have happened," Melissara said.

"What do you mean?" Rahg asked.

"I mean, they should have been able to smell us, but they didn't. And I know they tried because I saw one trying to find us."

Melissara continued watching the dorgans as they disappeared. "The only explanation is that your power has increased," she said.

"Increased? How?"

"I don't know how, but it happens. At the strongest level, like the level Aentarra had, you can't be seen, or heard, or tracked, or even Sensed by those with that power."

"I don't have that—"

"You must. Let's try it."

"I'm not getting near them again," Wisp said.

"You don't have to. Use Stealth, and once you've disappeared, make noise. Talk, cough, anything. If we can hear it, we'll know you don't have that part of the power. If you can't . . ." Melissara stopped. "Wait. Once you disappear, not only talk, but walk around, and we'll see if we can spot your tracks."

"Okay," Wisp said. "But give me a minute to rest."

Once he rested, Wisp announced he was ready, and in a moment, he disappeared. He waited a few seconds, then he said, "Hey, Rahg. Hey, Darstan. Can you hear me?" Then he said it louder. All the time, he stepped heavily on the ground surrounding them. After another moment, he reappeared. "Well?"

Melissara smiled. "Didn't hear a thing. Did you talk?"

"A lot. And loudly," he said. "And I stomped all over the ground." He looked where he had stepped as he said it. "Not a mark."

"Looks like we have our answer," Melissara said. "And it's a good answer."

She turned to Darstan. "Once I asked you how you stopped the Slicers from entering your mind and—"

"And I told you I had no idea," Darstan said.

"I know that, but how did you discover you had FearMist as a power?"

Darstan bolted up, embarrassed. "How did you know about that?"

"Aentarra told me long ago. And don't be embarrassed. It may prove valuable. We have never seen anyone with that power."

"Not even your father? Or—"

"Or *your* father?" Melissara said. "No, not even them."

"Valuable or not, I'm never using it again. After seeing the damage caused, I can't."

"That's a good vow to make, but don't be so hasty. There may come a time when you need a power such as that."

"I won't do it," Darstan said.

"We'll see. I understand your position, but between Wisp's

Stealth and your FearMist, I'm already feeling better about our chances against the Lights." She looked at Rahg and said, "Rahg, anything you're not telling us about the things you can do?"

"I wish there were," Rahg said. "But I'm afraid not."

Chapter Nine

THE JOURNEY CONTINUES

Wisp led the way from the hiding spot, and he set a brisk pace. "What do we do now? We can't risk too many encounters because I can't use Stealth that often."

"We need to do a better job of watching out for them," Melissara said. "Every time you take a step, look to the side or behind you. And listen at all times. If you listen well, you'll hear them from far off. Also, learn to *feel* the ground as you walk and especially as you sleep. If you pay attention, you'll soon be able to detect them from far away, and that's what we need."

Rahg moved alongside Melissara. "I'm not sure I want the amount of experience it would take to get good at recognizing them. I'll stick with trying to spot them in the distance."

"That's fine," Melissara said. "I'll bear the nighttime burden. You and your brother watch during the day."

"I guess that leaves me joining you at night," Wisp said.

After walking all afternoon, Darstan found a place to stop for supper. "Just ahead there's a small stream. Not much to eat, but I spotted some berries, and I think there are enough to make dinner if we have to."

"We've got plenty of bread," Rahg said. "I could live off bread for days."

"Good for you, brother, but I prefer something more solid. I'd love some meat."

"If we go another day with no sign of the dorgans, we'll try to get fresh meat and risk letting Darstan cook it."

"Sounds good to me," Darstan said. "Now I'll be on the alert for game as well as dorgans."

"Just remember that the dorgans take priority," Melissara said. "Game won't kill us."

After suffering through intense heat the following day, Melissara suggested they look for game since there had been no sign of the dorgans. Before long, Rahg spotted a few deer grazing in a small canyon to the west. "Doesn't get much easier than this," he said. "They're boxed in."

"I'll leave the task of securing the meat to you and Darstan," Wisp said. "I'll remain with Melissara."

Darstan and Rahg returned shortly with a large doe, more than enough for a few meals. "Shall we build a fire or—"

Melissara shook her head. "No fire. Darstan and I can cook it. If any dorgans are close by, they may not see our Fire, but they'd surely smell a campfire."

As they ate supper, Darstan looked at Melissara and posed a question. "Tell us about the Lights. How strong are they? How do you plan on killing them?"

Melissara finished chewing, wiped her hands, then paused before speaking. "The Lights are the ones who exiled us to this horrible place we're in right now. It's how we came upon your world."

"Your world connects to this place?" Rahg asked.

"Our *worlds*. There are seven of them, which is why there are seven Lights—one for each world. My father was the head one—the Light of Lights, he was named."

"What happened?" Wisp asked.

"To shorten the story, Lukaan and my father disagreed, and they started a war. That war lasted more than a hundred years, wreaking destruction on all the worlds. There was no neutrality; you were either for one and against the other, or you were the reverse."

Melissara stopped, but Wisp urged her on. "And . . ."

"And it continued until Lukaan killed my mother. That sent my father to the brink of madness. He set in place an elaborate plot, the first phase of which involved using Slicers—which had been banned—to kill millions upon millions of people on one of the worlds—Nagassa, home of Bolledar. He was one of Lukaan's allies and had been part of the attack on my mother."

"Then what?" Darstan asked.

"The Lights wanted the wars to end, so under the guise of a treaty, they lured both Lukaan and my father to a meeting in the Great Hall, where they used the Book to kill my father before exiling us."

"The Book?" Wisp asked. "I've heard you mention it, but what does it do?"

"Don't ask me to explain it because I can't, but when someone uses it and joins forces with another, their power becomes magnified. In this case, all five Lights used it, joining forces, hence their power grew by tenfold or even a hundred-fold. I don't know how much."

"How does a book produce powers like that?" Darstan asked.

"How do you and I have powers?" Melissara asked. "I don't think anyone knows *how* it works, but I know it does. I saw it work. I saw the Lights use the Book to take off my father's head."

"And where does Anciara come into this?" Rahg asked.

Melissara sighed as she bit into her food. "Lukaan followed her, and he wanted everyone else to do so. My father didn't believe in her or her teachings. That's what started the wars."

"Why didn't she help Lukaan?" Darstan asked.

"That's the kind of person—or goddess—you're dealing with. She's not to be trusted."

"How is any of this going to help us defeat Anciara?" Wisp asked.

Melissara gestured to Rahg. "First, we need to kill the Lights so Rahg is freed of his oath. He took an oath of life and death, which means if he fails to keep the oath, he dies."

"How is that possible?" Darstan asked.

"The same way the Book is possible, and the Slicers, and anything else associated with all this. I don't have the answers. I just have experience in that I've seen it work."

"I still don't understand how killing the Lights will help us kill Anciara," Wisp said.

"It won't. But the Book might. And once we kill them, we take the Book."

"How far until we get to Nelstar?" Rahg asked.

She shrugged. "No idea. It could be a day, a week, or a hundred years."

She took a few gulps of cool water. "Worst of all, we have no idea what we'll find when we get there. It's been a thousand years since I left. I have no inkling what progress they might have made, so we need to be ready for anything."

"Progress? What does that have to do with anything?" Wisp asked.

Melissara grinned. "Wisp, when I left Nelstar, there were tens of thousands, if not hundreds of thousands, who had powers. People were accustomed to Shifting not only from place to place on their own world, but many of them were able to Shift to other worlds. Slicers were used at will as a means to send messages in the form of thoughts to others, even if they were worlds away, and they did it in seconds. Some people possessed the ability to propel objects across the ground and even through the air by thought alone. They commanded what were called 'moving carts' which held other people inside and were used for transportation."

Wisp shook his head. "This is all a little much for me, Melissara. I don't think I understand a lot of what you're saying."

Melissara smiled. "Don't worry, Wisp. You'll see when we get there. It might even be a revelation for me, depending on what's changed."

"We don't have any plan for killing them," Rahg said.

"That's because we have no idea what we face," Melissara said. "We have to see what obstacles there are before we can overcome them."

"And once we know the obstacles, how do we kill the Lights. From what you said, they were all pretty strong," Darstan said.

"It's true that they are strong, and I'm sure they're stronger now. But we have some advantages."

"Like what?" Darstan asked.

"Our biggest advantage may be Wisp and his Stealth. If things are the same as when I was last there, no one has Stealth, and if that's still the case, they couldn't possibly anticipate anyone having it. Not after more than a thousand years."

"And the other advantage?"

"You, Darstan."

"Me?"

"You are not only strong, you have FearMist, which they will *never* anticipate. I've never known anyone to have that power, and I doubt they have either."

"You think it will work on them?" Darstan asked.

"I see no reason why it wouldn't. It should be the same as all other powers, and all of them work on anyone. And as far as I know, there is nothing that could block FearMist."

"Suppose they surrounded themselves with a Shield that doesn't let the mist inside?"

"To do that, they would have to anticipate its use. Since they don't know it exists, they can't very well anticipate it."

"Those advantages seem hopeful at best," Rahg said. "I'd rather have something more definitive."

"Hopeful, yes. Maybe even promising. But those advantages—if they are advantages— are not a reason to shout for joy, as you so wisely stated," Melissara said. "I would also like to have something more definitive."

Darstan walked to the stream and washed up, then returned and sat on a rock between Rahg and Wisp. "There's no sense in discussing it until we get there. Let's focus on that."

"I agree," Melissara said. "Let's concentrate on getting to Nelstar safely. We can decide what to do after that."

"Don't let those dorgans get you, Melissara. We'll be relying on you for strategy," Wisp said. "I guess that means we'll have to protect you."

Melissara got up and made her way to the stream. She smiled, and said, "That's the way I planned it, Wisp."

"Good," Wisp said, "Then you take first watch—or listen—and wake me when it's my turn."

Chapter Ten

THE SEARCH FOR MIKKELLANA

The captain of the guard paced furiously while waiting to see Takar. After almost ten minutes, Takar's door creaked open. "You asked to see me, Brenner?"

Wiping sweat from his brow, Brenner stepped forward. "I did, Force Commander. I received a summons from Anciara, asking me —or should I say demanding that I visit her at her palace."

Takar thought for a moment before he spoke. "Do you still have family in the city?"

Brenner nodded. "A wife and two sons. And a sister."

"First, do not mention them under any means, not even the pain of torture. Not unless you want them to suffer a similar fate."

"But, sir—"

"I can only guess what you were going to say, but it makes no difference. If she wants to see you, there's not much to do. You can try escaping, but you'd need to take your family with you, and it's doubtful you'd be able to escape. Your best bet is to see her and tell the truth."

Brenner gulped and saluted. "Yes, sir. I'll do it."

As Brenner walked away, Takar shook his head and thought, *you've been a good soldier, Brenner. May the Maker watch over you.*

~

Anciara took her morning meal on a patio outside what used to be the king's palace. As she nibbled on fresh fruit, the guard announced Brenner's arrival.

"Captain, how nice of you to visit. How are you this morning?"

Sweat beaded on his forehead and rolled down his cheeks. "Fine, My Lady. I understand you wanted to see me."

Anciara laughed. "Indeed, I did. I am curious as to the whereabouts of Mikkellana and those who travel with her. In case you're not familiar with their names, they are the ones with powers."

Brenner suddenly felt feverish, and the sweating increased. "I don't know, My Lady, and that's the truth. We saw them here days ago, but they disappeared."

"And you don't know where they went?"

Brenner found the courage to look up. He almost got enough courage to look into her eyes. "No, My Lady, I don't."

"Such a pity," Anciara said. "For one so young that is."

Brenner gulped, not knowing what to expect. "My Lady?"

"Do you have family, Captain?"

Brenner wondered if she could determine a lie, but then he remembered what Takar told him. "No, My Lady, I was never so fortunate."

"That's odd. The people I spoke with said you had a lovely wife and two sons. One said you even had a sister."

"My Lady, I—"

"Note that I said *had*, Captain. I paid them a visit this morning. They were sorry to hear of your passing."

Brenner gulped, then he turned and ran. He didn't make it five steps before he was wrapped in a shield, unable to move. Anciara finished her fruit, then walked past him. "I was going to strike you with Lightning, but I think I'll just let you suffocate. It's much more painful."

Tirzinitzia met with Anciara at the next intersection of hallways. She shook her head.

"You have nothing?" Anciara asked.

"I have a plan, but nothing solid."

"I would have preferred a solution, but I'll consider a plan to be better than nothing." She nibbled on another piece of fruit Tirzinitzia brought in from Khatara. "I hope this is better than this morning's selection. Now tell me of this plan you think so much of."

Tirzinitzia walked faster while focusing her power on controlling her trembling. "We know that they are hiding, and it's likely someplace neither of us has been to before, which means we can't Shift there."

Anciara nodded. "I agree. The logic makes sense."

"Since that must be the case, I suggest we go to all the major cities and question people. A demonstration must be made in each city to show the people that you are serious—intent on discovering our quarry's whereabouts."

"A demonstration?"

"Kill a few, or a few dozen, citizens. Enough to make an impact. Mikkellana would likely have put fear into them, but I doubt she did anything other than display her power. I'm almost positive she didn't harm anyone."

Anciara smiled. "I think I like you. I may heed your advice. When people see others die, they grow afraid, much more afraid."

"In that case, I suggest we begin in Khatara—maybe Jattan Kir —then go to Pomanda, followed by Genda. If we get nothing, we visit the smaller towns. Sooner or later, someone will tell us."

A servant opened the gates, and Anciara walked through. "Let's begin, then. You'll have to provide the Shift points."

"I think Jattan Kir may be a good place to start. It's the farthest away, and not many people have visited there. In fact, I don't even have a Shift point, though we could go to Khatara and then Sight Shift."

"Let's go then," Anciara said, and reached her hand out. Tirzinitzia took it, then Shifted to Khatara, reappearing near what had been the guard's barracks in the northern part of the city.

Tirzinitzia looked around, pausing for thought. "We might hold off on going to Jattan Kir. I thought of something while we Shifted. There are a lot of people at the port. If we go there and question them, we may find some who saw Mikkellana or the rest of her group. It's possible they used the seaport to leave instead of Shifting."

"Lead the way," Anciara said.

Tirzinitzia Shifted by sight until they got to the port. Crowds of people were already gathered at the markets nearby and at the docks where workers loaded cargo onto waiting ships.

Tirzintizia struck a nearby building with a bolt of Lightning to draw the crowd's attention.

Within moments, a large number of people gathered around her. Anciara stepped forward. "I know you are familiar with the people who were here before, the ones with powers. I'm not blaming you for any assistance you provided. I am, however, asking for your help. I need to find these people, and I'm sure you can steer me in the right direction."

Many in the crowd turned and looked at each other, then back at Anciara. "We have no idea," a guard who stood at the front said.

Tirzinitzia glanced at Anciara and nodded. Anciara wrapped the guard in a thin covering of Shield and squeezed. Within moments, the man gasped, then collapsed. Soon after, he died.

Anciara took a step forward. "I think the rest of you need to give more thought to your answers. That man's response was unsatisfactory."

"But we don't know where they went," someone in the crowd

said.

Anciara spun toward the sound of the voice. "Who said that?"

When no one admitted to saying it, she asked again. "*Who said it?*"

She waited a moment, then glared at all of them, fixing the crowd with her gaze. "If the person who said it doesn't step forward, I'll be forced to kill all of you."

An older man near the center of the crowd slowly made his way forward. He walked up, stood before Anciara, and said, "I said it, but it was true. We don't know where they went. The last we saw, they were here fighting Lukaan, then they either sailed away or just disappeared. We haven't seen them since."

Anciara stared. She looked at Tirzinitzia, eyebrows raised.

"Please, My Lady. Spare us. We told you what we know."

Anciara paced, hands folded behind her back. "I think you may have told the truth. I am inclined to believe you." She turned and paced north and south, stopping in front of the man who had spoken. "I'm going to allow you to live, but if I find you lied, I'll be back to kill all of you."

The man gulped. "Yes, My Lady. If we hear anything, how do we get a message to you?"

Anciara laughed. "Now you have confirmed my decision. I know it was the right one. In the event anyone hears *anything*, get a message to Sykor. It will reach me."

The man bowed low and backed toward the crowd where all the people stood with heads bowed.

"And remember, from now on, you worship me. No other." Anciara turned to Tirzinitzia. "Take us to the next location."

"Where do you want to go?"

"The closest large city to Sykor," she said. "We'll go through all the cities until we find them."

Tirzinitzia took hold of Anciara and Shifted to Pomanda, appearing in the central plaza.

Anciara moved to the sculptures, standing in front of the

Goddess of Death, where a small crowd stood. "I'm thrilled you admire my likeness," she said, "though I'm not fond of how it depicts me."

People faced her, some gasping, others looking on with curiosity. "Now that I have your attention," Anciara said, "I want to know where Mikkellana and her followers went. And I *do not* want to hear 'I don't know.' That answer is not acceptable."

"But we don't know," one man said.

Anciara lashed out with a narrowly shaped strike of BlackFire. He fell immediately, screaming as it burned through him.

"I'll ask again," she said. "Where are they?"

The crowd quieted down, followed by silence. Anciara glared, and she waited for answers. After several moments, she raised her hands and was about to strike when a man stepped forward.

"Genda," he said. "Don't blame us because we really don't know, but I heard the people of Genda know; they're the ones who took her to sea on their ships."

Anciara let the people go, but not before issuing a warning. "Be advised that if I don't get what I need in Genda, I'll be back, and when I return, all of you will suffer. The whole city will suffer."

"Genda knows," a woman shouted. "All you need to do is force them to tell."

"Let's go, Tirzinitzia. Genda awaits."

Anciara and Tirzinitzia Shifted to the docks, which were bustling with activity—people loading and unloading cargo, rigging sails, and corralling feedstock on board.

Tirzinitzia approached a large group and again issued a bolt of Lightning. Once she had their attention, Anciara took over.

Anciara moved alongside Tirzinitzia and stared. "I have it on good authority that one or more of you know how I may find Mikkellana. I need to know." She lowered her voice. "If you tell me, nothing will happen. If not . . ."

One of the older sailors stepped forward and spat to his side. "We don't know nothin'. None of us do."

"So sorry to hear that," Anciara said. "In that case, I'll have to kill you." She fired a shaft of Fire at him, causing him to fall quickly, wailing as he did.

When he stopped moaning, Anciara addressed the men. "Now that you have seen I expect results, make sure you do not fail me. I will ask again. Does anyone know where I can find Mikkellana and her friends?"

No one stepped forward, and Tirzinitzia took hold of a large sailor in the front row. She walked him toward Anciara, but before they reached her, he bolted. Anciara cut him down, but this time she used Lightning, not Fire.

She turned back to the crowd. "I'll ask one more time. If I don't get the answer I want, all of you will die. *All* of you."

Anciara paced. "I will walk from one end of the dock to the other. When I'm done, I'll start the killing. I'll wrap a Shield around you, then fill the Shield with Fire. It's not a good way to die."

She walked to the end of the dock, then started back. When she hit the other end, she turned and surrounded the men with a shield. "I'll count to five," she said.

"One. Two. Three."

"Okay, hold it, a voice from the last row said."

"Step up here."

The man moved through the others, drawing glares as he did. Eventually, he reached the front. "She's in Entiria."

"Where is Entiria?"

He gestured toward the sea. "Way out there. Across the Sea of the Lost."

"That's good. But how do I get there?"

The man shrugged. "I don't know, and that's the truth. Some of the men here took her, but I don't know how to get to it."

He trembled. Tears dripped from his eyes. "Somebody here knows. A lot of them were involved. Ol' Crazy led them, so he knows for sure."

"Ol' Crazy?"

"Jacopo Sennaro. He's a captain. Used to be a good one. He was still good enough to take her to Entiria."

"Where can I find Ol' Crazy?"

The man turned and pointed to the far left. "Right there. Next to the last one."

Anciara pointed at Sennar, her finger beckoning him forward. "How do I find her?"

"No idea," he said. "I don't know what he's talking about, and I'm guessin' he don't neither."

"I'll ask once more. How do I find her?"

Sennar rubbed his hand against a cheek that had scarred and burnt for years. One that was now smooth and clean because of Mikkellana. I'm not about to give up the good Lady. "I still don't know," Sennar said. "Nobody's told me since the last time you asked."

Anciara issued a thin stream of Fire at his side, searing a deep gouge. Sennar winced, and his knees buckled, but it didn't break his resolve. He glared at Anciara and gritted his teeth. "You old witch. If ya think a little fire is gonna pry somethin' from these old bones, you don't know Jacopo Sennaro. I been burnt before; in fact, I eat fire strikers to win wagers."

"In that case, I'm sorry," Anciara said, and she struck with Lightning and then a ForceBolt, dropping Sennar in less than a moment.

He tried to strike her before he fell, but it was too late.

Afterward, Anciara faced the crowd. "I'm going to close the Shield now. When it's done, I'm going to fill it with Fire. If I have a satisfactory response beforehand, everyone lives. If not . . ."

The Shield began to close around the men standing on the docks. Just before closing, one of them hollered and moved toward the front.

"I can take you there," he said. "I was with Sennar the first time."

Anciara looked left and right, her gaze settling on a ship being loaded with cargo. "We'll take that one," she said. "Gather a crew. We leave in the morning."

"What time?"

"Dawn," Anciara said. "Not a moment later. And I better have a deluxe cabin prepared for me when we leave."

"Don't worry, My Lady, we'll be ready."

Anciara walked away, followed by Tirzinitzia. They went to a local tavern that offered rooms for the night. "Two rooms," she said. "And they better be clean."

The innkeeper looked as if he might say something, but Tirzinitzia, standing behind Anciara, shook her head as a warning. The man scowled but said no more, just handed the room keys to Anciara.

Once inside the room, Anciara addressed Tirzinitzia. "You have no problem doing what has to be done to your old friends?"

"I wouldn't call them friends, My Lady. They are acquaintances at best." Tirzinitzia moved to let the light from the window strike her face, and she turned her cheek to face Anciara. "You see this?" she asked, and then turned to the other side. "And this?"

Anciara nodded. "I've wondered about them."

"Courtesy of Lukaan, but I strongly suspect Melissara played no small part in making it happen. There is no love lost on her."

Anciara smiled. "That warms my heart, Tirzinitzia. I always worry about past friends or acquaintances, but knowing that gives me assurances."

"You need not worry, My Lady."

"Are there any of them worth worrying about?"

"I am intimately familiar with Melissara and to a lesser extent, her sister. Neither of them are strong enough to be trouble, however, the boy, the one who used the ColdFire against you, *he* is strong. Very strong."

"How strong?"

"I doubt you knew her, but he single-handedly killed Sendra, who was as strong as I am, if not more so. And I heard he did it without straining himself."

Anciara nodded. "Indeed. I can confirm his strength. His is the only power that felt to be a threat." Anciara poured a glass of wine for each of them and handed one to Tirzinitzia. "Mind you, I never felt vulnerable, but then again, I had been prepared. If he had caught me unaware, it may have been different. He's one who will have to go first."

Tirzinitzia drank her wine, then walked to the door. "If My Lady has nothing else for me, I am going to retire. It will be a long day tomorrow."

Anciara brushed her hand in the air. "Go on. I will be waking you early."

Anciara rapped on Tirzinitzia's door just after dawn. "Time to go," she said, then proceeded down the stairs.

Tirzinitzia appeared a moment later and quickly caught up with her. "It looks as if it will be a good day for a sea voyage."

Anciara approached the docks, walked to the ship they planned to use, and called for the captain. "You're ready?"

He bowed low. "I am, My Lady. We're packed with supplies and loaded with livestock."

She started up the ramp that led to the ship. "Let's be off then. I despise wasting time."

As Anciara went aboard, the captain shouted orders. "Raise them sails, ya old tars. I want 'em full mast before the next rays of that warm sun strike us. And haul up that anchor before I toss ya to the sharks. Ya need to listen to what I say, and ya need to figure out what I'm gonna say. Else you'll be scrubbin' decks instead of eatin'. That much I can promise."

Tirzinitzia rested on the rail alongside Anciara. "Sounds as if you may have gotten a good one to captain your ship."

"Too early to tell," Anciara said. "We'll see."

Chapter Eleven

ANOTHER VISIT WITH THE GODS

Rahg approached Melissara as she finished her breakfast. "I know you're in a hurry, and no one wants to get to Nelstar sooner than I do, but I need to make a stop."

Melissara set her mug on a flat rock and looked up at him, apparently bewildered. "Stop where? And why? What could you possibly need to stop for in this place?"

Rahg hesitated, then he spoke in a voice barely above a whisper. "To see the gods. I—"

"What? Are you insane? We're in the middle of battling one of them, and you want to stop and have a friendly visit?"

Rahg nodded. "I understand, and I know what you're thinking, but it's something I have to do. It may even help us in our struggle against Anciara."

"How so?" Melissara asked.

"I've been here before," Rahg said. "The three gods are against Anciara, and they helped me grow my powers. They also provided information that helped us."

"You think they'll help you?"

"I do. It's worth a try. The only thing at risk is my life, and that's mine to risk."

"I'd let him do it," Darstan said as he stepped forward. "The last time they gifted him some good powers."

"Do you know where to go?" Melissara asked.

Rahg grabbed hold of the amulet around his neck. "This will tell me. It hasn't been wrong yet."

"I hate to spend any more time in this place than we have to, but I guess we can spare the time if you think it will be useful."

"I'm sure it will," Rahg said, and pointed to the west. "We have to go that way."

After breakfast, Rahg led the way west and, for the rest of the morning, all went well. Sometime around noon, Rahg spotted the mountain. "There it is," he said. "That's where we need to go. To the top of that."

"The top? What's up there?"

"They are," Rahg said. "There is a cave with paths inside that lead to the different gods."

"Darstan and I will go with you."

Rahg shook his head. "I have to go alone. No one else may enter. Aentarra tried once, but even she couldn't get in."

Melissara looked at Darstan, and he nodded. "Rahg's right. We have no choice."

By supper time, they reached the base of the mountain. Rahg stopped and built a fire. "I need to eat before I go up. One time, I was gone for days."

"Then let's eat," Melissara said. "When we're finished, I suggest you rest for the night and eat a meal in the morning before continuing your journey."

R ahg ate breakfast, then started his long climb up the mountain. He dreaded making this journey, had no desire to see the gods despite them having granted him powers when he visited before. No matter how they presented themselves, Rahg didn't trust them.

Hours after starting the climb, he reached the top. As he scaled the last hurdle, the gaping maw of the cavern awaited, standing before him as if he had been expected. With much reluctance, he slowly made his way toward the entrance. No light emerged from the cave, but still Rahg moved forward. This is the first time he wasn't afraid. When he entered the cavern, the dragon was gone. It wasn't guarding the entrance as usual.

He paused to compose himself before going in, then took one step at a time, expecting to encounter the dragon at any moment. After going far enough to be surrounded in darkness, he once again slowed his pace.

Rahg breathed deeply and slowly, but he continued, though his pace had slowed to almost a crawl. Just as he was about to turn around and go back, a light shone from ahead. He followed the beacon until he arrived at a familiar juncture—the merging of the three paths he'd encountered previously. Now all he had to do was decide which one to take.

With only short deliberation, Rahg opted to take the path leading straight ahead, and as he progressed, the light at the end increased, lighting the way even more.

At the end of the path, a door with light emanating from underneath stood as the only way to proceed. He reached for the handle, hand shaking, and pressed the latch to open it. A blinding light forced him to close his eyes, and then he raised his hand to provide a shield for them.

Once inside, the door closed on its own, shutting as if someone slammed it. Rahg jumped, startled by the sudden closing.

Rahg felt a powerful presence, but he saw nothing. *"Is this the dragon? Is it you?"*

"What makes you think so?"

"I always encounter the dragon first," Rahg said.

"The dragon is but an illusion placed by another to keep

people from seeing us. Now that you've conquered your fear, the dragon will no longer appear."

"*Who put the illusion there?*"

No one answered him, but the voice of one of the gods reverberated in the small room. The echo produced was so loud it proved painful. "***Why are you here again?***"

Rahg focused on the spot where the voice came from. Three images appeared on the cavern's wall, each of them wearing a frightening scowl. "*I came to ask for help so we can defeat Anciara.*"

"***What kind of help?***" It was a different voice this time, but which god had spoken, he didn't know.

"*As I said, help to defeat Anciara. She's been freed, and we need to stop her.*"

Laughter erupted from one of the gods, and a moment later, the others joined in. "***We heard what you said. What we want to know is what you think you can do to stop her?***" one said.

"***There's nothing you can do,***" said another.

"***Set us free, and we will do more than help. We'll defeat her ourselves.***"

Rahg shook his head. "*No. I can't do that. But if you help us defeat her first, then—*"

"***If we help you, you'll free us?***"

Rahg thought for a moment, then nodded. "*If you help, I'll think about it.*"

The one in the center, spoke. "***I am Zukar. We are going to put a shield around you so we may discuss things.***" After he said that, all sounds faded, then disappeared.

~

The gods conferred with each other, while Rahg waited. It seemed as if hours passed, though it may have been days. The light grew blindingly bright, then Zukar spoke again.

"***We have decided. You will be granted more help.***"

Rahg felt relieved. "*Thank you. What suggestions do you have on how to defeat her?*"

"**Before we grant you aid, there are things you must agree to.**"

"*What?*"

"**If we give you power to help defeat her, you must return to set us free.**"

Rahg thought for a moment, but only a moment. "*I can't swear to that. I'll need to talk to Darstan and the others. If they agree, I'll do it, but if they don't, I can't.*"

"**Defeat her yourself, then.**"

Somehow, Rahg found the courage to say, "*Free yourself, then.*"

"**We can kill you right now,**" Zukar said.

"*And how will that help you get free? If you kill me, you will still be stuck here with no one to help you get free.*"

The cavern floor rumbled. Even the walls shook. "**Very well, you shall have your power, but we expect to be freed. You better be persuasive when you discuss this with your friends.**"

Rahg bowed his head. "*I will,*" he said. He waited for a chance to speak, then addressed the gods. "*If my friends agree, how am I supposed to set you free?*"

The floor again rumbled under his feet, almost making him stumble. Zukar spoke. "**You need to enter the bottom floor of the obelisk in Entiria. In the deepest part of the room in the far north, there is a portal to this world. We can access the obelisk, but the door was made to seal us in. You must open the door so we may be free.**"

"*I can't promise you anything,*" Rahg said, "*but if my friends agree, I'll do it.*"

"**Then make sure your friends agree,**" Zomnel said.

"**We will grant you the ultimate in strength for a Shielder. You will now be able to use Spirals.**"

"*What are Spirals?*"

"**Spirals are the utmost in offense. They can go through**

almost anything. Very little can stop them. They are equivalent to ColdFire."

"Can Anciara can stop them?" Rahg asked.

"You will penetrate her shields as if they weren't there," Zukar said.

Rahg bowed low. *"Thank you. I'll make good use of this."*

"That's not all," Zomnar said. *"You will surely suffer casualties during the battle. To deal with them, we grant you the ultimate in Healing."*

Rahg appeared stunned. *"Healing?"*

"Brace yourself," Zomnar said.

Rahg placed one hand against the wall behind him and his other hand against the wall to the side. No sooner had he done it than the pain began. His skin felt as if it were being peeled off, and his bones cracked and seemed to move inside him. Rahg screamed as his knees buckled, feeling as if they'd been struck by a mallet.

"No," he yelled. "I don't want it."

His cries fell on deaf ears as the agony continued. His eyes bulged, and at one point, he felt they would be expelled from their sockets. When he thought he couldn't take it any more, it stopped.

Rahg fell to his knees, his hands running over his body to check that all was still there. *"What . . . what was that?"*

"Nothing worthwhile comes without pain," Zomnel said. *"What you felt was the consequence of absorbing new powers so quickly—Healing and Spirals. Now go and finish your mission. Then, return and free us."*

"Don't make us wait long," Zukar said.

Rahg bowed as he backed up, then he left and went back down the mountain. He surprised the others when he entered the camp.

Melissara stood and greeted Rahg. "You were gone for six days! Did everything go all right?"

"It did," Rahg said. "In fact, they gave me new powers. Something called Spirals, and new powers of Healing too."

Melissara spun around, looking in all directions. "Spirals! I thought they were only a legend."

"You've heard of them?" Darstan asked.

"I've heard of them, but only in children's tales and legends from ages ago. Some say the First Ones had Spirals along with Fear-Mist and other powers, but I've never known anyone else who had those powers."

"They said I was to set them free when we're done."

"You can't do that," Melissara said. "Setting them free may be as dangerous as facing Anciara, something we can't afford to risk. It's questionable if we can beat Anciara; I doubt if we could successfully do battle with three of them."

Rahg nodded. "All right. There will be time to consider that later. For now, let's focus on what we have to do on Nelstar."

Chapter Twelve

NEARING NELSTAR

Wisp rubbed sleep from his eyes and looked at the others, all tucked into their bedrolls. He gathered some wood in the hopes Melissara would okay a fire to cook breakfast, and he kept as quiet as he could while doing so. On the third excursion, as he returned with an armload of twigs, Darstan greeted him.

"Being a little optimistic, aren't you?"

"Those without optimism have no hope," Wisp said.

"You sound like a scholar," Darstan said. "But I know you're not, so quit trying to fool me."

"Don't fool yourself. Opinions are usually formed on how a person acts, not who they are."

Darstan laughed. "Wisp, you can act like a scholar all day long, but you'll still be a thief."

Melissara stirred. "I'm amazed that you two have lived as long as you have and not been killed."

"For what?" Wisp asked.

"For making so much noise when people are sleeping. Have you never heard of whispering?"

"Whispering is for secrets," Wisp said.

Melissara glared. "Then consider it a secret that you are up when I'm sleeping."

"No sense in keeping it a secret now," Wisp said, and kicked Rahg's leg to rouse him.

Darstan laughed and kicked Rahg's other leg. "Get up, brother."

Wisp made a pleading look to Melissara. "Well, My Lady? Is a fire in order?"

Melissara laughed. "For mercy's sake, why not? If the dorgans find us, so be it."

"Darstan, get the meat ready. We're going to eat like kings today," Wisp said.

Darstan placed the twigs in an ordered style topped by larger pieces of wood, then he lit the fire by issuing a flame from his arm. They had gathered dry wood so it would minimize smoke, but a small amount still rose from the campfire.

After eating her meal, Melissara stood. She looked in all directions, then said, "I think we should go east."

"Any reason for that decision?" Rahg asked.

She shook her head. "A hunch, that's all. No reason."

Darstan said, "I think we should go north."

"And the reason for that decision?" Melissara asked.

"The Slicers," Darstan said.

"Slicers? What about them?"

Darstan hesitated, then said, "I know this sounds crazy, but last night they told me where to go."

Melissara stared for a long time before saying, "If the Slicers said go north, let's go north. I'm not going to argue."

They walked until it was time to eat, then sat to share a meal and some water. "Tell us more about powers," Darstan said. "Like what?" Melissara asked.

"Like what determines the powers a person gets. For example, you said Wisp and Rahg were both offspring of Aentarra. Why do they have different abilities? Wisp has Stealth, and Rahg has Shielding."

"The short answer, Darstan, is I don't know. I've seen many people who *did not* have powers their parents possessed, and other people who had the same. An example is my own family. I can't use Shield, but Mikkellana has extensive Shielding, although she has no offensive powers. At the same time, Aentarra possessed both. No one but Mikkellana had any degree of Healing though."

"If you can't heal, and Lukaan couldn't heal, how is it that I healed Mikkellana?"

Melissara mulled the question as she finished eating. "It's a question I've been pondering since I heard about it from my sister. You shouldn't be able to heal unless you got it from my father, which means the ability is within me, but has never shown itself. Then again, you shouldn't have the ability to use FearMist either. All I can say is that since Healing was in the bloodline, it came to you that way. Following the same logic, I presume that someone in my past, at some time, had the ability to use FearMist. The only other option I can think of is that FearMist is an extension of another power, one that no one else has reached."

Melissara took a few more bites, then broached the subject again. "I can see the Healing because it was in the blood; my father could heal. But no one I know, or even heard about, could use FearMist, so I think it has to be an advanced stage of another power."

"So I should be thrilled about that?" Darstan asked.

"I don't know if I'd be so hasty as to say 'thrilled,' Darstan. Some powers, especially the more powerful ones, take something from you. ColdFire is one of them. Every time it's used, it takes something from the user. What FearMist does, I don't know. But I'd bet it does something, and I'd bet it's something that's not good."

"I think we've discussed this more than enough," Wisp said. "Let's move on and find our way to Nelstar."

Melissara stood and brushed off her clothes. "I agree. We need to go."

They walked the rest of the afternoon and well into the evening. As they were about to stop for supper, Wisp held up his hands, signaling them to stop.

"What is it?" Melissara asked.

"I feel something, that familiar rumbling. It's far off, but it's definitely there."

Melissara put her ear to the ground and listened. "Don't make any noise," she said. "Let me listen."

Darstan and Rahg remained still, as did Wisp until she rose. "You were right, Wisp. No doubt it's them, and they're coming fast. We need to move quickly."

Rahg's voice contained panic. "Which way?"

"I say we go north, but that's just my opinion," Darstan said. "Melissara?"

"I'm not going to argue," she said. "I haven't heard differently, so let's move it."

Wisp moved forward at a quick pace, followed by the rest of them. "We can't stop for anything. Keep moving."

"If they get too close, you're going to have to use Stealth."

"As tired as I am, it won't last long."

"That's fine. We may only need a moment," Melissara said. "If we're lucky, that is."

Darstan pointed to a thick copse of trees a short distance away. "They're going to catch up regardless of what we do. I say we hide in those trees. If they get close, Wisp can use Stealth."

"Sounds good to me," Rahg said, and turned toward the trees.

"Go in as deep as you can," Melissara said. "We need every advantage we can get."

They ran deep into the trees and hid behind a few of the larger ones. "No noise," Melissara said. "Get next to Wisp, and if they enter the trees, take hold so he can hide us."

The dorgans approached the trees, circled them, then started to move away. After only a few paces, one of the dorgans stopped and turned, sniffing.

"Don't move," Melissara whispered.

After a moment of sniffing, the dorgan turned back toward the stand of trees. Half a dozen others followed.

Melissara took Rahg by the hand and edged closer to Wisp. "Take hold, Rahg. You too, Darstan."

All of them took a firm grip on Wisp and waited.

Seven of the dorgans entered the trees, searching behind each one as they slowly made their way deeper into the copse. When they got halfway in, Wisp Cloaked.

The dorgan in the lead stopped and lifted its head. The ones following did the same, glancing about and sniffing, definitely searching.

The dorgans continued moving deeper, causing Wisp and the others to stir nervously. "Keep still," Melissara whispered. "I know Stealth protects us, but let's not trust it entirely."

The lead dorgan got to within a few steps before turning west. It stopped in a small clearing, raised its head, and sniffed the air. A moment later, it turned, growling loudly. The growl must have been a signal because it drew the others to its side.

They moved forward, seven abreast, in a slow, methodical fashion and headed straight toward Wisp and the others.

"I think they sense us," Wisp said. "I don't know how, but I think they do."

"Prepare to attack," Melissara said. "Rahg, you erect the best shield you can. Use the trees to brace it. Darstan, wait until they're bunched together, and then use ColdFire; I'll use BlackLighting and BlackFire."

"What about me?" Wisp asked.

"The best you can do is to rest up and recharge your Stealth. I'm sure we'll need it."

"Rahg, put up your shield, and when it's done, let me know so Wisp can drop the Stealth. Darstan, prepare. As soon as the dorgans bump into Rahg's shield, attack."

The lead dorgan walked headfirst into the shield, causing it to step back. When the others came to investigate, Melissara instructed Rahg to drop the shield, then she fired a wall of Black-Fire at the dorgans. It was wide enough to cover the entire group. Simultaneously, Darstan issued ColdFire.

The Fire struck with a roar, setting two of them aflame and bringing down one of them. The ColdFire did better, toppling two of the dorgans and injuring two others.

The lead dorgan let out a howl that shook the limbs from the trees. In the distance, another group of dorgans stopped and turned. They seemed to listen, then rushed to aid the others.

"Wisp, are you almost ready?" Melissara shouted.

Wisp focused on using Stealth, but nothing happened. "Not even close," he said.

"Then run," Melissara said. "We can hold them for a few moments, not much longer."

"I'm not leaving."

"There's nothing for you to do here," Melissara said. "Go."

As the second group of dorgans entered the trees, an arrow struck the frontrunner's throat. More arrows hit the necks of the others. Before they went ten steps further, two of them fell, frothing at the mouth.

"Kyra!" Rahg shouted.

To the left of the dorgans, a band of krengs hid behind the trees, shooting arrows at the dorgans and dropping them as if they were deer.

Melissara fired BlackLightning at the few remaining in the first pack and looked to Rahg. "How is that possible?"

"Kyra was with us in Sethia," Rahg said. "When we got out,

Rhaven gave her jars of his poison to use with arrows. It kills anything. Remember, we left more for her at the portal?"

"Thank the gods," Melissara said. "I've never seen anything but brute force kill them."

Darstan and Melissara resumed their attacks, but this time on the new group of dorgans. Before long, between the poison from the arrows and Melissara and Darstan's attacks, the dorgans had fallen.

Kyra approached, trailed by ten of her pack. She bowed to Rahg. "How is my friend?"

Rahg didn't know if she meant him or Rhaven, but since he was the one here, he assumed it was him. He bowed even lower than she had. "I'm fine, Kyra. And I'm glad to see you are doing well."

A guttural growl came from her. "Rhaven's gift has been more than a blessing from the gods. By using it, we can defeat the dorgans."

"As I saw," Rahg said. He spread his arms wide. "And we thank you for your help. It was timely. We left you more poisoned darts where Rhaven said we would. Enough for many arrows."

Kyra bowed low. "Your friend is true to his word. But tell me, why are you here? Do you hunt the same one as before?"

Rahg smiled. "No, he's dead, Kyra."

Kyra bowed again. "The news pleases me. But since you are here, there must be something of import. Be careful on your journey. The dorgans present much danger, and we may not be nearby the next time."

"We'll be off then," Rahg said, and bowed to say farewell.

As they walked out, still heading north, Melissara asked Rahg, "Do you know much of this poison that beast spoke of?"

"We've seen Rhaven use it more than a few times," Darstan said. "It is very effective on people, and obviously on dorgans. I don't know how it would work on others."

"You mean like Anciara?" Melissara asked.

Darstan stopped, smiling. "That hadn't occurred to me, but it is a thought. Why wouldn't it work on her?"

"How do we test it?" Wisp asked.

"If we had some, we could test it on the Lights. Since we don't, we'll have to wait until we return."

"We do have some," Wisp said. "When we visited the Lorns, they gave me some of the darts Rhaven uses and some poison to use with them. I have enough to try."

Melissara smiled as broadly as she had for ages. "That may be good, Wisp. If it doesn't work, we've lost nothing. If it does . . ."

"Now all we've got to do is make it to Nelstar alive," Rahg said.

Melissara sobered up. "There is that."

WE NEED ANOTHER SHIP

Captain Fernando did the last checks to ensure all was ready. He had no desire for anything to go wrong with his benefactor aboard. *If she can be called that.*

"Keep the sails at full mast till I say otherwise," Fernando hollered.

One of the old-time sailors objected. "But what if—"

"Unless sharks start flying, keep those sails up."

Anciara came up behind Fernando. "Trouble, Captain?"

Startled, he spun quickly. "No, My Lady. Nothing different than any other trek. There are always a few that voice a complaint or two. It's my job to keep an ear open for them that's complainin', then squash 'em."

Anciara smiled. "Be sure to tell me if you need any help."

"Yes, My Lady. I'll be the first one to call your name."

Three of the sailors waited for her to leave, then they approached Fernando. "Where are we headed, Captain? You told us a quick run to nearby isles. Now it don't sound like it."

Surna, an old-timer who'd been on runs with almost everyone, spoke up. "I've been on a hundred runs, probably more. Not much scares me, but I *do* like to know where I'm going."

Fernando looked around, then got close and whispered. "Suppose I told you we were going to the Sea of the Lost."

"Sea of the Lost? What for?"

"Ships don't come back from there," Surna said.

Fernando stared at him. "You did. You were with Ol' Crazy when he did it. I know. I saw you when he returned."

Surna shook his head and turned to the left, then right. "Right you are, Fernando. I was with Ol' Crazy, and he did a job like no other captain. I was proud to serve aboard his ship."

Fernando took hold of Surna's shirt and pulled him forward. "And that's what I need you to do for me—serve me like a good sailor. We've got a witch on board who's likely to kill us all if we don't do as she says, and what she says is she wants to go to the Sea of the Lost. So the Sea of the Lost is where I plan on takin' her."

"Why's she want to go there?" Surna asked.

Fernando kept his voice low, maybe even lower than he had before. "She said she wants to go to Entiria."

Surna stepped back. The shocked look on his face betrayed his fear. "You can't do that, Captain. Sennar did it, but he had coordinates from Malakai. We don't have that advantage. And sure as sharks eat fish, we're gonna need every advantage we can get our hands on."

Fernando balled his fist and shook it at Surna. "That witch wants to go to Entiria, and I intend to get her there. Since you're on board, you can either help me or start swimming back to Genda. I don't see another choice."

Surna's grim look told his mood, but he nodded. "All right, Captain. Ya have me in a spot. I'll try and get ya through this, but yer not gonna like what ya see. First'll be the doldrums, then winds that'll tear yer sails to shreds. Along with the winds will be waves big enough to flood the second floor of the Hawk's Edge up on

Fannel Street. Finally there's the Narrow Straits, where you'll think some demon with jaws of death is after you. If you survive all that—which is sayin' a mouthful—then you'll find Entiria."

"You make it sound unlikely," Fernando said.

"I'm bein' kind," Surna said. "It's weighin' heavy on me whether I should keep goin' with you or slit my wrists. How's that for soundin' unlikely?"

Fernando nodded. "Surna, I'll ask you as a decent man not to say anything to the others."

"Ya got no fears there, Captain. I don't want them so scared they can't do their jobs, 'cause without them performing near perfectly, we're all lost—just like the name of the sea says."

They found the doldrums first—or the doldrums found them. The winds were nonexistent, not so much as a whisper, and the heat was unbearable. Sweat formed in big, thick beads on men before breakfast and only got worse as the day lingered. It took two days to break free of the curse, and for another two days all seemed well, then the winds picked up.

Fernando stared into the horizon, seeing nothing but gray. The howling of distant winds grew ever closer, and what Surna had told him clattered in his head, a warning of what was to come.

Before he gave orders to lower sails, the first gusts of wind arrived, tearing at the sails and ripping some from the masts. The next few moments brought shrieking winds accompanied by waves the likes of which Fernando hadn't seen, only heard of. *Surna hadn't exaggerated.*

The third wave that hit the ship took one of the men with it when it washed over the deck. Fernando issued orders, but he couldn't be heard over the shrieking winds and howling of the waves.

Men scrambled to safety, eager to avoid the sure death of

staying above deck. "Stay on top," Fernando yelled. "Strap yourself to a mast or something else, but man your positions."

Despite the orders, the majority of sailors abandoned their posts and went below. A moment later, Anciara came alongside Fernando. "Are we getting through this?"

"My Lady, I couldn't say. Right now, it doesn't look so good. You better go below though. If not, the next wave might have ya greetin' a shark with teeth as big as my dagger."

"I'll remain here until all is lost," she said. "Besides, I need to safeguard you. If this fails, I'll still need a captain."

Fernando looked at her and raised his brows. "I'm strapped down," he said, and lifted the rope that tied him to the main mast. "It's you I'm concerned about."

Anciara reached down and untied the knot, despite Fernando's feeble attempts to stop her. "What are you doing? Don't do that."

When the knot was undone, Anciara held onto his arm, and then she Shifted to the docks in Genda. Tirzinitzia was already there.

Fernando's jaw dropped. "What! How did we get here?"

"I wouldn't argue if I were you," Anciara said. "I saved you."

"My ship. My men. What about them?"

"I'm afraid they're gone or soon will be. They didn't stand much of a chance *with* you to lead them. Without you, they stand no chance at all."

"Why didn't you help them? Couldn't you have saved them too?"

Anciara shrugged. "I imagine I could have, but I didn't need them. Thinking back on it, I should have saved the one who'd been there before, but you'll just have to find someone else."

"What?"

"Just because this voyage failed doesn't mean I've given up. You need to find another crew and make sure at least one of them knows where to go."

Anciara turned to leave. "We leave in two days, so be ready."

Fernando reluctantly recruited a new crew, working diligently, day and night, to find enough men. He fought with telling the truth when men asked him what happened on his first voyage, and how he escaped with his life, but his crew didn't.

He was about to give up when, from the corner of his eye, he spotted Anciara watching him.

"I'll be telling ya for the last time, mates, we hit a bad storm, and the sails went down. After that, we lost more than a mast or two, and after that . . . well, the men just gave up. Plumb quit and let the sea take 'em down with it."

"How did you get out?" someone yelled.

"Told ya three times now, and I won't be doin' it again. I was lucky enough to grab onto a lifeboat that I put the good lady in, then a kindly pirate ship picked us up. I thought we was good as gone when that happened, but it was one of Malakai's old ships, and they proved to be good, honest men. Brought us back here safe as can be and with full bellies to boot."

"I thought Malakai quit all his pirating ways," another sailor said.

"Thought he did too," Fernando said. "I guess I was wrong. But I'm glad I was wrong, 'cause I wouldn't be here if not for them scalawags. Fact is, I plan on drinkin' a toast to 'em tonight. Any man with an inkling to sail can join me."

"Your treat?"

Fernando smiled. "My treat," he said. "I'll buy two vidda for any man who signs on, and I'll promise five more when we return."

The last promise drew a roar from the crowd, and they hoisted him on their shoulders and carried him off to the tavern.

"Looks like our captain has done well," Tirzinitzia said.

Anciara nodded. "Indeed. He performed very well. I may not have to kill him after all."

"When do you want to leave?" Tirzinitzia asked.

"Before that pack of sots lose their courage," Anciara said.

Chapter Fourteen

WELCOME TO NELSTAR

Melissara led the way for most of the day with Darstan keeping pace beside her. Wisp and Rahg kept watch from the back, continually looking and listening for dorgans. Just before supper, Melissara stopped, staring ahead.

"What is it?" Darstan asked.

Melissara sighed. "It's Nelstar! After all these years, I can't believe we're here already. Darstan, I guess the Slicers were right; they did know the way to get here."

"Remember what you told us, Melissara. A lot may have changed."

Rahg moved alongside her. "I can't believe we're here either. Do you know where this portal leads?"

Melissara nodded in a slow, methodical rhythm. "Unfortunately, I do. It leads to the lower part of the Great Hall—where the Lights are."

"What? How are we going to get through there?" Wisp asked.

"Fortunately, we have you, Wisp. I'm going to presume that if the dorgans can't detect us while Cloaked, the Lights won't be able to either."

"What does that have to do with anything? I can't Cloak us for that long."

"If the Lights or any others are in there, we'll have to sneak through. The only way I know of doing that is with Stealth. The Great Hall is big, but not so big that you can't protect us while we traverse it. It won't take us as long to get through the hall as it did for you to protect us against the dorgans."

Wisp stepped close to Melissara. "You better tell me what you expect. I need to know beforehand."

"I don't expect much more than I did with the dorgans—for you to use your skill to keep us undetected. The portal ahead opens to the Great Hall, as I said. Once we go through the portal, there will be a large door that we'll need to open. It can only be opened from the other side though."

"How that's going to work?" Darstan asked. "We can't just knock on the door."

"That's precisely what we do," Melissara said. "We'll go through the portal, then make a ruckus at the door, enough of one to get the attention of those inside. They'll wonder what could be clamoring from the Forsaken Lands. Once they open the door, they'll see nothing because Wisp will be protecting us with Stealth. At that point—while they are investigating—we will have the opportunity to sneak past the ones sent to check on us, then up the stairs and out the front door."

"That sounds like a lot of things could go wrong," Wisp said.

"A lot of things *could* go wrong," she said. "But we don't have much of a choice—unless you have a better idea. I know of no way onto Nelstar other than this."

"Maybe we should take some time and think it over," Darstan said. "I'm with Wisp. It sounds pretty risky."

Melissara looked them over and nodded. "All right. Let's eat something and give it thought. If we don't have another solution by the time we're done, we'll go with what we have."

They ate supper in near silence, and when they were done, no alternative had been agreed upon. "Looks like we go with what we have," Melissara said. "I see no other way."

"No sense in delaying," Wisp said. "How do we get through the portal?"

"We just walk though," Melissara said. "The portal presents no problem. The problems don't begin until we hit the door."

Darstan headed toward the portal. "Be prepared to use your shield, Rahg. Just in case. And those Spirals too."

Melissa stopped a few steps in front of the portal. "We need to step through at the same time," Melissara said. "I still don't understand how these portals work, so we're better off being cautious. If we go through together and something happens, at least we'll be facing it together."

"Let's go, then," Rahg said, and grabbed hold of Melissara's hand.

They stepped through the portal while holding onto each other and reappeared at the back entrance to the Great Hall, facing a door that hadn't been opened since Melissara and her companions had been exiled more than a thousand years before.

Melissara paused for a moment, then unleashed a barrage of BlackLightning against the doors. Afterward, she spun to face Wisp. "Now," she said. "And make sure to keep quiet. I have no idea what powers the Lights may have now."

After a few moments, the doors creaked open. A handful of guards stood inside, backed up by two of the Lights. Melissara kept everyone still until there was enough room to squeeze by into the Great Hall. Once inside, she hurried up the stairs and across the main floor.

It took less than a minute to reach the front entry, where she waited to ensure there was no one nearby, then she opened the front doors, and they sneaked out, hurrying down the steps and into the street.

"Keep it up, Wisp. I want to get far away from here before we're seen."

As they crossed one of the main thoroughfares, something sped by, giving Rahg a start. "By the gods! What was that?"

Melissara stepped on the walkway and glanced about. *Moving carts. It has to be.*

"Do you know what that was, Melissara?" Wisp asked.

She nodded slowly and then continued staring while nodding. "As I mentioned earlier, those are *moving carts*. And I haven't seen them in more than a thousand years. Much more."

"How are they possible?" Darstan asked.

"I told you of the people who could move things just by thought. That's how they work. I saw them many years ago, but the Lights had banned them."

"I guess the ban is no longer in effect," Rahg said.

"I wonder what else has changed," Melissara said. "A lot, I'm sure."

They walked for a short distance, then noticed a man lying on the ground holding his leg and moaning. Rahg rushed to aid him. "What's the matter?"

"I fell down the steps," the man said. "I can't stand up. I think my leg is broken. Take me to the Hall, please?"

Darstan knelt beside him and looked. He pressed on the man's shin, drawing a yelp. "Don't touch it. If you want to help, get me to the Hall and an approved healer."

"We can heal this," Darstan said, and turned to face Rahg. "Brother, weave a protective shield around the broken bone so this man can walk."

"No! Don't. You can't do that," the man shouted.

"Can't do what?" Darstan asked as Rahg worked on him. "He's healing you."

"You're not allowed to do that. Hurry and get out. They'll be here any moment."

"Who? What are you talking about?"

"Don't you know? Powers! You can't use powers. Not unless you have permission. I thank you for what you did, but if you value your life, you need to run and hide."

Melissara grabbed hold of Darstan's sleeve and tugged. "Hurry. I see a moving cart coming. It might be them."

"I'm sure we can handle whoever's in there," Darstan said.

"I'm not concerned with who's in there. I'm more concerned with who gave the orders. If anything happens, that's who will show up, and quickly."

"Do we just leave him?" Wisp asked.

"We have no choice," Melissara said. "Wisp, Cloak us so we can get out of here."

Wisp took hold of the others, and in an instant, they disappeared. Once Cloaked, Melissara led them south. "This way. Hurry."

The moving cart halted where the man lay, and two guards got out. They scanned the area, then picked up the injured man and placed him in the back of the cart. One guard examined the man's leg, frowning. "Who did this?" the guard asked.

The man in the cart hesitated before saying, "I don't know. There were four of them. I told them not to do anything, but they didn't listen. I don't think they were from around here."

"Around here or not, they should know the law." The guard turned to the one he arrived with. "Stay here and search the area. I'll take this one to the Hall."

The cart sped off, leaving the other guard alone on the walkway. He walked slowly along the path, checking alleys and side streets as he did. After a few moments, he left, returning along the route the guards had taken to get there.

Melissara waited until the guard was out of sight, then she signaled to Wisp that it was okay to remove the cloak. They became visible seconds later.

"What was that about?" Wisp asked.

"I don't know. Judging by what the injured man said, healing is forbidden unless it's sanctioned. Something to remember while we're here."

"I wonder what else is forbidden," Darstan said.

"We need to find out," Melissara said. "And there's no better way than asking."

She approached a couple prepared to cross the street. "May I ask a question?"

When the couple nodded, she continued. "We are from far away—originally Runella, and have been traveling about. We are not familiar with the rules here. Can you tell us what is forbidden and what is allowed?"

The man stepped forward. "Good that you asked," he said. "You can't use any powers unless approved by the Council. I mean *any*. You can't heal, use carts, Shift, Shield, or anything else."

"You're not allowed to Shift?" Melissara asked.

He shook his head. "And if you do, they'll know. The slightest indication of using powers alerts them, and they'll send a guard or a whole patrol of guards right away. Punishment varies from draining your energy to death."

"Death?"

He nodded again. "I've seen them do it."

"What if you need to Shift?"

"You can do that, but only with someone who's approved to do so. And it will cost you a good bit of energy for each Shift, so where you want to go better be important."

Melissara bowed. "I owe you a debt, sir. I didn't know the restrictions. It's not so strict on Runella."

"You must not have been back in a while. The Lights made this rule effective for all worlds. None of them are exempt."

"We offer our thanks once again. And now we'll be on our way. It looks as if our journey may be a long walk."

After a few moments, Wisp said, "What now? It looks like shifting is out of the question, even if we had somewhere to shift."

Melissara nodded. "We need to find someplace to rest and settle in for the night. I don't think remaining on the streets is a good idea."

"We'll leave that decision to you," Darstan said. "None of us have any idea where to go."

"Then follow me," Melissara said. "And remember not a hint of powers."

Chapter Fifteen

SOMEONE NEW HAS POWERS

Vellana called a meeting once she arrived at the Hall—a mandatory-attendance meeting. By noon, all the Lights were seated at the table in the Great Hall. Servants shuffled about, busily attending to each of their whims.

She waited for the servants to leave, then stood to address her fellow Lights. "In case you haven't heard, there is someone using powers on Savar."

Doranna appeared shocked. "Who? Do we know who it was?"

"We don't know yet," Vellana said. "We don't even know if it's one person or more than that, although initial reports indicate it may be more than one or at least the one using powers is traveling with others."

"What *do* we know?" Xeter asked.

"What we know is that *someone* or several *someones* used power last night."

"For what purpose?" Chandra asked.

"The purpose doesn't matter," Vellana said. "What matters is that power was used against the rules. That kind of insolence cannot be tolerated. It must be punished."

"Surely, the type of crime makes a difference. If someone were—"

"The *type* of crime makes no difference whatsoever," Vellana said. "If someone commits a murder, we don't ask whether it was against a thief or a lover. Or if it was done with a knife or a Lightning bolt—it's a murder, pure and simple. The same applies here. Someone used powers without permission, and they must be punished for it."

Chandra rose and scanned those sitting at the table. "I concur. The reason has no bearing on the crime. The offenders must be found, and they must be punished."

"Who would be so defiant as to use powers after all this time?" Ebransco asked. "It must be someone from one of the other worlds. If it is, perhaps they haven't heard of the ban."

Chandra sipped from her mug. "And perhaps it's someone from farther away than that?"

"Like where?" Xeter asked. "Who wouldn't know of the ban?"

"I didn't say they weren't aware of the ban," Chandra said. "I said perhaps it was someone from farther away."

"Who could be farther away than the farthest world?" Ebransco asked.

"Someone who's been in exile," Chandra said, her voice lowered.

Vellana laughed. "Chandra, you give too much credit to legends. No matter how powerful the du Savarras were, they couldn't have survived the Forsaken Lands, not to mention, they couldn't have gotten back in here if they did survive. You were there when we opened the seal; no one entered. No one was in sight."

"Then what made the noise?" Chandra asked.

"I don't know what made the noise, but did you see anyone?"

"No, I didn't, but I also didn't see anything else that could have made the noises we heard. So I'll ask again—*what* made the noise?"

Vellana stood, shaking her head. "I don't understand what you're saying, Chandra. We saw nothing to indicate it could have been anyone, let alone one of the ones we banished so many ages ago."

Chandra smiled. "I'm using your own logic, Vellana. Since you state it couldn't have been the ones we banished because you didn't see any evidence, I'm simply stating it couldn't have been *anything* because we saw no evidence. And since we both know the noises didn't occur out of thin air, then there must not have been any noise. However, we all heard the noise, which negates that argument."

Vellana sighed, then took her seat. "All right, Chandra. All right. I'll concede *something* made the noise—or *someone*."

Chandra nodded slowly, then adjusted her pacing, though she let her gaze linger on each of the Lights. "You may be right, Vellana; in fact, you are more than likely right. I presented my logic as caution. I haven't lived three thousand years by being careless. Whether it's a miracle survivor of the Forsaken Lands or a previously unknown distant relative of the du Savarras, I think it would be prudent to check it out. Everyone knows how vengeance-driven they were."

Chandra started to sit, then stopped. "And let's not rule out that it could be something different altogether. Perhaps there are other worlds like ours, maybe even ones that banished people as well. It could be some of them that came calling."

"Then where are they?" Doranna asked.

Chandra shrugged. "I don't know, Doranna. Do you? I say we investigate further."

"I won't argue what Chandra mentioned, or that it may be the du Savarras," Doranna said. "I've never seen anyone as committed to vengeance as that family. I'll vote with Chandra. It won't hurt to investigate things."

"I'll vote with Chandra," Xeter said. "Besides, there is still the question of what happened to the people who purchased Antar's old manor—the ones who died on the first night they stayed there."

"The tales are all legends and stories meant to frighten children," Borrik said.

"Really?" Vellana said. "I've never heard of legends killing people."

"Enough," Chandra said. "Whether we believe or not makes no difference. I think the vote is to investigate, so the only thing that remains is to decide who to send to the manor."

"And it's a question that needs much deliberation," Vellana said.

"Five people have tried taking over the manor only to die, and we still don't know how. Legends say it's cursed, and while I don't believe in curses and hauntings, *something* killed them. And whatever did was strong. These were not kittens who attempted this. One of Therram's sons was among them."

"We could all go and do the inspection," Ebransco said.

"I'm not walking through that door first," Chandra said.

"Then we draw straws," Vellana said.

"Or we get someone else to do it," Doranna said.

Chandra looked at her, then the others. "Shall we vote?"

Chapter Sixteen

A LONG TIME GONE

They spent the night sleeping in a nearby forest, using leaves as cushions. In the morning, Melissara awoke earlier than normal, not to mention stiffer than normal. "I now appreciate my soft beds much more than before," she said.

Darstan stood, stretching as he did. "Let's hope that's the last time we find it necessary to sleep in the woods. My back is killing me."

Wisp laughed and moved about spryly. "After you've spent a few nights sleeping in alleys or on rooftops, those leaves feel great. I think you two are just complainers—old ones at that."

"Are we going to eat something here?" Rahg asked. "Or are we going someplace?"

Darstan laughed. "Leave it to Rahg. He's *always* thinking of food."

After leaving the forest, Melissara led them through the city, then down a wide street to the south, which was busy with moving carts. Every time one of the carts passed them, Rahg and Darstan craned their necks to get a look, though the spectacle didn't seem to affect Wisp in the same way.

"I can't believe they can do that," Rahg said. "I never imagined such things."

"I'm sure you'll see more wonders, Rahg. Just keep your eyes open."

"Do you know anyone who can do that, Melissara?" Darstan asked.

She shook her head. "I knew someone long ago, but only one. At that time, it was a rare skill." She looked at two of the carts as they sped by, one beside the other. "It doesn't seem so now. It looks as if half the populace has that ability."

"What else does that power allow you to do?" Wisp asked. "And one more thing. If they are allowed to use power to run the carts, what else can they do?"

"I don't know much about it, but as far as I *do* know, people who possess that skill can propel objects at will, but how and why they're permitted to do it, is beyond me."

"You mean move things without touching them?" Wisp asked.

"Much more than just move, Wisp. I mean, they can hurl them and at good speed as you can see with the carts. They can use almost any object as a weapon, but one with a sharp point can be lethal, even the smallest ones, like the utensils you eat with."

"None of this sounds good," Wisp said. "So we may as well discuss a plan. Let's assume something happens and the guards question us or want us to come with them. What do we do?"

"Good point, Wisp. If *anything* happens, draw close to me and take hold. There are points I can Shift to."

"Where? We haven't been anywhere yet."

"I lived here, Wisp. Though it's been a long time, I still remember some Shift points. Not indoors, because they may have changed, but special spots we used that would remain the same— like hiding places underneath huge boulders. Or caves within a mountain of granite."

.   .   .

They continued the walk along the street at a slow but steady pace. As they came to the end of the developed part of the city, shops and eateries disappeared and even taverns faded from view. Only houses remained, and within a few more moments, they became the occasional manor in the countryside.

"Where are we going?" Rahg asked.

"To someplace I hope will be a refuge," Melissara said.

"What could be a refuge in *this* place?" Wisp asked.

"My childhood home," Melissara said. "It's likely gone, but we'll see."

Darstan scoffed. "Even if it is there, what good will it do? Your family has been gone for a thousand years. Whoever lives there probably doesn't even know you."

"That's a possibility, Darstan. In fact, it's a probability, but we don't have many options, so we need to check them all."

They continued to walk for half an hour, but now they were walking down seldom-used streets lined with trees supported by large, thick trunks. Moving carts were noticeably absent; in fact, life signs of any kind were noticeably absent.

"These houses are like palaces," Rahg said. "They're huge."

"Look at that one," Wisp said, pointing to his left. "It's the size of any two of the others."

Melissara turned onto the walkway leading to the house Wisp mentioned. "Where are you going?" Darstan asked.

"This house is mine. At least it used to be."

"*This* was your house?" Rahg asked.

The manor sat behind a manicured lawn dotted with luscious fruit and nut trees and was surrounded by well-tended gardens. It was three stories high with a steep and varied roofline punctuated with half a dozen chimneys billowing smoke and another half a dozen that sat idle.

An older gentleman stooped to clip a few flowers. As Melissara got closer, she increased her pace. When she got within two spans, the man stood and turned. She ran to him and embraced. "Benna! Benna! I never expected to find you here."

Benna lifted his hand and ran his slender fingers along her jawline, then traced her facial features. "By all that's holy, it's Lady Melissara."

Melissara's tears rolled freely down her cheeks. "How are you still here? What—"

Benna started for the manor's front entrance, limping so badly his bones creaked. "Enough time for that later. Come in and let me fix refreshments for you and your guests."

He led them inside, then to a waiting room. "Sit here while I fix tea."

Melissara jumped up and went past him. "Nonsense. I still know how to fix te, and just the way you taught me to prepare it. Take a seat with the boys while I make it."

Moments later, Melissara returned with te for everyone. She passed it out, then sat in a soft-cushioned chair across from Wisp. "First, introductions are in order. Benna, this is Wisp, Rahg, and Darstan." She leaned over and kissed Benna on the cheek. "And this," she said, "is Benna. He's been with my family since . . . I don't even know how long, but it's been more than two thousand years."

"Sit, Miss Melissara. I have so much to ask. Tell me of Mikkellana and Lady Aentarra. How are they? And how did you get back here?" The cup shook as his hand trembled. "There is so much to learn."

"I think there is much to learn on both sides, Benna. I see many things have changed in Nelstar."

Benna shook his head. "And not for the better. The people aren't happy, and everyone knows the Lights are to blame, but who will stop them?"

"We ran across some of the changes on our way here," Darstan said. "We helped a man who hurt his leg, and almost before we finished, guards arrived and took him away, but they left one guard to search for us."

"I'm surprised you had time to get away," Benna said. "They're usually quicker than that."

Melissara hesitated, then said, "They would have spotted us but Wisp has a few special skills."

Benna smiled and reached to touch Wisp's hand. "So you are one of Aentarra's children?"

Wisp's eyes shot open wide, as did Melissara's. "What do you mean? How did you know?"

"I presumed you meant he had Stealth. Aentarra was the only one I knew of with Stealth, so it wasn't difficult to make that leap of logic."

"You knew she had Stealth? For how long?"

The old servant laughed. "Since you were children and played hide-and-seek," Benna said. "If you remember, none of you could ever find Aentarra. There was a reason for that."

Melissara looked aghast. "And you never said anything?"

"It wasn't my place to tell," Benna said. "Besides, that would have taken all the fun out of the game. What's the sense in playing if you can find someone?"

Melissara laughed, and when she finished, Benna looked in her direction. "Where is the world you live on?"

"It's too difficult to explain," Melissara said. "Suffice it to say it is somewhere on the other side of the Forsaken Lands."

Benna shuddered. "Enough said." He fixed more te and some khaffe for them, then resumed sitting. "Enough of my questions, I'm sure you have more than a few of your own."

"We do," Melissara said. "To begin with, what happened after we left Neltsar?"

"After your father died, the Lights took over everything," Benna said. "They forbade the use of power, and anyone who used power was punished severely or killed. It didn't take long for people to accept the inevitable. Within a few generations, powers were eliminated from those who didn't practice it anymore. Soon, only those who used powers on a regular basis passed the ability on to offspring. And when I say only those who used powers on a regular basis, that means only the Lights—and a few families who randomly retained the abilities."

"How do they know if people practice? And why are the carts allowed?" Darstan asked.

"They have abilities to detect if powers are being used. Similar to Sensing, but those abilities have increased in sensitivity over the years. They allow people to use carts, but that's all, and they can detect what power is used for—whether it's Shifting, Healing and more."

"That's how they found us in the city," Rahg said. "And that was just a minor healing."

"Exactly," Benna said. "They can detect the slightest hint of power." He brushed his hand in the air. "But enough of that, Melissara. Sit and tell me of these children. Who are they, and more importantly *whose* are they?"

Melissara smiled and sat on the sofa. She pointed to Rahg and said, this is Antar's grandson by Aentarra."

Benna got up and wrapped his arms around Rahg. "Oh my goodness. I always loved Aentarra. She was a little wild, but funny. Always playing tricks on people."

He turned to look at Melissara. "How is Aentarra?"

"Dead," Melissara said. "Killed while fighting to save the world we live on."

"Oh no," Benna said. "What a tragic end."

"And this," Melissara said, pointing to Darstan, "is my son."

Tears formed in Benna's eyes. He repeated his embrace with Darstan. "Forgive my emotions," he said, "but I never expected to see any of the du Savarra offspring. It truly is a pleasure."

Darstan patted Benna's back with his one good arm. "No apologies are necessary. Those kinds of emotions are always welcome."

"If you don't mind my asking," Benna said. "What happened to your arm?"

Taken aback at first, Darstan quickly regained his composure. "Fighting with Lukaan did this."

"Disgusting man!" Benna said. "Where is he now?"

"Dead," Melissara said. "As is almost everyone else. Mikkellana is still alive, though she lost the use of her legs for a while. She's walking now, but I don't know if it will last."

Benna turned to Wisp. "And I already know this young man's heritage. Welcome to Nelstar, son of Aentarra."

Melissara cleared her throat and stood. "Benna, I hate to interrupt the reunion, but we need a place to stay, at least until we learn the rules and learn how to get around without attracting attention. Do you mind if we stay here?"

Benna remained silent for a long time, then he held Melissara's hand in his. "My Lady, this is your home. Of course you can stay here; however, I might suggest you stay at my manor instead. It's not nearly so spacious as this, and it's all the way down by Lago Mago, but it is quite comfortable, and it is well-maintained. I spend two days a week keeping it clean."

Melissara leaned back, her hands folded on her lap. "Benna, I know it's been a long time, but I've found people don't change. Why are you suggesting we stay at your manor instead of here?"

He scooted his chair close to Melissara and leaned in to whisper. Melissara stopped him. "Benna, there is nothing you can't say in front of our guests."

Benna scooted his chair back in place, then sipped on his te. "The manor may not be a safe place to stay, My Lady."

"Not safe how?"

"The manor has been sold five times, and all five times the people who purchased the manor died the first night they stayed here. Another time, the Lights had three of the guard leaders spend the night in preparation for an important purchase by a nobleman from Nagassa. All three died."

The story grabbed Melissara's attention. "How did they die?"

Benna shrugged. "I don't know. Nor did the healers the Lights sent to investigate."

"Benna, did any of the people who stayed here have powers?"

He nodded. "All the guards did, and supposedly they were strong. And one of the merchants who bought it did."

"And you have no idea how they died?"

Benna gulped and stared ahead. "None."

"We can address this later, Benna, but I find I don't believe you. And I don't know why you'd lie to me."

Benna trembled so badly he had to sit. Tears formed and streamed down the creases in his cheeks. "My Lady, I don't want to hide things from you, but —"

"But what?"

"I'm sorry, Lady Melissara, but I made a promise to your father not to mention it."

"Mention what?" Melissara asked.

"I can't swear to it, but I think it's the Light Serpents."

"The what?" Rahg asked.

"Light Serpents?" Darstan said. "What are they?"

Melissara stood, her nerves on edge. "As far as I knew, they were only legend. Are you telling me they're real?"

"No one has ever seen them, and no one can swear they're real, but I've heard them at night. And I've *sensed* them. It's the same feeling I got the night your mother was killed. And the following morning, we found four of the soldiers who attacked her dead."

"But I thought—"

Benna shook his head. "It wasn't your father, as many speculated. I knew your father for centuries. If he had caught them, there would have been much more damage. He would have left nothing but ashes."

"And you think the Light Serpents did the attack the night my mother died?"

"I think they did that, and I think they are still guarding the manor which is why no one may stay here."

"But I stayed here many times, and so did my sisters."

"You were Antar's blood."

"No one who is not his blood has ever stayed here and lived."

"You've seen them?" Melissara asked.

"No. As I've said, I've never seen them, but I know they're here. I believe they live in the cellar, in the farthest room, deep under the ground."

"That door was always locked," Melissara said.

Benna nodded. "They can go through ground, and they go through steel, all without a sound."

"What is steel?" Darstan asked.

Melissara turned to Benna. "We do not have steel on the world we came from."

"What is it?" Darstan asked.

"It is a process of using iron and other material and burning it under high heat. It produces a new metal called steel that is even stronger than iron."

"What is it used for?" Wisp asked.

"Beams to hold things up, the strongest doors, swords, spears, and almost anything where strength is needed."

"And these Light Serpents can go through this steel?" Wisp asked.

"I've never seen them do it, but I know they can," Benna said. "And so do the dead who tried to stay here."

"Considering that we can't shift and that your manor is some distance from here, I think we will stay," Melissara said.

"But, My Lady, remember what I said."

"I'm not forgetting, Benna. But you also said that my sisters and I were not harmed because we were of Antar's blood." She spread her arms, the gesture encompassing all the boys. "They are of Antar's blood. Two of them—Rahg and Wisp—are Aentarra's, and

Darstan is mine. If the blood kept my sisters and I safe, it should keep the boys safe as well."

Benna looked toward the boys, though he could barely see, and nodded. "You always did present a good argument, Lady Melissara. I'll show you to your rooms."

Chapter Seventeen

MIKKELLANA'S INTUITION

Mikkellana walked across the room with only a slight limp. "What bothers me is how long it's been."

"How long what's been?" Tobias asked.

"How long since we left Sykor. I thought Anciara would have found us by now."

"Why should that bother you?" Rhaven asked. "We're here because you said she couldn't find us. I'd say your plan is working."

"I know what I said, but I didn't necessarily believe what I said."

"There goes more of that double-talk," Tobias said. "I wish you would speak the truth for once."

Mikkellana laughed. "Tobias, I realize that I haven't always spoken with complete honesty, but things are different now."

"How's that?" Tobias asked. "If she hasn't been here before, how's she gonna know where it is? And that's if she figures out where we are to begin with."

"I know it seems unlikely, but I understand Anciara—at least a little. It won't take her long to find someone who knows, or guesses, where we are. It could be someone who knows, such as Talanvar or his help. Or it could be someone who guesses, and can show her how to get here, such as one of Sennar's men."

"That would mean she'd have to sail here," Tobias said. "Not many would risk that. You remember how hard it was for us to find a captain."

"But we weren't threatening to kill; she will be. Not many sailors will buckle to her threats, but once they see her kill one or two people, they'll quickly reconsider. And believe me, she *will* kill."

"What's to be done?" Rhaven asked. "We can't just leave here."

"I need to check on her," Mikkellana said. "We shouldn't decide on a course of action until we know what she has in mind."

"I'll get ready," Rhaven said.

Mikkellana stopped him. "You'll stay here. I'm taking Aenaila."

"Aenaila? What for?"

"Because if something happens, she can Shift back here. Can you?"

Rhaven nodded slowly. "All right. But be careful. Take no chances."

Mikkellana reached over and kissed him. "I'm not a fool. I'm going to check, and that's all; besides, you want me to get Argus, don't you? That's a job that will be easier with Aenaila along. And don't worry, Argus listens to me."

Mikkellana explained the situation to Aenaila, and they prepared to leave after Aenaila gave Adju instructions to stay with Rhaven, an order neither one of them were thrilled with.

Afterward, Mikkellana took Aenaila's hand. "Ready?"

When Aenaila nodded, Mikkellana Shifted to the alley where she first encountered Sennar. "If Anciara has any plans, the place to find out would be the tavern just around the corner, the Gull's Gut."

"Let's go," Aenaila said. "I'm ready."

"You can't go in looking like that," Mikkellana said. "You're going to need to do something with those looks before we go in. If not, every sailor in there will be drooling and spilling ale to get to you. You'll spend so much time fighting them off, we won't get anything done."

Aenaila almost panicked. "What should I do?"

"I don't know. Use Illusion. Make yourself look . . . different. You don't have to be ugly, just less gorgeous. Mikkellana shook her head and held up her hand. On second thought, don't," Mikkellana said. "Anciara will surely Sense you using Illusion; in fact, I shouldn't have Shifted here. She may have Sensed that." Mikkellana grabbed hold of Aenaila's hair and mussed it up, then wrinkled her clothes and made her appear disheveled.

Aenaila blushed, then did a few more things to disguise her beauty. Afterward, she and Mikkellana entered the Gull's Gut.

It was crowded with sailors drinking ale and vidda. The backroom gaming tables were full and had long lines of people waiting to play.

Aenaila tapped Mikkellana's arm and gestured toward the tables behind her. "Second one over," she whispered.

Mikkellana scooted her chair closer and listened.

"Don't know if I trust all that Fernando's saying," one of the sailors said.

"He sounded good to me," another said.

"Sounded good, sure, but how did he sail all the way to the Sea of the Lost and back again in that amount of time? It's not possible, I tell you."

A third sailor nodded. "I been there. I was with Ol' Crazy when he sailed. Can't be done."

Aenaila leaned in toward Mikkellana. "Sounds like she's planning a trip to see us."

"Sounds like she already tried," Mikkellana said, and grabbed hold of Aenaila's sleeve. "I think we need to go."

Once back in the alley, Mikkellana and Aenaila Shifted back to

Sykor to pick up Argus, then to Entiria. Rhaven waited like a faithful dog and Adju sat by his side.

Rhaven shot up from the chair, nervousness showing. "What happened? Is Argus all right?"

Mikkellana raised her eyebrows. "So nice to see your concern, Rhaven, but yes, I'm fine as well."

Rhaven laughed. "But he is all right?"

"Yes, Rhaven, he is fine. He's with the Entirians, and he's being fed and watered. You may visit him if you like, but know that we'll be leaving soon. No hurry, but no delay either. Anciara is coming on a ship, though it will take her a while to arrive."

"Where will be go?" Adju asked.

"You'll know when we get there," Mikkellana said. "I don't want anyone on Entiria to know where we are. If no one knows where we went, no one can say even under torture. And believe me, there will be torture."

The following day, Mikkellana prepared for the journey, as did all the others. No mention was made to the Entirians of them leaving, despite pleas from Tobias to do so. "These people have been good to us. We should at least tell them what to expect."

Mikkellana closed her eyes and sighed. "No one is less pleased than I am, Tobias. But if we hope to live, we can't let them know we've even gone, let alone where we're going."

"Maybe we could take them with us?"

"I would if I could, but there are too many of them; besides, I doubt if they'd go."

Mikkellana sat Tobias on the sofa. "Tobias, no one feels as badly about this as I do. The Entirians were nice to us. They welcomed us with open arms, but if we tell them we plan to leave, and if that news is somehow relayed to Anciara, she will know we went somewhere safe, somewhere she didn't know about. Once she knows that, she'll torture as many Entirians as she needs to until one of them tells her what she needs to know."

"She'll know that anyway, once she sees we're not here," Tobias said.

Mikkellana shook her head. "Not necessarily. She may think we saw her coming at the last minute and Shifted back to Genda or Sykor or anywhere else, but if she thinks we planned this, she'll suspect it was to go to another place she isn't familiar with."

Tobias nodded. "All right, I don't like it, but I understand."

"I'm glad, Tobias. Now, gather everyone else and bring them back here so we can leave. We're not being rushed, but I'd rather be gone and have it behind us."

Chapter Eighteen

A NIGHT AT THE MANOR

Benna limped to the stairs and started to go up, but Melissara stopped him. "Don't think about going up those stairs, Benna. I know where the rooms are. I'll take the room my mother and father used, and I'll give the boys the ones my sisters and I had. You can sleep down here where you always did."

He nodded, then looked to the boys. "I don't know what to say. If you see anything enter the room, it will be too late. Are you sure you want to stay?"

Darstan took a few steps and turned. "We're staying, Benna, but thanks for the warning."

Benna opened the door beside him and entered the bedroom, shaking his head. "You won't be thanking me in the morning. Not if you're dead."

"We won't be dead," Wisp said. "We've faced more than a couple of snakes before."

Wisp and Rahg joined Darstan in his room, where they sat and talked. "This is a strange enough world," Wisp said. "Those moving carts took me by surprise."

"I'm glad to hear you say so, Wisp. You fooled me with your reactions to seeing them. It was like you'd seen them all your life."

"That was just me hiding my feelings, Rahg. I was plenty surprised."

"They surprised me too," Rahg said. "I've never dreamed of such things."

Darstan rose from the bed and paced. "Right now, I'm not worried about the moving carts. But those Light Serpents are another thing entirely. The way everyone talks about them seems threatening."

"You heard Benna," Rahg said. "No one has ever seen one. I wonder if they even exist."

Wisp smiled. "I guess we'll find out tonight. I just hope I really am Aentarra's son."

They talked long into the night, the discussion focusing mainly on Nelstar and how things were so different.

"It's difficult to believe Melissara is that old," Rahg said. "She doesn't look as old as Mollie or Tobias."

"I still can't believe the moving carts," Darstan said.

"And I'm having a difficult time realizing the concept of seven worlds," Wisp said. "It's tough enough to think about Shifting from Sykor to Pomanda, let alone from one world to another."

"Now that you mention it, that is difficult to grasp," Rahg said. "I wonder how far away they are." He moved to the window and pulled a curtain aside, then looked out. "I can't see anything."

"I doubt if you'd know another world if you *did* see it," Darstan said, then he covered his mouth and yawned. "It's time for me to sleep," he said. "I'll see you in the morning."

"Are you sure you don't want me to stay with you? At least if Benna is telling the truth, maybe I can Cloak us."

Darstan laughed. "I'll be fine, Wisp. Don't worry."

～

An alert sounded, forcing Chandra to go to the Great Hall. "This better be important," she said as she entered. "I was playing games with my grandchildren."

"It is, My Lady. One of the guards—Duskar—has reported an infringement, and it's one that hasn't been resolved."

Chandra examined the report, her frown growing deeper the further she read. "Alert the others and inform Duskar to attend as well. And mention that attendance is both required *and* immediate."

"Yes, My Lady."

Chandra sat at the head of the table, her dark-brown eyes burning into the guard who stood before her. "I expect the full report in the morning. In the meantime, tell us what happened."

The guard, Duskar, swallowed hard. "An alert sounded on the thoroughfare by the fruit market. Sousl and I rushed there, but by the time we arrived whoever had used powers was gone."

"What were the powers used for?"

"A man fell down the steps and hurt his leg. Someone healed it."

"The level of healing? Was it good or that of an unskilled person?"

Duskar kept his gaze on Chandra. "They were skilled, My Lady Chandra. There's no doubt about that. They had a shield wrapped tightly around the break. It was even difficult for the healer to remove it."

"What did you do with the man who broke his leg?"

Duskar appeared confused. "We dispatched him, My Lady. Isn't that the standing order?"

Chandra flashed a quick smile. "Yes, Duskar. Don't worry. You did well in that regard. However, regarding the other matter . . ."

"Yes, My Lady?"

"You couldn't find the one, or ones, who healed him?"

"No, My Lady. And it was definitely more than one of them. The injured man told us there were four of them."

Chandra stood. "My question, Duskar, and the one the Council is sure to ask tomorrow, is how did four people with powers escape? Why didn't you find them? Where did they go?" Chandra placed her finger under his chin and lifted it. "And most importantly, *where* are they now?"

Duskar stood stiffly, staring in her direction. "Yes, My Lady. I'll have answers."

"I'm sure you'll have answers, Duskar. But answers are no good unless they are the *right* answers. Keep that in mind as you rest tonight."

Chandra began to turn away, then stopped. "Just so you know, we've already had reports of an infraction which made Council wonder why you hadn't reported this earlier. In light of that failure, you may want to expedite your investigation. In fact, Duskar, you may want to call on your partner, Sousl, and begin your search tonight. If the Council isn't satisfied tomorrow, who knows what the verdict will be."

Beads of sweat formed on Duskar's head. He bowed low and stepped back. "Yes, My Lady. I'll do it at once."

After Duskar left, Chandra addressed the other Lights. "This is the second report today. The other report indicated someone using a consistently low level of power in the same vicinity."

"Did they track it?" Vellana asked.

"They tried," Doranna said, "but it disappeared as quickly as it appeared. Much like the one Duskar reported."

"If it was a low enough level, and the person left the vicinity, it would no longer be traceable," Vellana said.

Chandra placed her palms on the table and leaned forward. "But that leaves me to question why did the trace disappear suddenly, as if shut off, instead of fade? Something isn't right."

Doranna nodded. "All monitors are to be alerted. Everyone—and I mean everyone—needs to keep a cautious eye until we find out who is using this power."

Ebransco slammed his fist on the table, almost spilling his

drink. "I agree that it must be put to an end. If for no other reason than to allow me to rest. I don't want any more disturbances like tonight."

"It's settled then," Chandra said. "Alert the appropriate monitors of the breaches and remind them of the consequences of failure."

Darstan lay in bed dreaming of many things, but especially of how life would have been different if Mirana had lived. He would have probably been living in Cartena with her by his side and at least a couple of kids to raise.

"You need to see the Mother."

Darstan turned from side to side. He heard a voice, but it wasn't a voice. Still, it startled him enough to cause him to sit up. He looked around and wondered. If it wasn't a voice, what was it? He'd heard something—or thought he had—and it had said something about a mother.

But what mother? The only mother I know is in the other room.

A smell like burnt metal tickled his nose, and it was then he realized it had not been a dream nor his imagination. He sat up straighter in bed.

He stared at the corner, then he turned his head slowly, searching every part of the room. When he reached the center, he almost jumped up.

At the foot of the bed sat a serpent with scales as black as the darkest night, but with tips that glistened like diamonds. A thick forked tongue flickered as if striking the air.

As Darstan sat mesmerized, another serpent slithered down the bedpost from the ceiling. It was as thick as a man's leg and just as black as the other one.

The first serpent opened its mouth wide, baring fangs like daggers. As it slithered closer, so did the other one.

Darstan focused, prepared to use his ColdFire, then thought better of it. If the legends Benna spoke of were true, he doubted his power would do any good.

He sat as still as he could while they continued slithering up the bed. When they reached the top, one serpent crawled onto him until it was so close its tongue could have kissed him. It stopped and stared into his eyes. The tongue flickered, as if tasting or sensing him, then the other one did the same.

After what seemed like a lifetime, the serpents returned to the bottom of the bed and faced him. Once again, he heard a *voice*, and he realized it was coming from them—their thoughts.

"Seek her out. Seek out the Mother."

A moment of silence, then, *"She will know what to do."*

After that, the serpents disappeared. One exited through the ceiling, like it had entered, and the other left by way of the door, sliding through it as if there were no door.

Darstan took a moment to compose himself, then he got out of bed, dressed, and went to see Melissara.

After several knocks on her door, she answered, opening it quickly and appearing frustrated. "What is it?"

Darstan stood in the hallway, looking shocked. "They came."

"Who came?"

"The Light Serpents. They came to my room."

Melissara grabbed his arm and pulled him inside. "What? You saw them? What happened?"

"Maybe we should go downstairs. I think I'd like something to drink."

"Of course," Melissara said. "What would you like khaffe?"

"I think I'd like wine," Darstan said. "A lot of wine."

"Fine, get Rahg and Wisp. I'll get Benna."

Darstan sat on the sofa by himself. He still trembled. "I was almost asleep when I heard something. I thought it was part of my dream, but then I smelled something like burnt metal."

"Burnt metal?" Melissara asked.

"Yes, it reminded me of the way the swords smelled when Lukaan's BlackFire struck them in Khatara."

"Go on," Wisp said. "Where were they?"

"I didn't see them at first, but after I sat up, I saw one on the bottom of the bed, then the second one came through the ceiling. It was just like Benna said. Nothing stopped them."

Darstan sipped his wine before continuing. "My first reaction was to attack, but then I decided to sit still. They crawled up the bed and sniffed my face. Their tongues almost kissed me." He shook his head. "I was terrified. Then, all of a sudden, they left. One through the ceiling and one through the door."

He gulped the rest of his wine, then said, "Oh, yeah. And they said to seek out the Mother. They said she would know what to do."

"*Said it?*" Rahg asked. "They talked?"

"No. No. They didn't talk like us. But I heard their thoughts just as if they were talking."

"Good god!" Melissara said.

"What?" Wisp asked.

"That form of communication. The only ones I've known who could do that were Lukaan, my father, and the gods. No others."

"Camissa can do it," Rahg said. "She's done it with me a lot, and she's gotten to be good at it. When we were in Arangar the first time, she used it to contact Rhaven from pretty far away."

"I didn't know she could do that," Darstan said. "But the Light Serpents used it for sure. I won't soon forget that."

"I still can't believe it," Benna said. "No one has seen a Light Serpent except Antar, and I'm only going on legend to cite that."

"Who is the *mother*?" Wisp asked.

Melissara shook her head. "I have no idea." She faced Benna. "Do you?"

"Not a clue, Lady Melissara. I wish I did, but I don't."

Duskar roused Sousl from sleep by pounding on his door repeatedly. "Sousl, get up and do it now."

A moment later, Sousl opened the door, appearing more than groggy. "It better be important, Duskar. I was almost asleep."

"It's more than important. We have to report to the Council in the morning on the incursion we observed."

"Duskar, it was *not* an incursion; something triggered a monitor alert, and we investigated. We discovered someone healed a person. For the sake of all that's holy, healing someone is not a crime. At least it shouldn't be."

Duskar looked behind his back. "I know it shouldn't be, and you do, and most everyone else alive knows, but if the Council deems it a crime, it *is* a crime, and it's punishable by death."

"If you see it that way, so be it, but I'm tired and I need sleep. See me in the morning."

"Once again, you fail to grasp the seriousness, Sousl. If we don't find the ones who broke the rules, we'll end up serving their punishment. And the punishment is death."

"What!"

Duskar nodded. "I'll wait while you dress."

Moments later, Duskar and Sousl returned to the scene of the healing. They dispatched probes and issued sensors, but neither of them detected anything.

"How can this be?" Sousl asked. "One of them should have picked up something—some trace of scent."

Duskar continued scanning the area, searching in all directions. "You would think so, wouldn't you?" He pointed down a side street leading toward the section of city where the manors were. "Let's look this way, Sousl."

"You've not going to find anything there. None of the nobles are foolish enough to use powers, especially to heal a person like the one we found."

"You're probably right, but let's look, anyway. We're out of options."

Duskar and Sousl searched all night, but found nothing. When the first rays of Suvar's bright red sun brought the daylight, Duskar tapped Sousl on the shoulder. "Come on. I believe we've exhausted the trail by now. We'll have to report to the Council with what we have."

"But we don't have anything," Sousl said.

"That will have to do. For now, anyway. We can pick this up tomorrow night."

"You mean tonight?" Sousl asked.

Duskar shook his head. "Yes, I guess I do."

Chapter Nineteen

WHO IS THE MOTHER?

Darstan sat next to Melissara at breakfast, a break in his usual seating habit of being as far away from her as possible.

Melissara shot a few glances his way, then asked, "Were you able to sleep after the visit from the Light Serpents?"

"I slept, but barely," Darstan said. "I kept wondering what they meant by *mother*."

Benna stared across the table, his near-blind eyes not focusing on anything in particular. "You might find the answers at the Great Library. I can think of nowhere else. And I can't think of anyone alive who knows anything about the legends of old. Not anyone who would dare to tell you."

"Where is the Great Library?" Wisp asked. "Is it in the city by the Hall we came through?"

"It is," Benna said. "And it's not far from the Great Hall."

"I know where the Hall is," Wisp said, "but I have no desire to return. And considering how quickly the guards got to us when we healed that man's leg, I have little doubt they'd discover us if we went to the library."

Melissara interrupted. "If we don't use powers, they shouldn't be able to detect us."

Wisp sighed. "If you think it would do any good, Rahg and I will go. If anything happens, I can Cloak us."

"Fine by me," Rahg said. "If we're lucky, Wisp and I will find some answers to Darstan's riddle."

Melissara nodded. "I think it's worth it. And just the two of you will be less likely to attract attention. I doubt the library is accustomed to seeing groups of four adults browse the aisles."

"If you're going," Benna said, "I suggest you look at the histories of the seven worlds near the Beginning. That would be during the time of the Original Ones."

"When is the Beginning?" Wisp asked. "And who are the Original Ones?"

"The Beginning happened more than five thousand years ago, and it was created by the Original Ones. This person that you're fighting—Anciara—was a child of the Original Ones."

"What?" Darstan asked. "What happened to them, and how did she become so evil?"

"As far as I know, the Original Ones died long ago. As to how or why she became evil, I don't know. The same way anyone does, I guess. But if I were you, I'd start with the world of Asola, then move to Runella."

"And what are we looking for?" Rahg asked.

"I don't know. Anything that mentions the arrival of the gods or the Beginning, or any discussion of the first life on Nelstar—any of the seven worlds, really."

Rahg nodded and grabbed hold of Wisp. "I guess we better be off then. I'm sure there will be a lot of material to go through."

Melissara walked them to the door. "To get there, you —"

"I know how to get there," Wisp said. "I remember passing the library on our way here."

Melissara pursed her lips and nodded. "Impressive. Not many would recall that."

Darstan laughed. "Wisp remembers *everything*, Melissara. Nothing escapes his attention."

It didn't take long for Wisp and Rahg to get to the library. They stood around talking, then entered with a few other people to better blend in, although they separated once inside.

Wisp found several books to look through within a few moments, and he got busy browsing through them.

He and Rahg sat at a long table filled with other people, and turned the pages slowly, taking in all they could. Moments later, Wisp tapped Rahg's leg and gestured toward the front where four guards had entered and were crossing the floor in their direction.

"Let's go, Rahg," Wisp said. "Those guards look to be on a mission, and I think we better move quickly."

Wisp and Rahg moved behind a large shelf stacked with books, and he Cloaked them. "Time to go. Remember to keep hold of me."

In a Cloaked state, they slipped past the guards and exited the front door. Then they raced across the street and down a series of side streets until they were far away. Wisp dropped the Cloak, making the two of them appear fully visible.

"How did they know we were there?" Rahg asked.

"That's what we need to figure out," Wisp said. "In the meantime, let's get back to the manor. We need to report this to Melissara."

Wisp and Rahg entered the front door of the manor and walked directly to the kitchen.

Melissara stood. "Well? What happened?"

"They knew we were there," Rahg said. "We hadn't looked through two books before they came, and they were ready for trouble. There were four of them."

"You cloaked?" Melissara asked.

"They were coming across the room directly toward us. I knew we had to get out of there quickly."

Melissara paced slowly. "And neither of you used powers?"

"Nothing," Wisp said. "Not until I had to Cloak us."

Benna cleared his throat. "If I may, My Lady?"

Melissara turned. "Go ahead, Benna. What is it?"

"When your father was alive, he once told me that he couldn't hide from any of the Lights who had Sensing because he had a continuous emission of power in the form of a shield. Perhaps —"

Darstan almost leapt from the chair. "Rahg, the power from the gods. Your shield."

Melissara stared. "What's he talking about, Rahg?"

Rahg hesitated, but after regaining composure, he spoke. "When I went to the Paaren, one of the gods gave me a power that protects me even when I'm sleeping. It's a shield, not much, but a shield all the same. If someone stabs me or even shoots me with an arrow, it will stop it."

Melissara slammed her hand down. "That's got to be it. They must be able to detect that despite it being a low level."

"Then why haven't they come here?" Darstan asked.

"Probably because they can't sense his power so far away," Benna said. "When Antar was alive, he said they could only feel his presence when he was close."

Melissara tensed. "Perhaps we should move him someplace farther out? Someplace away from the city."

"I'm fine here," Rahg said.

"I don't know," Melissara said. "Now that they've Sensed you in the city, combined with our Sensing the other night, they may send people searching for us; in fact, I'm sure they will."

"There is a spot deep in the woods north of Gorshan that would be near impossible for them to Sense him," Benna said. "Best of all, Antar told me something in the rocks that forms the caves prevent others from Sensing you."

"I've never heard of that," Melissara said.

Benna nodded. "Antar used to take me there when he wished to relax."

"We should get supplies and go," Melissara said. "It will be a long trip."

"Not so long if we shift there," Wisp said.

Melissara shook her head. "We can't risk Shifting. They'd know."

"Not if we do it my way," Wisp said. "I'll Cloak us, and afterward, you can Shift without them knowing you Shifted. Since we'll be cloaked, they won't know where we shift to either. I'm assuming we'll be far enough away that they won't notice me uncloaking either."

Melissara looked to her side. "Benna, will they be able to detect him Cloaking?"

Benna seemed to give it thought, then shook his head. "I doubt it. I think we're far enough outside the city to be safe. Besides, I think the young man has a point on what he said about you Shifting. But the question is—do you have a Shift point in Gorshan?"

Melissara smiled. "I do, a cave on the northern edge of the lake."

"I'll prepare a day's food for all of you and at least a week's worth for Master Rahg."

After Benna finished with the supplies, Melissara and the rest of them walked a distance away to be safe, then Wisp Cloaked everyone. Melissara Shifted to the cave she spoke about in Gorshan.

Before becoming visible, she reminded them not to use powers. Wisp released his Cloak, and Melissara instructed Rahg on what to do.

"You've got enough food until I get back, and nothing should present any danger, so there is no reason for you to use powers."

She gestured to the back of the cave. "You'll find more than enough water back there thanks to canals that connect different parts of the lake, and there are numerous rents in the ceiling that provide light. In other words, Rahg, there is no reason to leave here."

Rahg nodded. "I understand. I'll be fine. This isn't unlike some caves we had in Twin Forks where I grew up."

"Good, stay put and keep quiet. I'll be back soon."

Melissara held out her hand to Wisp. "If you're ready, good sir. I suggest we go back to the city so nothing is detected at the manor." When Wisp nodded, she said, "Grab hold, Darstan. You too, Benna."

Wisp smiled and Cloaked them. They reappeared in the city, after which, while still Cloaked, they made their way back to the manor.

"Now what?" Wisp asked.

~

Chandra reached behind herself and scratched her neck. "There it goes again. I distinctly feel someone using powers, yet I can't pinpoint it."

"This is a growing concern," Doranna said. "The other night was bad enough, but now we've got this."

"And don't forget this morning," Vellana said. "There was a similar disturbance near the library this morning. Four guards were dispatched to investigate, but when they got there, they found nothing."

"And not once was anyone even spotted," Chandra said.

The seal on the front door opened, and Ebransco's heels clicked as he crossed the marble floor. "And don't forget the library."

"If you got here on time, you'd know we already discussed that." Chandra said.

"Not the one I have to report. There was one *near* the library, and there was one *inside* the library. I haven't reported the inside one yet, but I am now. The most interesting—or should I say disturbing—part was when the guards investigated, no powers were detected."

"How can that be?" Xeter asked.

Parron shook his head as he spoke for the first time. "Chandra, we can't waste time with these imbeciles. And we can't wait to find out about these powers. A deep investigation must begin. I say we put Salinas on it. He's the best we've got."

"Salinas?" Borrik seemed to object. "You know what he'll cost us?"

"Price is not the primary concern, Borrik. "To you it may be, living way out on Nagassa, but we can make up the price by raising taxes."

"Raising taxes on what? The people on Asola and Runella are already complaining."

Chandra smirked. "The people on Runella and Asola have always complained."

"They don't complain when the tax money taken from Sunnara and Taragon feed them during the long winters," Xeter said.

"All right, enough discussion," Parron said. "Put out a summons for Salinas. Everyone knows he has the best Sensing on all seven worlds. If anyone can find this stranger, it's him. Let's get this done."

"I second Parron's suggestion," Doranna said. "He's also the best warrior. I'd be torn which way to wager if it were a fight between Salinas and Xeter."

"Enough of this," Chandra said. "Summon him."

It took nearly two hours for Salinas to show up, but when he confronted the Council, he looked ready.

"Do you feel that aura about him?" Vellana asked of Doranna.

Chandra approached him, her dark robe dusting the floor. "Salinas, we have need of your services."

"Explain."

"For two days, we have Sensed a new power in the city, but

when we investigated, whoever created that power was gone, however, they didn't have enough time to have traveled so far."

"Where did this occur?"

"At first, on the street not far from the library, then nearer the Great Hall, then inside the library. After that —"

"Enough," Salinas said. "I'll look into it. Do you want this person or persons alive or dead?"

"Dead, of course," Xeter said.

Salinas nodded "It will be twenty thousand *renta*."

"Twenty thousand *renta?*" Vellana shouted her objection, but Chandra calmed her down.

"Twenty thousand *renta* will be fine, Salinas. Five thousand now and the remainder when you finish."

Salinas nodded and held out his hand. "It's done. I'll be back when I have finished."

Salinas returned an hour later. "Whoever it was has left the city, and they left no trace. They must have Shifted somewhere."

Doranna shook her head. "They couldn't have, or we'd have Sensed it."

Salinas, in a matter-of-fact manner, said, "They did."

"If they Shifted, it would have had to be to another world, and if they did that, we'd have surely noticed," Chandra said.

Salinas looked from one Light to the other. "Perhaps I didn't ask for enough."

Doranna stood and walked to Salinas. "I think that whoever we detected is no longer in the city. And if they haven't left this world, it means they are somewhere far outside the city. We need to find them."

Salinas bowed. "Consider it done."

Chapter Twenty

SALINAS HAS A MISSION

Salinas walked stiffly out of the Great Hall, his boots slapping the marble tiles as if angry. He ignored those who nodded as they passed by and continued toward the front of the hall where he exited onto the street.

Three soldiers waited at the corner. They greeted Salinas when he arrived. "Your orders, sir?" the tallest guard, Petr, asked.

"We have an assignment to find a stranger in the city. It's someone who is using powers."

"Do we know who he is or where he is or even if it *is* a he?"

Salinas shook his head. "No, and I even misspoke when I said 'In the city.' Whoever it is may have left Suvar for another world. The Council didn't know; in fact, there may be more than one—as many as four."

"How will we find him, or them, if we don't even know which world to search on?" This question came from the newest member, Sinta.

One of the guards lowered his head and chuckled, and Salinas glared at Sinta. "We do what we do. If finding someone who secretively and illegally used powers was easy, they wouldn't have to hire us, would they?"

Salinas shook his head and pursed his lips. "The first use of power was detected right there," he said, and pointed across the street. "Moments later, when the response team arrived, the offenders were gone, vanished as if into thin air."

"They?"

Salinas nodded. "As I said, The Lights believe there were more than one. Doranna said she detected two definitive signals, and the man who was healed identified four people."

"I can't believe four people would use powers," Sinta said.

Once again, Salinas glared. "Two people, or more, *did* use powers. If we believe Doranna, there is no question, so we'll take that as truth. And I said the man who was healed identified four people. He didn't say all four used powers." Salinas held his gaze on Sinta. "I'm beginning to think I erred when admitting you to the team. Did I?"

Sinta gulped. "No, sir. My apologies."

Salinas led the way across the street and stopped at the spot where the man had broken his leg. He stooped to the ground, sniffed, and removed his gloves, then felt the ground.

"Was it here?" the tall guard asked.

A nod from Salinas was all he got for an answer. Petr turned to the others. "Spread out. Go as far as you need to, but find another location where powers were used. Doranna said they were here."

Salinas continued to evaluate the scene while his guards searched the nearby areas. After several moments, he stood. "Anything?" he hollered to the guards performing the search.

The guards shook their heads or responded with a "no" even while they searched on.

Half an hour later, one of the guards—Edgar—called out. "Found it."

Salinas and the others rushed to the guard's side. "What have you got?"

Edgar saluted Salinas, then reported. "Trace evidence from several days ago. It seems like a Shift, but something's different."

Salinas knelt and examined the site, rubbing his fingertips over the area, though he was sure to use his other hand, not the one he'd used at the first site. He lifted his hand, brought it to his nose, then continued rubbing the site. After a few moments, Salinas stood.

Sinta looked questioningly at Salinas. "Why did you use different hands?"

Salinas sighed, then patiently explained. "Anytime someone uses powers, it leaves a trace, similar to residue on the ground where the powers were used. And each type of power leaves a different trail of evidence, not to mention that each person leaves a distinct signal."

"How does that help us?"

"We already know that two people were involved and that they used two different powers. Now we have to continue locating sites where they used powers to narrow it down further so we can see which one used which power."

"Do we have any more leads?" Edgar asked.

"The library and another spot not far from it. I suspect at least one of them is a Shift point, but I can't imagine what the other is."

"Was this one a Shift point?" Edgar asked.

"I don't know that either," Salinas said. "And it makes me wonder because it's such a short distance from where they healed that man's leg."

"What did the man have to say about them? Is he sure there were only four? Were they all men or were there women too?"

"Unfortunately, the Council carried out punishment hastily. They didn't wait for answers."

"Where does that leave us?"

"The same place we were before, Edgar. We must find the answers."

"Suppose we can't?"

Salinas scoffed. "Not an option, Edgar. Remember what happened to the man who was healed? His only transgression was being healed. If we fail the Lights, they will deem it a far greater sin."

Petr, who stood at the front of the group, stepped forward. "Shall we continue spreading the search?"

Salinas nodded. "As far as you need to. We'll find them, eventually."

Edgar mumbled as he moved to the north. "Let's hope 'eventually' is soon enough."

"Everyone move out. Don't stop until you find something, and, when you do find it, don't touch the scene until I get there."

An hour later, the guards regrouped with Salinas. Petr shook his head. "Nothing. Not a trace."

"Same here," Edgar said, and Sinta echoed him.

"It's on to the library, then," Salinas said. "I want to look at the inside before the steps, but I *do* want someone to guard the second location." He pointed to Edgar. "That's you."

"What should I do?"

"Nothing. Guard it, and nothing else."

Salinas entered the library and moved to the table where Rahg and Wisp had researched books. He then followed the Sense of their footsteps to the aisle behind the shelf of books. Salinas knelt on the floor about halfway down the aisle. "It was here," he said. He brushed the floor with his fingertips, then brought them to his nose. "It's the same person as whoever was at the second site, but I still have no idea what power this person used."

"Isn't that unusual?" Sinta asked.

Salinas nodded. "Let's go see the other site," he said, and led the way outside. He walked up to Edgar, knelt, and examined the ground. After a short evaluation, he stood. "Same as in the library. Same person and same power, but the mystery remains."

"Which power?" Petr asked.

Salinas shook his head. "That's what's puzzling. I can't tell."

"That's odd," Petr said.

"What's more strange is trying to determine why someone

would use powers inside the library, then again right here. It couldn't have been Shifting. If it had been, they wouldn't have gone so short a distance."

After searching for blocks, they came up empty. "I want everyone to think of why someone would do this. There's got to be a reason, and I want to know why."

Melissara returned from a trip to the city, an information-gathering event. She walked into the manor and took a seat. "Benna, would you please ask Darstan and Wisp to join me."

Moments later, Darstan walked in, followed by Wisp. "You wanted to see us?" Darstan asked.

"Sit," Melissara said. "I just returned from the city."

"And?"

"And it's common gossip that the Council has hired Salinas to find us."

"Who's Salinas?" Wisp asked.

"He's the worst," Benna said. "As bad as Lukaan was."

"What makes him so bad?" Wisp asked.

"He takes assignments from the Lights and asks no questions. And he never quits hunting until the job is done."

"Let him find us," Darstan said. "I'll teach him—"

"And even if you could defeat him, it would take using a lot of power, which would bring the Lights quicker than you can imagine. I know you're strong, Darstan, but you can't defeat all the Lights. I doubt you could defeat one of them."

"There's no sense in speculating on it," Wisp said. "Whether he could or couldn't, we're not going to risk it. And that means we have to figure out another way to approach this."

"We can just stay here," Darstan said. "If we don't use powers, they can't find us."

"Don't be too sure," Melissara said. "Someone talented in Sensing can do amazing things with tracing."

"What you need to do is figure out what the Light Serpents meant by the Mother," Benna said.

Darstan laughed. "Benna, even if I knew how or where to find them, I don't know if I'd go. Not much frightens me, but they did."

Benna was near blind, but he had an uncanny way of knowing who spoke and where to focus on them. "You said they sent you their thoughts when they came to you?"

Darstan nodded. "They did."

"Then do the same. When you go to bed tonight, think of the Mother and of the questions you have about her. Perhaps your thoughts will reach them."

Melissara almost leapt from her chair. "Benna, that's a wonderful idea. I like it."

Darstan frowned and shook his head. "I don't know if I like it, but I'll try it. If they didn't kill me the first time, I imagine I'll be safe again."

Benna smiled. "If they had wanted you dead, you'd have been dead. I have no doubts about that."

"With that frightening thought in mind, I think I'll retire," Darstan said.

"One more thought, Darstan. Instead of thinking about '*who* is the Mother?' think of '*where* is the Mother?' It seems as if they want you to find her. I don't know if they wish you to know who she is."

Darstan hesitated before closing the bedroom door, but when he finally did, he quickly prepared for bed, though he dreaded what may happen.

He removed his boots and clothes, then got under the covers and lay down to sleep. He closed his eyes and began thinking, much the same way he focused on accessing the palace in his mind, the one that held all the secrets.

Before long, his eyes closed and sleep overcame him. It wasn't long after that, his mind shook with the reverberations of a distant voice.

She wants to see you, and you need *to see her. Follow the path past Runella and search the worlds beyond.*

Do not *let anyone follow.* Do not *take anyone with you. She wants to see you. No one else.*

Darstan tossed over in bed, then he rolled to the side, almost falling off. *How will I get there?*

Be ready in the morning. We will take you. Come see us.

Darstan arrived late to the breakfast table, well past the serving of food and khaffe.

"Sleep well?" Melissara asked.

"I had visitors, if that's what you mean," he said.

Startled, Melissara turned. "Them? They came?"

Darstan nodded. "I did what Benna suggested, and they came just like the last time. They said the Mother wants to see me—"

Melissara got up from the table. "Then, I'll—"

"Me alone, they said. I'm supposed to go to them, and they'll take me."

"Go where? That's crazy," Melissara said.

"The basement," Benna said. "There is a room no one enters. I'm sure that's what they mean."

"When are you to go?"

Darstan picked up the mug of khaffe Benna placed in front of him. "This morning. That's all they said."

"One of us should go with you," Wisp said.

Darstan shook his head. "They said 'alone,' Wisp. I'm not going to argue."

Benna moved into the kitchen. "I'll fix you some food, Master Darstan. What would you like?"

"Thanks, Benna, but I'd rather go on an empty stomach. Let me finish the khaffe, then I'll ask you to walk me to the room.

IT'S TIME TO HIDE AGAIN

They gathered in Mikkellana's room after lunch, and after everyone connected. They were about to Shift when Mikkellana broke the link.

She had been prepared to Shift, then thought of something. "I'll be right back," she said, and exited the room in a hurry. She found the shulan and asked to speak with him privately. Once his aides left, she started. "Shulan, we are leaving, going back to Sykor to see if we can help some of those who need help the most."

"What can I do to assist?"

"We know that Anciara is on her way here. If she finds us gone, she will torture every one of you until she gets what she wants or until you're all dead."

The shulan kept his stoic composure. "What can I do for my people?"

Mikkellana smiled. "I hoped you'd see the problem. I suggest everyone—and I mean *everyone*—leave on ships and sail to Arangar."

"Why Arangar?"

"Because she won't know how to get there without being guided by someone. If there's no one to guide her, she won't be able to get there at all, or at least for some time. Perhaps enough time to give us a chance to find a plan to defeat her."

The shulan nodded. "I'll put out the word at once. I am sure there will be many who object, but I promise we will be gone in days."

Mikkellana placed her arm on his shoulder. "I thank you, Shulan. Your help is much appreciated."

Mikkellana rejoined her companions, then she and Aenaila Shifted, reappearing outside Chingua, the capital city of Arangar.

Rhaven looked toward the city gates, then in back of him and up the hillside. "What are we doing *here*? Isn't this Arangar?"

"It is," Aenaila said. "It's Chingua, the capital city. Mikkellana and I both felt Anciara wouldn't be familiar with this place, nor would anyone she could torture. Even if she got to Arangar by way of ship, it would be a long way to get inland to Chingua and would take a long time."

Camissa finished brewing khaffe while Tobias cooked biscuits. When she finished, she poured a mug for herself, then sat on a nearby stump to enjoy the drink. "I'm sure glad we're finally safe and sound. Anciara can't find us here."

"Don't be so sure," Mikkellana said.

"What do you mean by that?" Tobias asked.

Mikkellana finished chewing a biscuit, then said, "I mean just what I said—that you shouldn't be so sure she can't find us."

"How would she?" Tobias asked.

Melissara stepped up alongside her sister. "I don't know if *she* could or not, but I know Tirzinitzia could."

"How do you know that?" Camissa asked. "I thought it was everyone's opinion we'd be safe here."

"And I think we *will* be, at least for a while. As to Tirzinitzia, when we were trapped in Sethia, I saw what she could do with Sensing. She can Sense what power was used and often who used it just by running her fingertips over the ground. Combine that ability with Anciara's fondness for torturing people, and it may not take much for them to get here. Don't misunderstand me; it will be a while, but not forever. Not long enough for us to forget we're in hiding."

Tobias nodded. "It's like waitin' for a bear to wake from sleep. While he's sleeping you're safe, but when he wakes, watch out. In other words, we still need a way to beat her."

"Exactly," Mikkellana said. "As my sister said, we can't let our guard down because it's only a matter of time."

Camissa drained her mug. "Even if she can find Arangar, what good will it do? She doesn't know where we are, and Arangar covers a lot of land."

"You're right, Camissa, she doesn't know where we are," Mikkellana said. "But I have no doubt she'll find someone from Entiria who will guess where we went, and she'll search until we're found. And even though I advised the shulan that everyone leave, I doubt they will. There are always a few who refuse to do the sensible thing. If that happens, it won't take her long to find someone to lead her here."

Camissa raised her head and looked at Mikkellana, a question in her gaze. "I understand that, Mikkellana, but like I said, Arangar is huge. We could avoid her for years."

Mikkellana nodded her head. "I know it seems as if it should be that way, but I'm sure that Tirzinitzia is able to Sense power over far distances, and assuming they're close enough, that Sensing ability may very well determine our fate."

"What can we do?" Camissa asked. "We're running out of places to hide."

"I have one idea, and I know just who can help." Mikkellana rose and walked to Aenaila. "We need to talk. I have an idea that may help us remain hidden. Not forever, but for a good while."

Aenaila nodded, rose from her seat, and followed Mikkellana to a place they could speak privately.

Aenaila spoke as Mikkellana sat. "I'm up for anything, so tell me about your idea and how I might help."

Mikkellana sat upright. "I have no doubt that sooner or later, Anciara will find someone in Entiria, or somewhere else, who will mention Arangar. Before she does that, however, she may consider we returned to Genda or Sykor or any other of the cities. As far as we know, she isn't even aware of Arangar and if we give her other options, she may *never* know."

Aenaila scrunched her brows. "I'm not sure I follow what you're saying."

Mikkellana patted the log next to her, one which could serve as a seat. "It's a detailed strategy, but, if it works, it will be more than worth it."

"What's the strategy?"

"First, Shift back to Entiria. Once there, find Anciara'a ship and sink it. Destroy it by setting fire to ambergis or anything you can think of. After you destroy it, Shift to Genda, then wait a while."

Aenaila tightened her brow. "How will this help? She can shift to Genda as well."

"True," Mikkellana said. "But there are two possibilities. First, if they shift to Genda and you're still there, take that opportunity to shift to Sykor or Pomanda or Khatara. After you've done that, Shift back here. I'm betting that either Tirzinitzia or Anciara will detect your presence in Genda which will lead them to search the other cities."

"And if that doesn't work?" Aenaila asked.

"If it doesn't work, it means they have to get another ship and start over."

Aenaila nodded, then smiled. "I like that, Mikkellana. I like it a lot."

Mikkellana took Aenaila's hands in hers. "There's another piece to this puzzle. It's more dangerous, but it's potentially more effective as a strategy."

"Let's hear it."

"Let's assume she finds out we're in Arangar. That does her no good as far as Shifting goes. She'll still have to sail here. If she takes another ship, and if we can get a Shift point on that ship, we wait until she gets as close to Arangar as possible, Shift aboard the ship and destroy it, then immediately Shift to another location. Unless they want to drown, they'll have to Shift to Genda or Entiria or someplace."

Aenaila smiled. "I like that plan even better. The best part of that plan is we can delay them forever."

Mikkellana's smile matched Aenaila's although she advised caution. "I don't know about forever. After a few times, I'm sure Anciara will figure out a way to set a trap, but it should work more than once or twice, and even that will buy us months."

"I think it's a good plan, especially since there is no one left in Entiria to guide her here. Without them, I don't know who could guide her, but even if she finds a way, this plan will stop her."

"In that case, you should take your leave," Mikkellana said, and she stood to hug her. "I wish you luck though I doubt you'll need it. I've seen how good you are."

"I'll be off as soon as I say goodbye to that little rascal, Adju. Will you make sure to have someone look after him?"

"Of course. I'll have Rhaven watch him. He acts as if he minds, but he doesn't. I think he likes it."

Aenaila smiled. "I know what you mean. Wisp was the first one to fall for his charms. Now he's lost without that little troublemaker."

enaila Shifted to the back alley in Genda where she and Mikkellana had gone before. After checking to ensure no one was nearby, she meandered to the docks to look for Anciara.

She didn't see her at first and asked a few sailors if they knew if her ship had sailed yet.

"If you're talkin' about that witch, she's gone, and not a minute too soon. Left with a full crew, one of them my wife's cousin. I told him not to go. Told him it would likely be his last voyage, but he wouldn't listen."

The man turned his head and spit a wad of tobacco on the dock. "Been tryin' to teach that lad all my life, but he never listened. Always thinkin' about gold and the promise of riches."

He picked up a bale of hay and carried it toward a ship about to sail. "Told him all the time that you can't sail with the captain who promises you riches; you gotta go with the one who promises to bring you home safe. Go on enough of them voyages where you come home safe and the riches will follow."

"Did they say where they were headed?" Aenaila asked.

"Far as I know, back where they lost their other ship—the Sea of the Lost. I'm wagerin' two vidda against a mug of ale they don't return from this one either. Take my word for it, lass. They won't be comin' back; leastwise, the crew won't be."

"I thank you for your wisdom, good sir, and I wish you well on your journey," Aenaila said.

Chapter Twenty-Two

SALINAS PAYS A VISIT

S alinas sat on the steps by the library, waiting for his team to show. After a few moments, Edgar and Sinta returned, and they were followed closely by Petr.

"Well?" Salinas asked.

All of them shook their heads. "You know we'd have gotten here earlier if we had anything," Petr said.

"Nothing?" Salinas asked.

Despite the pressure, Edgar answered *no*, and it was echoed by the rest of them.

"It's time we take the search farther out," Salinas said. "If they aren't in the city, we'll begin searching the outskirts, then even farther to the surrounding areas, then to the countryside, and then to other cities and worlds. One way or another, the ones doing this *will* be found. And they'll be found by us."

"Suppose the ones doing this are strong?" Edgar asked. "The man who was healed said there were four of them. There are only four of us. Perhaps we should recruit a few others."

Salinas paced in front of the guards. "Edgar, I've known you most of your life. You're not one that typically shows fear." Salinas faced Petr and Senta. "I haven't known you two as long, but you've served me for a while, and I've never seen signs of reluctance when it comes to a battle."

He clasped his hands behind his back and continued pacing. "If anyone has hesitation, the time to show it is now. If I see any form of reluctance during battle, you won't have need to fear the enemy, I'll kill you myself."

Salinas stopped pacing and faced them all. "Is that clear?"

"Clear," they all said.

"Good, then let's get to work. Petr, go with Edgar and take the western part of town. Sinta and I will take the east. If you find *anything*, you're to notify me at once. That means *do not* touch the crime scene; in fact, do not contaminate it in any way."

"Clear," Edgar said.

Edgar and Petr went off to the western part of town, careful to meticulously examine each street, especially the intersections. By mid-afternoon, they'd found no clues and hunger had made a comfortable home in Edgar's stomach.

"I need to stop, Petr," Edgar said. "I'm starving."

Petr pointed ahead. "There's a fruit stand up there, and it's got fresh goods. I've eaten there numerous times."

"I'm elated to hear the fruit is fresh, Petr, but I was thinking of something more nourishing. Fresh game and some ale, perhaps."

Petr smiled. "I see. In that case, a tavern lies only a short distance farther. It will have what we need."

"Lead the way, then," Edgar said.

After eating a hearty meal, the soldiers picked up tracing. A slight Sensing near the library led them to another slight Sensing a few streets away.

"Isn't this where Salinas picked up the scent earlier?" Petr asked. "It led nowhere."

Edgar nodded. "You're right, Petr. We've already followed this, but I have to wonder again, why it stopped here, and with no trace of them having Shifted. It's almost as if they disappeared."

Petr laughed. "No one can disappear, Edgar. It must be something else."

Edgar glanced in all directions and used all his Senses, then he dispatched Probes in each direction. "I know that people should not be able to disappear, but the question is *can they?*"

"What does that mean?"

"Keep alert, and we may soon find out," Edgar said. "The evidence of our Sensing says the trail stops here, but we know they didn't. Since evidence doesn't lie, we're left with a quandary. Where did they go, and how did they get there?"

"We'll have time to figure that out later," Petr said. "For now, let's keep moving west."

Edgar shook his head. "No need to. The trail from the library shows them heading east, then it disappears. I'm going to assume that however they managed to vanish, they continued going east."

"What do we do, then?"

"We rejoin Salinas," Edgar said. "This is going to require more thought."

Petr shook. "And what do we tell him?"

Edgar grinned. "Relax, Petr. We'll tell him what we know, which is a lot more than you seem to think it is."

"What do you mean? We know *nothing*. Nothing at all."

Edgar sighed and sat on a bench used by people awaiting moving carts. "Sit, Petr. And *try* to learn."

Petr sat beside Edgar. "I'm listening."

Edgar faced him. "You said we know nothing, but let's review that. We had a report of low-level power being used in the library. When we arrived, there was nothing, but the trail led to an aisle between the bookshelves where power was once again used."

"Yes, but we have no idea what kind of power," Petr said.

Edgar smiled. "Precisely. And that tells us a lot."

Petr scoffed. "How does not knowing tell you anything?"

"I know if someone has used Shielding, or Fire, or Lightning, or *any* of the offensive powers. I know if someone has Shifted or used Illusion. I can even tell if someone has Healed another person. But they can all be eliminated because they weren't detected. That doesn't leave us with much, Petr."

"What could it be?"

"I don't know, but it can't be much. We'll leave the clever parts up to Salinas, which means we better go see him soon."

Melissara pressed her finger to Wisp's mouth just as he was about to speak. "Let's be cautious," she whispered. "Check the house first."

Darstan nodded. "I'll take downstairs while Wisp does the main level and you do the rest, Melissara."

She nodded. "Agreed," she said, and trod lightly as she climbed the stairs.

Thirty minutes later, they rejoined in the kitchen. "Sorry for the alarm," Melissara said, "but it is better to be cautious."

"It's not a problem, My Lady Melissara. When caution gets into an argument with carelessness, I *always* choose caution."

Melissara scrunched her eyebrows and stared, but Darstan pulled her aside. "Pay him no mind. He often utters nonsense like that. I quit listening to him long ago."

Melissara shook her head. "Wisp, Darstan, we need a plan. If you're to visit the Mother, Darstan, you should get a full night's rest because I have no idea what you'll face. And we should rest also, Wisp, because regardless of logic, I'm sure the Lights or Salinas or both will find their way here in due time. If they do, we need to be prepared."

"Are you sure you're going to be all right?" Darstan asked.

Melissara smiled. "No, Darstan, I'm not. But we have no choice. You have to visit the Mother which means we have to wait here."

"I'll pack food for you, Master Darstan."

"No need, Benna. I doubt if they would try killing me by starving me. I'm sure there will be *something* to eat even if I don't like it."

Melissara leaned over and kissed Darstan on the cheek. "Sleep well and good luck tomorrow."

Chapter Twenty-Three

THE MOTHER

Once again Darstan refused breakfast, so Benna walked to the door leading down to the basement, and Darstan followed closely. Benna stopped and turned before proceeding. "This way, Master Darstan. If you want to visit them, we have to go this way."

Darstan set his mug on a table they passed and continued to follow. "Lead on, Benna. I'm as ready as I'm going to be."

Benna held onto the railing as he led the way down a long flight of stairs, treading carefully. "Don't worry, Master Darstan, if they didn't bother you the two times they visited you, I'm sure they won't bother you now."

"How are they going to help me? What are they?"

A shake of Benna's head answered Darstan. "I have no idea how to respond to either question. I will lead you to the entrance, but after that, it's up to you."

Benna stopped in front of a large steel door near the end of the hallway. He gestured in that general direction. "In there is where you will find them. I think."

"You *think*?"

"Exactly. I don't know for sure, but I think you will find them inside. Master Antar always warned me to avoid this room, so I'm only guessing." He turned to leave, walking down the darkened hall without a light. "May good fortune walk through the door with you, Master Darstan."

Darstan took a deep breath, then slowly opened the door. He stepped inside and looked around, but nothing was there. Nothing. The room was large, as big as the kitchen and dining area together, but it was empty—no furniture, no other walls, not even support beams—just a mud floor with a few rocks jutting out.

He called out a few times, but nothing happened, then he thought about how he contacted them the night before—by focusing on his thoughts. With that in mind, he closed his eyes and focused all thoughts inward in an attempt to reach them.

"You told me to come, and I am here."

Within moments, the massive head of a serpent breached the surface of the ground near the side wall. A moment later, the other serpent rose from the ground, its forked tongue tasting the air rapidly.

"It is good you are here. Prepare yourself with Fire. Where we are going, it is too cold for your body."

Darstan was about to speak, then thought better and focused on thinking. *"Should I get a cloak or something warmer?"*

"It is too cold for a cloak or anything else to help. You must use Fire. Nothing else will keep you warm—no matter what you wear. Do as we say and prepare yourself with Fire."

Darstan did as told, calling Fire to the forefront and letting it sizzle inside him. *"Ready."*

Both Light Serpents leaned against him, then the three of them disappeared, only to become visible again at the entrance to a darkened cave somewhere in the mountains.

Darstan looked up but saw no moon or sun. His Fire warded off the cold surrounding him, but even that seemed difficult. Cold and night were everywhere. *"Where are we?"*

"We are home. You are at the home of the Mother. Now you must see her."

Darstan looked at the Light Serpents. *"How do I see the Mother?"*

"Enter the cave and go all the way to the rear. Don't stop or take any turns along the way."

"It's too dark in there. I can't see," Darstan said.

"That will be taken care of. Just go."

Darstan walked toward the cave. He trod slowly, both because of the dark, and because he was leery of the Light Serpents. After six or seven steps into the cave, a few dozen Slicers came from the rear. They glowed enough to light the way and allow Darstan to see, and, being able to see, he quickened his pace.

Several times, Darstan focused on his thoughts, but the Slicers didn't answer him. A few moments later, a bright light emanated from the end of the path. His instinct advised him to turn around or at least slow down; instead, he moved faster toward the glowing object. A moment later he stepped into a large cavern, empty but for a column as big across as several men and taller than four of them, and the light that emanated proved strong enough to make him shield his eyes even when looking away.

Something slammed into Darstan's mind, causing his body to vibrate as if someone hit him. Then a thought—a strong one—reverberated inside his head.

"Have you come here to kill the Lights?"

The feeling was similar to when the Light Serpents contacted him, but this was stronger and clearer.

Darstan didn't know what to say at first, so he thought he better stick to the truth. Besides, he wasn't sure if they could determine a lie or not. *"I came to get something called the Book. My brother came to kill the Lights."*

"It's good that you work together on this, for to get the Book, you must kill the Lights. Your brother is not strong enough to do that. And neither are you. To kill the Lights, you must listen to me."

"I've heard better threats from ones stronger than you," Darstan said. *"You don't know how strong I am."*

Before Darstan could form another thought, a thousand Slicers appeared and hovered a hair's breadth away from him. Then the Mother glowed like never before. The cavern lit as if it were day, and the Slicers vibrated rapidly. Darstan could *feel* them pulsing.

He laughed. *"You can't scare me with Slicers; they won't enter me. They've tried before."*

Sounds of laughter echoed through the cavern, then Darstan staggered as a lone Slicer pushed through the nape of his neck and dug deeply into the base of his skull. He stumbled until he fell against the far wall, but he managed to keep standing by holding onto protruding rocks.

"When the Slicers wouldn't enter you before, it was my *doing. I told them not to harm you because I needed you for other things. More important things."*

The revelation shocked Darstan, but it also stirred his curiosity. *"What other things?"*

"Exactly what you're here for now—to kill the Lights and retrieve the Book."

"I didn't come here for that. I only came for the Book."

"You can pretend to fool yourself, Darstan, but you can't fool me. Whether you realize it or not, the reason you came here is exactly what I said—to kill the Lights and get the Book. And you won't leave here until the job is done—or you won't leave here. And once you finish, you'll go back and kill Anciara."

The Slicer flew from Darstan's neck and joined the others hovering next to the column of light.

Darstan struggled to stand straight and stable himself. Once he did, he cautiously made his way back to where he'd stood before.

"I don't know who you are or where we are, but before I do anything, I'd like answers. To begin with, what are those snake things that brought me here?"

"Very well. I will address your concerns. As to where you are, you are on the eighth planet of Nelstar."

"I thought Nelstar only had seven worlds."

"Were there places on your world that you didn't know existed?"

"Of course. I didn't know of everyplace."

"Then why should it surprise you that there are places here that you don't know exist?"

"But Melissara—"

"Melissara is but a youngster. I was here long before Melissara. Even before her father."

"What about those serpents?"

"They are my children."

"Children? What do you mean? How is that possible; they're snakes? Who are you?"

Darstan waited for almost five minutes before he was addressed. *"I am the Mother, the one you seek."*

"The Mother? Mother of what?"

"Of everything you call Slicers."

"How is that possible?"

"Sit and listen." The Mother waited for Darstan to sit on the ground, then she continued. *"In the beginning, a god and goddess ruled all the worlds—they were known as the Original Ones. The number of worlds ruled by them were too many to count. After many thousands of years, the gods produced four children—three males and a female—the female you know as Anciara.*

"The children often played on many worlds, and the parents wanted them to have a means to communicate, so they created the Slicers. I was the first of the Slicers, and I produced many children—billions of them.

"Our mission—our sole purpose in life—was to be a messenger for transmitting thoughts between the young gods. We were given speed greater than that of light, and we were given the ability to change our make-up so that we might go through anything without stopping: rock, dirt, water, glass, wood, and more.

"As all things do—even gods—the Original Ones died, and as the chil-

dren grew older, their boredom overcame common sense, and they began using us for other purposes. At first, the uses were minor variations of messaging: make a suggestion, then make a strong suggestion, convince *a person to do something, make a person do something, harm a person, and at the end—kill a person.*

"We performed as expected until the requests were meant to harm or kill others, then we established rules stating that we refused to enter another person's body if they had a mental block in place. If there was a block, a battle must ensue, and it was to be to the death. This was meant to deter harmful use.

"This worked until man came along and began using Slicers even more recklessly than the gods."

Darstan moved to the side and leaned against a large boulder. *"Why didn't it work?"*

"It may have worked but for men. Too many of the men did not have the ability to block their minds, which allowed those who used the Slicers to do so with no repercussions. Slicers were used as pure weapons, like an arrow, a spear, or a dagger."

"What happened then?" Darstan asked.

"The gods once again grew bored, and since they couldn't spar with each other, they did so using the humans, choosing sides and fighting as if they were them.

"Eventually, they were tricked by Antar and Lukaan into being held captive on your world, in the obelisk in Sethia and in the Forsaken Lands, inside the mountains. The real entrance to that is sealed inside the obelisk in Entiria.

"Now that Anciara is out, the world is no longer safe. There is no one to balance her power."

Darstan stood and stretched. *"What can I do? We tried fighting her, and our powers did nothing. Even the Slicers I used did nothing."*

"You'll never defeat her without three things: you'll need—"

"I'll need what?"

"Never mind. You have to get back to the manor. Melissara is in trouble."

"*What? How can I make it from here?*"

"*My children will take you. Go to the entrance and tell them. Hurry. When you return, I'll tell you the rest.*"

Darstan raced to the entrance to the cave and approached the Light Serpents. "*The Mother said—*"

"*We know; Mother told us.*" One of the Light Serpents latched onto Darstan, then they Shifted.

Chapter Twenty-Four

A VISIT TO THE MANOR

"Petr, Edgar, have you found anything yet? "Salinas asked.

"Nothing we haven't seen before. But I wanted to talk about what we saw at the library. We reviewed the evidence by the library again, as well as the street across from it. That same evidence can be traced to locations a few streets away, but then it stops dead. Dead. No Shifting, no fading. It stops dead when it shouldn't."

"How can that be?" Salinas asked. "People don't just disappear."

"We both know that as true, Salinas, but in the library, they did it; they disappeared."

"Explain."

"We went to the place where the low-level reading originated, then we followed it to the aisle between the stacks. At that point, power was used, but I couldn't determine which power, and the trace of them disappeared."

"That's impossible," Salinas said.

Edgar stepped forward and cleared his throat. "I understand. I don't have an answer, but we did make note that all traces pointed in one direction. Every place we looked, when the trail disappeared, it led in that direction." Edgar pointed east. "The library's trace was the most distinct, but the trail from the man who was healed exhibited similar signs."

Salinas looked around the area. "I don't see much here except a few houses, and the farther we get from the city, the fewer houses there are."

"Then maybe we should go to each house and investigate," Petr said. "Isn't that the way you taught us, Salinas?"

Salinas gestured to the street on his left. "We'll start here and conduct a methodical search. If they're here, we'll find them."

Salinas and his men searched house-by-house down both sides of two streets for almost a league, but they found nothing.

"What now?" Petr asked.

"We do the same tomorrow morning, starting on the Way. Wherever they are, they can't hide for long."

I n the morning, Petr and Edgar took the east side of the street while Salinas and the other guard handled the west.

"At least the houses are farther apart," Edgar said. "It makes the job a lot easier."

"This job won't get easier until we find the ones using powers; in fact, knowing Salinas, it will get much more difficult."

"I don't see the big deal," Edgar said. "If we don't find them, someone will find them eventually."

Petr laughed. "I guess you didn't ask enough questions before you joined this branch of the guard."

"What's that supposed to mean?"

"It means, if we don't find the people who are using powers, we die. The penalty for failure is the same as the penalty for using the powers—death."

Salinas investigated two more houses, then met with Petr and Edgar before moving on. "If anyone is superstitious, now's the time to get sick and go home."

"Why did you say that?" Edgar asked.

"Because we're about to come to the legendary manor of the even more legendary Antar du Suvarra, Light of Lights, Keeper of the Flame, He Who Drank the Darkness."

"Antar! I've heard strange things happened in that house," Petr said.

"A lot more than strange things," Edgar said. "And from what I've heard, it's *happen*, not *happened*. Some people, people not prone to exaggeration, say there are Light Serpents in there."

"There are no such things as Light Serpents," Petr said.

Salinas grinned. "Don't be too sure. I've heard those rumors too, and as Edgar said, they originated with reliable people."

"Let's go," Petr said. "I'm not going to let fear of something that isn't real deter me from catching these people."

"I thought all the Du Suvarras were gone," Edgar said.

"They are. Antar was killed, and his children were exiled. I heard the only one living at the manor is an old blind servant."

"The thing that bothers me is that old blind servants don't look like Light Serpents. If he's the only one there, where did the legends come from? Legends usually have *some* aspect of truth to them."

Petr's voice quaked a little. "What *are* Light Serpents anyway? What makes them so dangerous?"

Salinas crept along slowly, glancing in all directions. "No one knows what they are, or what they're supposed to be, but if legend holds any truth, they are a formidable foe—more than a formidable foe. It's been said, nothing harms them. Not Lightning, Fire, or even ColdFire."

"Not ColdFire?" Petr asked.

Salinas shook his head. "Legend says that Lukaan tried the night he killed Antar's wife, but it didn't work. He had to hide on Runella to get away."

"If that's true, what are we doing here?" Petr asked.

"A job," Salinas said. "We took an assignment, and it must be finished. Or would you rather report your fear to the Council?"

Petr gulped. "Not much of a choice is there?"

"I disagree," Salina said. "We only *think* there may be Light Serpents; we *know* the Lights exist."

Chapter Twenty-Five

WELCOME HOME, MELISSARA

Melissara wiped her mouth after finishing breakfast, then stood. "Ready to go, Wisp? This world is no different than the one you come from: time doesn't wait."

"It will have to make the same exceptions my world did because I'm not quite ready. Go outside, and I'll join you in a moment."

"It better be only a moment. After that, I begin walking."

"The prospect of you walking doesn't bother me. I can catch up with you if you're walking. It's only you Shifting that worries me."

Melissara smiled, then opened the front door and stepped outside, only to be greeted by Salinas and his guards.

She recognized him immediately; he was once in her unit under Lukaan. She only hoped he didn't recognize her. "Good morning, sir. May I help you?"

Salinas stared, then stared some more. Finally, he smiled broadly. "Melissara! What an unexpected pleasure."

She raised her brows as if confused. "Melissara? I'm sorry, sir, but my name is Daniella."

"Shield her," Salinas said to his men, then, "That was a good attempt, Melissara, and it *has* been a long time, but I'd remember you for twice as long. You almost killed me on several occasions."

Melissara was about to lash out when she felt the shields closing in on her. She recalled enough about Salinas to know if he wrapped her in a shield, there would be no getting away, leastwise not before help arrived to assist him.

"What is it you want, Salinas?"

He smiled. "Now we're getting somewhere. Just tell me who has been using the powers, and we can be done with this. I don't even have to report you being back, though I would like to know how you managed it. And I'd like to know if Aentarra is with you."

Melissara smiled. "You should be afraid, Salinas. The last time I saw my sister, she was about ten times as strong as she was when she left Nelstar. More than strong enough to deal with you."

isp reached for the handle on the large double doors, then stopped when he heard voices from outside.

He peeked out the window and saw Salinas and his men, then he noticed Melissara, and she seemed to be held against her will. He suspected a shield but he couldn't see any.

Wisp sneaked out the back door, Cloaked himself, then crept around the manor house until he was almost on top of them.

id you Sense that?" Petr asked. "Someone used powers, and it wasn't far from here. Out back, I think."

Salinas gestured toward the back of the house. "Check it out quickly. We'll wait here." He turned back to Melissara. "Who was it, Melissara? Care to tell us now? If not, you'll make it worse for all of you?"

Petr moved toward the rear of the manor, passing within an

arm's length of Wisp, who stayed Cloaked. He went around the corner of the house and moved forward slowly.

Wisp waited until Petr got out of sight, then he pulled two daggers from sheaths at his side and approached Salinas and the other guards silently.

Once he was within striking distance, he jammed a dagger into Salinas's ear, piercing his eardrum while simultaneously doing the same to the other guard. He then slashed both their throats.

Edgar ran, but as he did, he let go the shield on Melissara, who immediately struck him with BlackLightning several times, dropping him to the ground. She then struck Salinas and the other guard for good measure and grabbed hold of Wisp. "We must leave quickly."

"Not yet," Wisp said, and he ran toward the back of the manor where Petr had gone.

Melissara Shifted in front of Wisp and seized him as he ran by. As soon as she had hold of him, she Shifted to a spot inside the house. She grabbed Benna to Shift, then thought of the bodies lying in front of the house. "We need to get rid of them," she said. "Come out front with me. We'll get the bodies, then Shift."

After taking hold of the bodies, Melissara Shifted to the caves where they'd left Rahg.

They reappeared deep inside the cave, and Melissara lit a wall lamp to provide light. "We should be safe here."

"You shouldn't have done that, Melissara. I could have taken that guard. Now, we've left a witness."

Melissara laughed. "You think all that use of power would have gone undetected? It doesn't matter if that guard is alive or not. The Lights will know what took place and where."

"But now they'll have someone to confirm it," Wisp said.

"My dear boy, they don't need someone to confirm it. If a Light suspects you, you're dead. That's how things work here."

Benna nodded. "Lady Melissara is right. It's how things have been for many years."

Melissara held Benna by the shoulders. "Benna, can you make it to your manor? And will you be safe there?"

Benna nodded. "Yes to both questions, My Lady." He leaned in and kissed her cheek. "That will have to serve as a temporary goodbye kiss. And tell Lady Mikkellana I send my love as well. Tell her I miss her."

"I will, Benna. Be assured of that."

Rahg walked in, surprise showing on his face. "Wisp, Melissara! What are you doing here? And what are these bodies doing here?"

"We ran into trouble," Melissara said. "And if you and Wisp don't mind, we have to bury these."

"I can handle that," Rahg said, "But where's Darstan?"

"Not back yet," Melissara said. "And we don't know when he *will* be back." Melissara then related the events at the manor to Rahg.

"What'll happen to Darstan when he returns? Won't he go to the manor?"

Melissara lowered her head. "By the blood! I hadn't thought of that, but you're right. That would be the only place he'd know to go to."

"Our only hope is the Light Serpents will take him to their room in the basement," Wisp said. "I doubt if anyone will look down there. At least not at first."

"We've got to do something," Rahg said.

Melissara held him in place. "There's nothing we can do, Rahg. If I knew where Darstan was, I could get a message to him, but I don't have a clue."

Wisp sat quietly for a few moments, then he said, "I have an idea. Suppose we Shift to the basement, the room where the Light Serpents were. Once there, I can Cloak us and we can go upstairs."

"I commend you for your brilliance, Wisp, but there are several problems with your plan. First, I don't have a Shift point to that room, and second, once the Lights know you're in their presence—and they'll know as soon as we Shift—they will spread Fire or Lightning or worse over the room until it consumes you. Being cloaked protects you from being seen and even Sensed, but not from being killed."

Wisp nodded. "I hadn't thought of that."

"My father taught us you must learn to think before you can fight. He always said the best thinker in the world will kill the best fighter."

Rahg seemed ready to panic. "Then what do we do?"

"We wait," Melissara said. "Darstan is strong. The strongest I've seen since my father. And don't forget, he has two Light Serpents with him. That's an advantage not many can boast."

At a long table in the Great Hall, Borrik and Exeter sipped on te while discussing the day's events. Borrik shook, spilling his drink. "Did you feel that?"

Xeter stood, nodding. "How could I not. It was much more than a minor transgression."

"Send for Salinas," Borrik said.

"We have no time for that. We'll do it ourselves."

Borrik and Xeter Shifted to the spot where they had Sensed the power, which brought them to the front steps of Antar's manor.

"This is Antar's manor," Xeter said. "What are we doing here?"

Borrik looked about cautiously. "Investigating a transgression. Or did you forget?"

"But I thought only the blind servant lived here."

"And so did everyone, but unless he has developed significant powers, another has taken up residence."

Borrik reached for the door handle and pushed, letting the door slide open. "Let's go. Somebody's going to pay for this."

Xeter followed Borrik inside, all the while remaining alert to danger. "Proceed slowly," he said. "Whoever did this may still be here."

"If they are, we'll take care of them soon enough," Borrik said as he moved into the next room.

~

The Light Serpents and Darstan reappeared in the basement room, seeming refreshed and energized.

"Make no noise," One of the Light Serpents said. *"There are strangers in the house."*

Darstan almost spoke, then remembered he had to communicate with thoughts. *"How do you know that?"*

"Because we do. Now be still while we investigate."

Darstan sat with his back against the wall while the Light Serpents slithered through the door.

A moment later, sounds of battle erupted from upstairs. Darstan stood and moved toward the door, contemplating whether to go up or not.

The ruckus continued, so Darstan exited the room and climbed the stairs. In the almost-empty room, two Lights battled the Light Serpents, Fire and Lightning raging.

The Lights issued all manner of attacks at the Light Serpents, only to see them disappear. They vanished under the floor or above the ceiling, reappearing again a short distance away. Each time they reappeared, they continued a relentless advance on the Lights.

"Nothing's working," Borrik said. "Retreat."

"I'm not about to go back like a whipped puppy," Xeter said. "Focus."

The Light Serpents appeared at that instant—one rose from the floor, the other descended from the ceiling. They coiled around the Lights, squeezing them until the Lights couldn't move. *"Now, Darstan."*

"You're in the way," Darstan said.

"It doesn't matter. Do it now."

Darstan wasn't about to give the Lights another chance. He focused his own power and unleashed a barrage of ColdFire, aimed at both of them. It shot forth from his left arm and raced across the room in an undulating wave. When it struck, the Lights shattered, pieces of them flying in all directions.

Darstan was stunned. He stopped and stared at what remained of the Lights. He was even more stunned when the Light Serpents rose from the floor and slithered toward him. As he wondered how that was possible, the Light Serpents sidled up to him.

"We must leave now. Others will be coming."

"How? What happened? Why weren't you hurt?"

"The Lights are dead. You killed them. It doesn't matter about us."

"Me?" Darstan asked. *"I killed them? I think you did all the work."*

The Light Serpents moved closer to him until they touched his skin, then they Shifted, reappearing in the same place they had taken him before—outside the entrance to the cave where the Mother was.

Darstan looked from one serpent to the other. *"Why weren't you hurt? I hit you with ColdFire."*

"Mother awaits."

"I'm to go back in?"

"Learn your fate. Only then can it be fulfilled."

ANCIARA CONTINUES HER SEARCH

Fernando got through the doldrums, and shortly afterward, he hit the storms that ravaged his ship on the last voyage. He ran below and sought Anciara. "My Lady, I know it's my responsibility, but we've hit the rough seas, and they're giving my men a hard time. If there's anything you can do to help, it'd be good; otherwise, I'm afraid we'll lose the ship."

Anciara pushed past Fernando and onto the deck where waves taller than three men crashed on board and threatened to capsize them. She looked about, then focused, placing a shield on either side of the ship, offering protection from the winds and the sea. She then erected more shields in front of them shaped like a pyramid so the ship had a safe channel to sail through.

She turned and scowled at Fernando. "There, Captain. You now have your protection. Make sure you use it well, as I won't be so forgiving next time."

Fernando blinked rapidly while staring at the safety provided by Anciara. "Yes, My Lady. I'll call you when we dock."

"It better not be before then," Anciara said, and went to her cabin.

Fernando managed to steer the ship through the straits while avoiding the rocks that jutted from the roiling sea. After an arduous journey, he breathed a sigh of relief as he anchored in a cove with calm waters.

Once secure, he knocked on the cabin door. "My Lady, we're here. We've arrived."

Anciara emerged moments later, followed by Tirzinitzia exiting her cabin. "I think we should see what's here," Tirzinitzia said.

"Remain here," Anciara said to Fernando. "Tirzinitzia and I will scout the area."

"How will you do that?" Fernando asked. "I don't see a way out of here."

Anciara's laugh held her scorn in check. "Do as I say, Captain." She turned to Tirzinitzia, grabbed her hand, then Sight Shifted to the top of the nearest mountain. From there, it was only three more shifts until they reached the city. "This has to be it," Anciara said. "I'd recognize that obelisk anywhere."

Tirzinitzia nodded. "As would I. But I see no one around. I wonder why."

Anciara and Tirzinitzia entered the temple, then searched diligently in every corner of the main building, then they continued with the buildings attached to it. "Am I to believe that all the people left this island? Every one of them? And if they did, why?"

Tirzinitzia paced the tiled floors of the room, her hands folded behind her back. "The only reason I can think of is that one or more of the Entirians knew where they Shifted to, and Mikkellana didn't want them telling us where that was. Mikkellana would know that the only way to ensure silence was to have no one here to tell."

"Where do you think the Entirians went?" Anciara asked. "Back to Genda?"

Tirzinitzia shrugged. "They could have gone anywhere. The logical guess is one of the larger cities like Genda, Sykor, Pomanda, or even Khatara, although they may know places we're not aware of. We should begin by searching the major cities, but even so, that will prove to be difficult, and it will take a lot of time."

"You heard what the sailor in Genda told us. He said there was another land the Entirians knew of. *He* didn't know where it was, but he said *they* did."

"If they sailed everyone away from here, they didn't do it from that cove," Tirzinitzia said. "That means they must have a port free from the deadly winds and the currents and rocks. There is no way anyone sails from where we landed, not on a regular basis."

"Then let's find it," Anciara said, and they began Shifting toward the western coast. Within moments, they identified the port, along with a few ships that remained tied to the docks. "Looks like we found what we wanted," Anciara said as Tirzinitzia walked the dock.

She boarded the closest ship and strolled about, examining the masts and sails. "Looks to be a well-built vessel," she said, then continued looking at the cabins and crew's quarters.

A moment later, Tirzinitzia stopped pacing and stared. "Wait, I Sense something."

"What?"

"The ship!" Tirzinitzia said. "We must get to the ship, now."

Tirzinitzia and Anciara Shifted to the harbor only to see the ship they used to sail to Entiria in flames. The crew was nowhere in sight.

"How did this happen?" Anciara asked.

Tirzinitzia walked closer to the flames, then reached out and touched them. "It was them. Someone Shifted here."

Anciara spun around, looking in every direction. "Are they still here?"

"They're gone," Tirzinitzia said. "I'm sure it was Mikkellana's strategy. Destroy our ship and force us back to Genda so we waste more time."

"Hurry and get to the other ships," Anciara said.

They Shifted back to the western ports, but all the ships were ablaze. "Effective," Anciara said. "I'll give her that."

"Effective, yes, but not foolproof. Every plan has a weakness. All we have to do is find it."

Anciara narrowed her eyes and glared at Tirzinitzia. "I suggest you get busy and find that weakness."

Tirzinitzia shot her a hard-eyed glare. "If you want me to get busy, let's go."

"Go where?" Anciara asked.

"I suggest we start in Genda. If they're not there, we'll check Sykor, Khatara, Pomanda, and then figure out where else to go. They can't hide forever."

"Every minute I don't have hold of them is too long," Anciara said.

Tirzinitzia nodded. "Then I suggest we do as I said and get moving."

On the docks in Genda, amid crowds of merchants and sailors, Tirzinitzia and Anciara reappeared. Both of them scoured the area, scanning for familiar faces.

"Use your Sense," Anciara said. "And remember, one of them has Illusion."

"If we plan on continuing this chase, we need to secure another ship," Tirzinitzia said. "We need someone who can get us back to Entiria, but we also need to be able to venture farther. If the Entirians left their home, I'm willing to wager it was to go someplace we're not familiar with."

Anciara smiled. "We have no reason to worry about getting to Entiria. Find me a captain with courage, and I'll do the rest."

"And what is that?" Tirzinitzia asked.

"I took a Shift point at the dock on the other side of the island when we searched for them. I can Shift the ship fully manned when we're ready."

Tirzinitzia smiled. "I hadn't thought of that. Very good. It will save a great deal of time."

"Speaking of which, let's not waste what little we have," Anciara said. She turned and faced a group of sailors. "I've got gold and lots of it for the first crew that volunteers."

"Volunteers for what?" a sailor yelled.

"How much gold?" shouted another.

Anciara smiled. "More gold than you will need in your life," she said. "As to the other question. We're sailing on the sea. Isn't that what sailors do?"

"Aye, Ma'am. But the sea holds a lot of danger, and, though we be sailors, we're not so foolish as to spit in the eye of a shark."

A sailor wielding a hook for a hand approached. "I be volunteering, My Lady. Barnell's the name, and I've sailed with Ol' Crazy himself, so I know how to steer clear of trouble, and how to handle it if it comes our way."

Anciara stepped forward. "Did you serve long enough to be deemed a captain?"

"I can captain any ship you give me, and any crew ya put together, and woe be the man who says different."

"Which ship is yours?" Anciara asked.

Barnell gulped. "Truth is I got no ship, but if ya get me one, I'll have it rigged and manned by morning."

Anciara looked around, spotting a ship fresh in port. "Consider that one ours," she said, then turned to Tirzinitzia. "Do what's necessary to secure that ship. And I mean *whatever* is necessary."

Tirzinitzia bowed. "Your will, My Lady."

A stack of crates sat ready to be loaded on the ships waiting to sail. Between two of the stacks, Aenaila peered through at the ongoings. *The Rusty Nail. So that's the ship they'll be on.*

She waited for Anciara and Tirzinitzia to leave, then she went on board and secured a Shift Point near the back of the ship and another one in the captain's cabin. After that, she Shifted back to Arangar.

Chapter Twenty-Seven

RETURN TO THE MOTHER

No more than a few heartbeats after Shifting to the eighth world, Darstan appeared at the entrance to the cave where he had first seen the Mother. He looked at the Light Serpents, got no response, so continued inside. He was still tentative, but more comfortable than before.

Once again, Slicers appeared and lit the way for him. They stayed by his side until he reached the cavern where the Mother was.

"Welcome back, my son."

"You wanted to see me? Why?"

"You have done well, but more needs to be done."

"What?"

"The goddess must be killed, and to do that, you must get the Book, and to do that, you must kill the rest of the Lights."

"And how do I kill the Lights?"

"One at a time, if you can. And be advised, you will grow stronger after each Light you kill."

"Two are already dead, thanks to the Light Serpents. But I don't feel stronger."

"*But you are stronger. You just don't know it yet. And once you kill the last Light, you will unlock the final door.*"

"*What door?*"

"*Don't act as if you don't know—the one at the top of the stairs, the one that was locked.*"

"*What's in there?*"

"*When it's unlocked, you'll know.*"

"*What does the Book do?*"

"*While connected, the Book allows the one who touches the Book first to increase their power by magnitudes—how much the power increases depends on who else is touching the Book when linked. But be warned, the Book drains those who use it, and it takes a long time for those people to regain energy.*"

"*What does that mean?*"

"*It is a warning, nothing else. But know you will need a lot more than the Book to kill her. You will need all the powers at your command—all of them. She is not just someone with powers; she is a goddess.*"

"*I heard what you said, but what does it mean? And does she have anything to do with what Aentarra called the Others?*"

"*No. The Others were my children. Special Slicers meant to stop Aentarra and her father from doing wrong things.*"

"*Rahg said he communicated with Antar while sleeping. How did he do that if Antar was dead?*"

"*He didn't. He spoke with my children, who absorbed Antar's thoughts when he died.*"

"*So Antar is dead?*"

"*Yes. He's been dead for many centuries.*"

"*Thank you,*" Darstan said. "*I'll be off now. It seems as if I have Lights to kill.*"

"*Wait. As I said, you'll need more than the Book. Your last power allows you to make use of my children. Use that power wisely.*"

"*What does that mean? Make use of your children? What are you speaking of?*"

"*The Book is only a reflection of Persuasion, although it is a strong reflection. Your last power, however, is the ultimate. It allows you to fully control the Slicers and Light Serpents. They will be at your command."*

Darstan turned to leave.

"One more thing, Darstan. Before you leave Nelstar, you must see me. You will need my children to accompany you."

"The Light Serpents?"

"They will accompany you along with others. Just see me."

Darstan exited the cave and approached the Light Serpents. *"I suppose we need to go back, but I doubt the manor is the place to go. Not now."*

"Then where?"

Darstan thought for a moment, then said, *"There is only one safe place I know of—where Melissara took Rahg. I can provide the Shift Point."*

"We will accompany you to ensure your safety, then we will leave."

Rahg fell back when the Light Serpents appeared but regained his composure when Darstan spoke.

"We've just returned from the Mother. Things are proceeding as planned."

"I'm thrilled to hear," Melissara said, all the time eyeing the Light Serpents. "I presume these are the famed serpents."

"They are," Darstan said. "They won't bother anyone."

"You appear to be comfortable in their presence," Wisp said.

Darstan mulled it over, then said, "I guess I am, Wisp. It's strange, but you're right. I feel comfortable."

"What are your plans, Darstan? It would be nice to be aware of them."

"I don't know the plans," Darstan said. "All I know is what *not* to do."

Melissara looked skeptically at the Light Serpents. "What do we do with them while we're gone?"

"Tell her we will accompany you."

Darstan raised an eyebrow, then turned to Melissara. "They said they'll accompany us. I don't know how they understood you, but they did."

Melissara, shocked, looked over to them. "They can—"

"I'm afraid they can," Darstan said. "I wouldn't argue. Besides, they killed two Lights at the manor in no more than a few heart-beats. I helped, but they did most of it."

Melissara pondered. "We can't go back to the manor . . ."

"What about my manor?" Benna said. "I doubt the Lights even know about that."

Melissara grinned. "I hadn't thought of that, Benna. And if Wisp cloaks us, they won't be able to Sense the Shift when we appear. And the power he needs to undo the Cloak isn't enough to be Sensed so far away."

"But how will we get there?" Darstan asked. "Does anyone have a Shift point to Benna's manor?"

Benna shook his head. "Master Antar always said that every plan had a problem."

"Which is why he instructed us," one of the Light Serpents said. *"He showed us your manor before he died. We can take you."*

Benna turned and stared at the Light Serpents, then he spoke to Darstan. "Did they say that to me?"

"I heard them too," Wisp said, then he addressed Darstan. "If we're traveling with them, they can link with *you* when I Cloak. *I'm* not touching them."

Darstan laughed. "That's fine, Wisp. I'm getting used to them. If they keep killing Lights, I may grow to like them."

The Light Serpents Shifted to Benna's manor, dropped them off, then said they had to return to Antar's manor.

"Won't the Lights detect you Shifting from here? If they do, they'll know power was used at this location."

"Then you and the one with Stealth must accompany us back to the cave. We'll Shift to the manor from there, and you can return here."

Darstan nodded. *"I think that will work."*

"Make certain to be vigilant. We must leave to maintain the sanctity of the home."

"What if someone is at the manor?" Darstan asked.

"Then they will die."

TIME TO KILL THE LIGHTS

Vellana sat at the center of the table, closest to the Book. The other four Lights occupied nearby seats.

"What now?" Parron asked. "We can't hide. We've got to draw them out so we can do battle."

"Bravery is a noble virtue," Chandra said. "Brave people have been admired for thousands of years. Unfortunately, it is usually dead people who are the ones being admired."

Vellana laughed. "I agree, Chandra. Bravery has its place, but I much prefer caution and wisdom."

"What do we do then?" Parron asked.

"We do what all wise people do," Vellana said. "We set a trap."

"However, before we set a trap, we must know what we're trapping," Vellana said. "All we know right now is that someone—likely more than one—is attempting to eliminate us. I suggest we go to Antar's manor to find out more."

"But we don't know what happened there?" Doranna said.

"Precisely," Vellana said. "All the more reason we need to go. We can't leave the investigation to someone else, and with Salinas gone, we are by far the best recourse."

"I second Vellana's suggestion," Chandra said.

"I'll go along as well," Doranna said. "When do we go?"

"It's too late today," Chandra said. "I say we leave after opening session tomorrow."

Vellana glanced around the table. "If there are no objections, I'll place it on the agenda."

Melissara walked from the kitchen to the sitting room in Benna's manor. After half a dozen times, she paused and rested her palms on the back of the sofa. "We can't stay here forever. Something needs to be done."

"I haven't heard a good plan yet," Wisp said. "I don't think it's wise to attempt to kill the five most powerful people on seven worlds without a good plan."

"Good plan or not, if the Mother said it has to be done, then it has to be done," Darstan said.

Melissara poured more wine for everyone, then handed the empty bottle to Benna. "It seems as if we need a better plan then. It's time we thought of one."

Darstan sipped a goblet filled with wine while Melissara walked circles around the table. "I'm all for better plans, but if we don't have one by morning, I'm going with what we have."

"Darstan's right," Melissara said. "We need to do something, and we need to be quick about it. We can't give the Lights time to plot, now that they know we're here. I'm also worried about what's happening with Mikkellana and the others."

"Let's just kill them," Darstan said. "We can do it."

"Darstan, 'Let's just kill them' is not the answer to everything," Wisp said. "There *are* other options, you know?"

"There may be other options, but mine is the simplest," Darstan said.

Melissara laughed. "I admire your enthusiasm, not to mention your bravery, but there are five Lights left. That's more than a chore for all of us, let alone you by yourself. At the very least, you'll need the rest of us to help you."

Darstan shook his head. "I can do it myself, Melissara. I don't need anyone to help."

"You may think you don't need help, and if it turns out you don't, that's fine, but if you attempt it and you *do* need help, you'll be dead. At that point, you'll be beyond help. I know of many illnesses that can be healed, but death isn't one of them."

Darstan thought for a moment, then smiled. "All right. I'll agree if you do it my way."

"There's no doing it *your* way," Wisp said. "We'll do it Melissara's way, or we won't do it."

Melissara circled the food Rahg was cooking. "Darstan, the Lights are not ones to trifle with; they killed my father in a heartbeat, and he was as strong as you and a lot more experienced. In addition, they trapped Lukaan, me, and my sisters. Yes, there was subterfuge involved as well as trickery, but there was also a remarkable amount of strength."

Wisp placed his arm on Darstan's shoulder. "You can't argue that, Darstan. It's crazy to try anything without help. I'm sure there will be more than one of them guarding the Book, and that's when we need to strike so we can get the Book."

Rahg looked up. "At least even the odds *some*. If you won't take all of us, take at least one."

"All right," Darstan said, "but we better come up with a plan quickly because I'm doing this tomorrow."

Melissara sat on the sofa, leaned forward, and stared. "Do what you need to do then because if it takes all night, we're coming up with a well-thought-out strategy.

During the night, they discussed all manner of plots: ambushing the Lights as each one left their manor, waiting for them at the Hall and doing a surprise attack, luring them away with a demonstration of powers, and more. None of them resonated with more than one or two people, though.

By late into the night—almost morning—they arrived at a plan. "I think we need to rest first," Melissara said. "Let's try to sleep and go at midday."

"How do you plan on getting there?" Rahg asked. "If they can Sense when you Shift, won't they know when we arrive?"

"That's a good question, Rahg, but if Wisp Cloaks us when we Shift to the outside of the Hall, they won't be able to Sense it when we arrive. After that, we can walk into the Hall and do what we need to."

"When do you think we should go?" Wisp asked.

"Midday, as I said. The Hall should be least crowded then, and there will likely be fewer Lights."

"And if there aren't fewer Lights?" Wisp asked.

"Then we proceed anyway," Melissara said.

"All right," Darstan said. "Let's hear the final plan so I can get some sleep beforehand."

Chapter Twenty-Nine

THE LIGHTS INVESTIGATE

The Council gathered for the first time since Xeter and Borrik met their demise at Antar's manor. Five of the Lights sat at the table, and, after erecting a Shield of Silence, they began discussions.

"How did this happen?" Vellanoa asked. "Both of them were in top shape and strong at that. I once saw Xeter do battle with almost a dozen guards on Asola, and he defeated them handily. It wasn't even a contest."

Doranna stood and waited for silence, then said, "And I witnessed Borrik fight three usurpers on Nagasha. He dispatched them without a struggle."

"I think the testimony from two of our senior members indicates we have trouble," Chandra said. "*How much* trouble can only be determined when we discover specifically what we face."

"What do you suggest?" Parron asked. "I know you have something in mind."

"What I suggest is the protocol for any transgression involving the use of powers. We all—and I mean *all*—go to the scene and conduct a complete investigation. We need to discover what powers killed Xeter and Borrik, and we need to know how many were involved in the attack."

Ebransco shook his head. "We better do it quickly. I heard more than a few mumbles on the way to Council. Many people are talking about what happened."

"You can't stop people from talking," Vellana said.

"I understand the talking, Vellana, but they're doing more than that. People are questioning how powerful the Lights really are based on what happened. Once our power is questioned, it won't be long before we see rebellion. It may not be a lot of rebellion, but some, and *some* leads to more."

Vellana refilled her mug of water. "We can't afford *any* rebellion, not one bit. Rebellion is like a disease; it spreads faster than the Runellan plague." She looked at each of them. "I trust you remember what happened with that."

"I don't remember," Ebransco said. "What happened?"

"Ten million people died in the span of a few moons. It might have been a hundred million or even billions if not for Antar and his mysterious Slicers. He used them to eradicate the disease."

"How?"

Doranna snickered. "Nobody knows how. Back then nobody cared how; they were just happy to have the plague gone."

"If whoever is doing this has Slicers, we could be in trouble," Vellana said. "Make sure your minds are blocked."

Chandra stood again. "All of which speaks to the urgency of the matter. I say we take what nourishment we need, then begin. The first stop needs to be the manor, and I suggest we take a contingent of guards with us—strong guards."

"Why?" Doranna asked. "Whoever did this was strong enough to kill Xeter and Borrik. Considering that, a few guards, no matter how strong, won't be anything but more fodder for them."

"But while they're busy killing the guards, it will give us enough time to do something, whether that be attack or escape," Chandra said. "I vote to bring them with us. At least ten of them."

Doranna shrugged. "I'll go along with that strategy. It's wasted effort as far as I'm concerned, but it's fine with me if you want to do it."

Chandra turned to the other Lights. "Send for ten or twelve guards and make sure they're among the strongest we have."

"When do we need them?" Ebransco asked.

Chandra shook her head. "Don't you listen to anything? Now! They are to accompany us to the manor."

The Lights—all five of them—Shifted to a spot not far from Antar's manor, and they brought twelve guards with them. Once they reappeared on the street, Chandra checked to ensure everyone was in attendance, then walked toward the entrance. "Be on alert. We've already lost two of the Council here. We can't afford to lose more."

Doranna signaled several of the guards to move in front of them and lead the way. She slowed her pace to allow them to advance.

"Letting them bear the brunt of any potential attack?" Parron asked.

Doranna nodded. "Caution is a part of wisdom. You should learn it."

Two of the guards slowly opened the doors to the manor and stepped inside. After checking the nearby rooms, they signaled the others to follow. "Looks empty to me," the first guard said.

Vellana walked into the adjacent room and knelt beside Borrik and Xeter. She reached down and ran her fingers across the spot where their bodies had been, though nothing remained but pieces. She then brushed her fingertips across the floor beside them. Her eyes widened, and her jaw fell. She turned to face the others and whispered, "ColdFire!"

Chandra shook her head. "Impossible. No one has ColdFire."

"Correction, fellow Light. No one *had* ColdFire. Someone does now."

"I agree with Chandra," Doranna said. "No one has had Cold-Fire since Antar and Lukaan, but it's obvious someone does now."

Vellana stood and took a step toward the other Lights. "Every one of you knows my Sensing powers, and all of you know that the only one who was more proficient was Salinas. With that in mind, I'm telling you that the traces are undeniable—ColdFire was used here."

Ebransco seemed to be shaken. "ColdFire? If that's true, we're facing more than we thought."

Chandra grinned as she turned toward Ebransco. "Perhaps you simply weren't thinking right. When I heard two of the Council members were dead, I knew something was amiss, something big, not just a random insurgent who got carried away."

"Why didn't you say something?" Ebransco asked.

Chandra scowled. "I ordered guards to accompany us, didn't I? Would I have done that if I hadn't anticipated trouble?"

She shook her head. "Sometimes I wonder how you got voted on the Council."

"Enough bickering," Vellana said. "We have yet to determine who has the ColdFire. After that, we must make a plan to find and kill them."

"And it *will* be a task to kill someone with ColdFire," Doranna said. "Remember how devastating it was when Antar and Lukaan used it?"

"How can I forget?" Vellana said. "If it weren't for them, none of us would be here. We'd be in a dorgan's stomach."

Chandra turned to the lead guard. "Search the rest of the manor for any signs of life. Make sure to be thorough and look upstairs and down."

The guard took two men with him and split the rest into groups of three, dispatching each in a different direction.

"Should we go with them?" Parron asked.

This time it was Vellana who shook her head. "If the one who has ColdFire is upstairs, do you want to be the one to face him, or do you want the guards to bear the brunt of his attack?"

Parron shriveled under her glare. "The guards."

"Then I think your question is answered," Vellana said. "Just remain alert to anything and warn us at the first sign of trouble."

For the next thirty minutes, the guards searched the upstairs, then they moved to the cellar.

～

"*T*hey *are coming*," one of the Light Serpents said. "*Should we kill them?*"

The second Light Serpent thought, then sent a message. "*No, we'll hide for now. We should let the young one kill them all. It will increase his power.*"

At that, the Light Serpents burrowed into the ground and disappeared.

～

A moment later, the guards entered an unlocked door at the end of the hall. "It's empty," one said. "Nothing here."

"Check it," the guard in charge said. "Search every corner."

Fifteen minutes later, the guards returned to the room where the Lights waited. "Nothing," the guard said. "We searched every room thoroughly, and we found nothing. Not even a trace."

"Then it's time to leave," Chandra said. "There's no sense in staying here." She turned to the guard in charge. "Lock the doors and seal them. Set sensors in place at every entrance. I want to know if anyone comes in here or tries to."

The guard nodded. "Consider it done, My Lady."

Chandra joined hands with the other Council members and Shifted back to the Hall.

"What now?" Parron asked.

"Now we wait for someone else to die," Chandra said. "Not a settling thought, is it?"

Chapter Thirty

THE FIRST ATTEMPT

"Are we ready?" Darstan asked.

"We haven't finished eating," Wisp said. "Don't be in such a hurry."

"Darstan's right," Melissara said. "We agreed to do this, so we may as well get it done. Is everyone clear on what to do?"

"We went over it enough times," Rahg said. "I'm good."

"I know Darstan's ready," Melissara said. "How about you, Wisp?"

"I'm as ready as I'll ever be," Wisp said. "Let's go."

Melissara stood and grabbed Darstan and Rahg's hands. "Wisp, take hold of us and Cloak so we can Shift. And everyone remember to stay linked afterward so we can enter the Hall undetected."

Rahg and Darstan nodded, then they linked with Melissara. "Let's go, Wisp," she said.

They reappeared near the front steps to the library, invisible to all around them. "This way," Melissara whispered, though she had no need to whisper as they were fully cloaked and couldn't be heard.

She led the way into the Hall while linked to the others. They passed numerous patrons as well as guards and made their way across the tiled floors until they stood no more than ten paces in front of the table where the Lights sat. A small contingent of guards stood between Melissara and the Lights. "There are two Lights" Melissara said. "Just remember to get the Book first."

As they slowly advanced, something caught Melissara's eye on the side where a few people were passing by. She held out her arms to stop everyone. "Don't go any further," she said, and caution tinged her voice.

"What's the matter?" Darstan asked.

"Something flashed while we were approaching," Melissara said. "It wasn't us, but I'm sure it was a Sensor or a Probe set off by something, probably those people who passed by."

"How will that affect us?" Rahg asked.

"If they have Sensors set, the moment we breach a certain point, the Lights will know. What that means is regardless of us being Cloaked, they'll know where we are. We won't have time to reach the Book, and if they have it under their control still, we won't stand a chance of defeating them."

"I say we try," Darstan said.

Melissara shook her head. "No. It's too risky. We need to regroup and come up with a different plan."

They walked a short distance from the Hall, and then Melissara Shifted to Benna's manor. Once inside, she continued her explanation, picking up where she left off.

"If they went to the trouble of erecting a wall of Sensors, I'm sure they backed it up with a Shield. Even if we could break the Shield, they'd have more than enough time to use the Book and attack us by the time we did."

"It looks as if a direct assault is off," Wisp said. "What do we do now?"

"We come up with a new plan," Melissara said. "And it has to be a good one."

"What about waiting outside the Hall and attacking when they come out?" Rahg said.

Melissara started to respond, but Wisp interrupted her. "Ragh, didn't you notice the number of guards near the entrance to the Hall? They weren't all wearing uniforms, but you could tell by the way they positioned themselves, and by the fact that they were the same ones who were there days before. It was fairly obvious they were guards."

Melissara smiled. "Well done, Wisp. I'm impressed."

Darstan sat and grinned. "I told you. He remembers *everything*."

"That's good," Melissara said. "There's not much that's more important than being observant and being able to put what you see into perspective."

Darstan lay down on the sofa, cushioning his head on a pillow. "Now that you say we can't attack them inside the Hall, and we can't attack them outside the Hall—where do we attack?"

"That's what we need to determine," Melissara said.

"Would there be a space between any shield they put up and the floor?" Wisp asked.

Melissara looked at him as if he were nuts. "Just when I was beginning to think you held promise, you ask a question like that. Do you intend to crawl *under* their shield?"

"But I asked for a reason," Wisp said. "If there is a gap, it may allow Darstan's FearMist to slip underneath. I've seen what it can do. It may not affect the Lights, but it should work on the guards."

"I take back what I said, Wisp. That's brilliant. And it just might work."

"The might is what worries me," Wisp said. "I like to *know* something will work before I try it."

"I don't want to be the one to sound defeatist, but neither of you have mentioned the obvious problem," Darstan said.

"That being?" Melissara asked.

"Whether the FearMist works on the Lights or just the guards, doesn't matter. If we use it, it will linger in the air for quite a while, long enough to affect Wisp and Rahg, and possibly you, Melissara."

Melissara lost her smile and sat in the chair opposite Darstan. "I hadn't thought of that."

"Now what?" Rahg asked. "I thought we had a good plan before."

"Tell me about this Book," Wisp said to Melissara.

"There's not much to say that I haven't already. It magnifies the power of the one touching it first by many times, depending upon who else has hold of the Book."

"How often do you think they'd use it?"

"The Book? I doubt if it would be once every ten years or more. Perhaps once in a hundred. Why? What does that have to do with anything?"

Wisp paced the floor. "Hear me out before presenting arguments."

"Go ahead," Darstan said.

"Suppose we use Stealth to get into the Hall before they arrive in the morning. I'm guessing there would be no shield or no sensors."

"There shouldn't be, no," Melissara said. "The guards would likely show up before the Lights, but not much earlier. Why do you ask?"

Wisp sat on the table between Melissara and Darstan. Rahg sat to his side. "Suppose we sneaked in and went to the table where the Lights deliberate and got close to the Book. Let me touch the Book first, then the three of you touch it, allowing me to use Stealth for a long time. I can keep us Cloaked until after they arrive, and once they're all there, we can switch, allowing Darstan or Rahg to use the Book and attack."

Melissara remained silent for a few moments, then a smile appeared. "I like it, Wisp. I like it a lot." She stood and poured a goblet of wine for each of them. "I think this calls for a celebration.

Now all we need to do is figure out what could go wrong with the plan."

"What if the guards are in place when we get there?" Rahg asked.

"Then we use Stealth to sneak by them," Wisp said. "They definitely won't be able to detect us."

"Suppose the guards have a shield up?" Darstan asked.

Melissara shook her head. "There'd be no reason to. Not when there's no one to protect. The guards would never anticipate an attack when the Lights weren't in attendance."

Wisp held up his hand as if signaling someone to stop. "I don't want to be the one to ruin my own plan, but what happens when we attack the Lights? Won't the guards immediately attack us?"

Melissara nodded. "You're right about that, Wisp. All we need to do is determine how to overcome that."

"I have an idea," Rahg said. "Once we switch to Darstan touching the Book, I'll put up a shield to protect us from the guards while Melissara and Darstan fight the Lights. I can hold them off for a long time, probably long enough for you two to dispatch the Lights."

Darstan sat up. "One thing to note. The Mother said the ones providing the source of power to the Book will be weakened, so your shield may not be as strong as normal, or it may not last as long."

Melissara nodded. "Darstan's right about that, but we can avoid that situation if Rahg doesn't touch the Book. Wisp and I can provide enough power for Darstan to be effective. I'm pretty sure of that. And that leaves Rahg to protect us from the guards on his own. He'll have no extra power, but he won't lose any either."

"I like it," Darstan said. "And after we're finished with the Lights, we can easily take care of the guards."

"I don't know about *easily*, but yes, I think we'll be able to overcome them with little trouble."

"When do we go?" Rahg asked.

Melissara stood. "I suggest we take plenty of nourishment today, get a lot of rest tonight, and go very early in the morning. Before dawn."

"Before we rest," Wisp said, "let me ask. How are we certain the Lights will be there every day? Why do they go to the Hall?"

"They have to go there to hold session. People voice their grievances, and the Lights hear them out, then decide on what to do. They also judge any transgressions such as the use of power illegally."

"Then I'd say we're ready," Darstan said.

"One more thing," Melissara said. "If something goes wrong, I'll call for a Shift. When I do, make sure to link immediately, so we can escape. And if anything happens to me, Darstan, you call for the Shift. Understood?"

Wisp and Rahg nodded, and Darstan said, "Understood."

"One final thing," Rahg said. "I want to kill at least one of the Lights. I don't know if I *have* to in order to fulfill my oath, but I want to anyway."

"Do you think you can do it?" Darstan asked.

"I guess we'll find out," Rahg said. "Just make sure to leave one for me."

Vellana appeared at the entrance to the Hall, then went inside. She stormed toward the Council's meeting area and faced those who were present. "What is the emergency? We just left here not long ago."

Chandra didn't bother to stand, speaking from her position at the head of the table. "The urgency is because we've had another transgression. Someone used powers not far from the Hall, and it wasn't long ago."

Vellana's look went from annoyed to serious. "Do we know what the powers were used for?"

"I haven't checked them myself, but one of the guards with strong Sensing abilities said it was definitely used for Shifting. Furthermore, he said it was one of the same ones who did it before."

Vellana bit her nails. "What's your suggestion, Chandra?"

"My suggestion is for everyone to find somewhere different to spend the night. Who knows what these people plan? They may be plotting an attack on us while we sleep."

Doranna stood and slammed her fist on the table. "Nonsense! We can't hide like sheep from the wolves. We are the *Lights*. We *are* the wolves. I say we fight."

"And fight we will, impatient one. But we'll fight on our terms." Chandra looked at each Light and let her gaze linger as she spoke. "Do as I say and find another place to spend the night, then we'll meet here early. At that time, we'll determine when and how to find and kill whoever is doing this."

Vellana nodded. "Agreed."

Her vote was echoed by the rest of them.

Chapter Thirty-One

WHAT NOW?

The following morning, Melissara and the others ate breakfast, then prepared to go. "Is everyone ready?" Melissara asked.

"Aren't we going to the cavern to Shift?" Rahg asked. "They'll detect us Shifting from here."

Melissara shook her head. "It won't matter. If they detect us, the worst that will happen is they'd send some guards to investigate, and that will only help us. Besides, we're not leaving the Hall unless *we* kill them or *they* kill us. Either way, the Shift point won't matter."

"In that case, let's go," Wisp said.

Everyone linked, then Melissara Shifted to a spot near the entrance to the Hall. No one was out; in fact, it was still dark. "This looks good," Melissara said. "Let's hope the inside is as empty as the streets are."

Before anyone could react, hundreds of Slicers appeared next to Darstan. He stared, then tried to communicate with them. "*Why are you here?*"

"*Consider us reinforcements. The Mother instructed us on what to do.*"

"And what is it that you're supposed to do?"

"Watch. Help when we can."

"Fine. But let Rahg and I kill them. Only interfere if you think you have to."

"Your will, young master."

Using Wisp's Stealth for concealment, they entered the Hall—along with the Slicers—and made their way to the table where the Lights met. No Lights were there, and no guards were standing duty. "So far so good," Wisp said, then he moved toward the center of the table where the Book was.

Wisp looked to Melissara and posed a question. "Should we wait to use the Book? I can keep us Cloaked for a while, so we don't have to use it yet."

She nodded. "I think we should wait a little while, not long, but a little. The longer we can go without using the Book, the better it will be; besides, I'm sure we'll hear the Lights arriving, which will give us plenty of time to act."

Within fifteen minutes, a ruckus sounded at the entrance. "Must be them," Melissara said. "Wisp, take hold of the Book, then we'll touch it. Rahg, remember not to touch the Book, but make sure you stay linked to Wisp so you're concealed. And, Wisp, make sure when I give the order, you switch, letting Darstan absorb the power. If you can maintain the Stealth, do so, but if you can't, don't worry about it."

~

A contingent of guards took their place watching over the Lights, then it took twenty more minutes for all the Lights to arrive, but once they did, each one of them took a seat at the table. Servants brought them pitchers of khaffe and te along with morning nourishment.

While this was going on, ten more guards lined up at the entrance to the alcove where the Lights held session. When all were in place, the lead guard nodded to Chandra, who erected a wall of Sensors and a Shield that spread across the opening from wall to wall.

"Do we have much business today?" Parron asked.

"Why? Have you something more important?" Vellana asked. "Besides, have you forgotten the business regarding the latest transgression?"

~

"Now!" Melissara said.

Wisp let go of the Book, but he was able to keep them Cloaked. Darstan and Melissara let go, then Darstan immediately placed his hand back on the Book and opened it. Like before, the Book unleashed a ferocious storm of lightning in chaotic, unrestrained power. Shards of jagged bolts erupted and raged out of control.

It settled down quickly, and Melissara and Wisp took hold. The power surged into Darstan, and he immediately issued ColdFire against Chandra. It struck with such force, she froze, unable to do anything. After a moment, her body shattered into thousands of pieces. Darstan wasted no time. He spun a little to the left and fired on Parron and Ebransco.

Melissara, though providing a source for power, used Black-Lightning against Vellana and Doranna, striking both of them simultaneously. It injured them, but not fatally.

Vellana and Doranna fired back, issuing Fire and Lightning against Darstan, but he absorbed the attacks and showed no effects.

The Slicers attacked the Lights, entering their minds and partially blocking their offensive abilities.

Rahg wove a shield behind the guards so they couldn't attack. Once in place, he turned and used his newly acquired power of Spirals against Vellana and Doranna. A dozen formations of Shield, pointed and twisting, flew at them with breathtaking speed. They struck at the same time as Melissara's Lightning, but the Spirals did far more damage, burrowing into the Lights and making holes that bored right through them. The Spirals continued after going through the Lights, boring holes in the walls of the Hall itself.

Rahg turned to the two remaining Lights, but as he did, Darstan's ColdFire finished them off. All that remained were the guards. Melissara spun to face them, and just then, Wisp lost his Cloaking ability, forcing them all to visibility.

"Prepare for an assault," Melissara said, but just then, a thousand more Slicers arrived, hovering near the guards, poised to attack.

"I suggest you surrender," Darstan said.

In response to Darstan's ultimatum, the guards attacked with Fire, Lightning, Shields, and more. Rahg's shield held, then Melissara signaled for him to release it. When he did, she and Darstan used all the power they had, but they didn't need to because the combination of Darstan's ColdFire and an attack by the Slicers took them out with the initial strike.

When it was finished, Wisp stood near the center of the table, shaking his head. "I can't believe you three did that so quickly. From what Melissara had said, these were strong individuals, but you defeated them in a few minutes."

Melissara nodded while staring blankly at the carnage. "I told you, the Book is powerful. When Darstan's ColdFire hit them, they had no chance; they simply shattered, like hitting glass with a mallet."

Wisp nodded. "And Rahg . . . whatever it was he did, those things he used went right through them. They didn't even have an opportunity to respond."

Melissara clapped Rahg on the back. "And that was *without* the Book. Imagine what it would be like with it."

Darstan whistled. "And considering what those Slicers did, I'm beginning to like our chances against Anciara," he said.

"Don't get ahead of yourself, Darstan. Anciara's power puts the Lights to shame—all of them. I guarantee she won't be so easy to do away with."

"There's only one way to find out," Darstan said.

"I know you're eager, Darstan, but your vengeance will have to wait. I must install some semblance of rule here before I leave; otherwise, chaos will ensue."

"What are you doing?" Rahg asked.

Melissara stepped forward and addressed the crowd gathered in the Hall. "Many of you just witnessed what happened. In case you didn't see, the Lights are gone. Destroyed. You can pick up the pieces when we leave."

A loud gasp rose from those who gathered.

"That *doesn't* mean life will continue under someone else's rule; in fact, life is changing for the better. There will no longer be restrictions on using powers, and you will be allowed to Shift wherever you want at will. I will put someone in charge of things until I return, so if any of you know where to find Yettl, tell me now. Or better yet, find him and tell him I'd like to see him."

An older-looking gentleman stepped forward. "I know him, and he's not far from here. I'll go get him. Can I Shift?"

Melissara laughed. "I just said there will be no restrictions on Shifting, and I meant it. Go. Retrieve Yettl."

T he man returned in moments with Yettl by his side. Yettl looked about warily, then approached Melissara. "You're a du Savarra, aren't you?"

Melissara nodded. "I hoped you'd remember, though it has been a thousand years."

Yettl smiled. "That it has, My Lady."

"Enough of the 'My Lady' nonsense. I asked you here to see if you would take charge of things while I'm gone."

"Where are you going?" Yettl asked.

Melissara paused. "It's difficult to say, but when we were exiled, we found another world and have been living there for many, many years. Now that world is threatened by Anciara, the goddess who once influenced a large number of our people. I must return to help them kill her."

"Who is *them?*" a voice from the crowd shouted.

Melissara stared and thought she recognized the one who shouted. "Is that you, Therrim?"

He stepped to the front of the crowd and stood alongside Yettl. "Who is helping you fight her?"

"It's good to see you again, Therrim, though the last time was not pleasant."

Therrim nodded. "As I'm sure you guessed, it had nothing to do with me or the others with me. The Lights controlled everything."

"I presumed as much. But to get to your question," Melissara spread her hands to encompass Rahg, Darstan, and Wisp. "These three—who are the ones who just defeated the Lights—along with my sister Mikkellana, and a small contingent of others, some who have powers and some who don't."

"And you think you can kill her?" Therrim asked.

"With the Book I do."

"If you could use some help, I'm sure I can muster up a few more men. We'd like nothing more than to see her defeated. The only thing I worry about—and I'm sure others will too—is going to your world and returning to ours through the Forsaken Lands. We've all heard the horror stories of what awaits people who go there."

Melissara's smile broadened. "You would be more than welcome, Therrim, as would anyone who comes with you. As to the Forsaken Lands, I can assure you we'll get through without long delays. I've been through it twice now, and while it's not been a vacation, it has been manageable."

"One more thing," Therrim said, "some of these men were marked as criminals by the Lights for using their powers—"

"They have nothing to worry about," Melissara said. "All transgressions for using powers are forgiven, and going forward, there will be no punishment. A new set of laws will be put into place. Yettl will initiate this, and when I return, I'll review it. Everyone will be treated the same. Things will go back to the way it was before the Lights, and before Lukaan."

Therrim bowed, then stepped back. "I'll get the men, and we'll return ready to go. You have my word."

"We'll wait on you, Therrim." Melissara turned to Darstan. "What do you need to do before we leave?"

"I need to see the Mother again, and to do that, I need the Light Serpents, which means I need to return to your manor to get them."

"I'll take you to the manor; the rest is up to you. Just don't be too long. I don't want to leave Mikkellana alone forever. She's just foolish enough to try something without us."

Melissara reached out her hand, then stopped. "Rahg, can you wrap the Book in a shield so it doesn't open? I think it would be safer that way."

"I'll do it now," he said.

Melissara then took hold of Darstan and Shifted to the manor. "You know the room, I guess?"

Darstan walked toward the steps leading down. "I do, and I'll meet you back at the Hall soon."

Chapter Thirty-Two

BACK TO THE MOTHER

The Light Serpents took Darstan back to the Mother, Shifting to the same spot as before—the entrance to the cavern. He didn't need to ask about instructions, just entered the cave and walked toward the rear, guided by a handful of Slicers providing light.

As he made the final turn, the brightness of the light forced him to shield his eyes. *"I've killed them,"* he said. *"All the Lights are dead."*

"Well done and long overdue. I've been waiting for aeons."

"Now what? You said to see you before we returned to our lands."

"I did, indeed," the Mother said. *"You now face your biggest challenge, and you'll need all the assistance you can get."*

"We've got the Book," Darstan said.

The light in the cavern flickered as the Mother vibrated. *"You'll need much more than the Book. My children will accompany you. They will guide you through the Forsaken Lands and help with your struggle against Anciara."*

"Who do you mean when you say 'your children'?"

"You have already met some of them. The ones who brought you here."

Darstan appeared puzzled. *"You mean the Light Serpents? How will they help?"*

"It won't be just them," the Mother said. *"I'll send others as well. Together they should be enough to ensure victory."*

"Who are the others you mention?" Darstan asked.

A blinding light crept forward from around the corner, then from both sides. The effect caused Darstan to cover his eyes and turn his head. *"I can't see,"* he said.

"Forgive me," the Mother said, and then the light dimmed. Darstan opened his eyes and stumbled backward. The cavern was filled, top to bottom and on all sides—with Slicers.

"What is this?" Darstan asked.

"These are my children also," the Mother said. *"And they will accompany you and help you."*

Darstan gulped. *"How many are there?"*

"More than a million," the Mother said. *"Enough to make a difference."*

A shiver ran up Darstan's spine. *"Enough indeed."*

"They will guide you through the Forsaken Lands, and they will protect you from the dorgans."

"What are *the dorgans? I've seen them, and they don't look like anything I've seen before."*

"That's because they're not like anything you've seen. The Original Ones made them to deter normal people from using the Forsaken Lands, which was a bridge between worlds. The problems happened when—over many hundreds of years—the dorgans grew so powerful that even those with powers couldn't traverse the lands."

"So how will your children help with them?"

"Just know that they will. With your new powers, they will listen to you."

"Is that all?"

"It is. My children will go with you, but don't fear about losing track of them; they have your imprint now, so they will be able to find you anywhere."

"I don't know if that comforts me or frightens me," Darstan said.

"Be comforted. And one more thing, tell Rahg not to let the other gods free. They're not to be trusted."

Darstan exited the cavern, then Shifted back to the Hall where he promised he'd meet Melissara. She waited near the entrance along with Wisp and Rahg, and they had been joined by Therrim and his volunteers.

Therrim backed up to the wall. Even Melissara took a few steps back. The entire plaza was filled with glowing shards of crystal, shining like the sun and reflecting its rays of light.

Melissara approached him cautiously. "Darstan, what did you bring?"

Darstan smiled. "An army of Slicers," he said. "One million of them."

The Slicers pulsed and vibrated, shimmering all the while. "Are we safe?" Rahg asked, his voice tremulous.

Darstan nodded. "Don't worry, brother. They won't bother you; they're here to help us, and as you can see, there are a lot of them."

Rahg continued to gawk at them. The sheer numbers were frightening, especially when he recalled the power of only a few of them. "That's what makes it scary," Rahg said. "I never even imagined so many Slicers."

"I don't want you or Wisp to become anxious about the journey, but the Light Serpents are coming too."

"Now you *are* making me nervous, Darstan. You know I don't care for those things," Wisp said.

"Get used to it because they'll be sleeping beside us as we travel through the Paaren."

"Just make sure they sleep next to you, not me," Wisp said.

"And the Slicers?" Rahg asked. "Where will they sleep?"

"From what I can tell, they don't sleep," Darstan said. "I guess that's a good thing, but I'm not sure."

Melissara moved closer to Darstan. "If we want them to keep a watch for us in the Forsaken Lands, it's definitely a good thing. It will allow us to sleep at night without fear of being attacked. I know from traveling with Aentarra, nothing—and I mean *nothing*—keeps watch like a Slicer."

With his back pressed against the wall, Therrim spoke. "When do we leave?"

"Right now," Melissara said. "Let's make our way to the portal."

They walked through the Hall and down the stairs to the portal. Melissara turned and took a moment to stare. "This is the second time I'm leaving this world, not knowing if I'll return. I hope I do."

She reached out and touched Darstan's hand. "Wait. I forgot to say goodbye to Benna. I'll only be a moment."

Melissara Shifted to Benna's manor and found him working the garden. She approached quietly, but he must have heard her footsteps. "You can't fool me now, Lady Melissara. I recognized the sound of your walk."

Melissara laughed and gave him a hug. "I came to say goodbye. I hope it won't be a permanent one, but the task we face is dangerous, so I don't know. In any case, I'll tell Mikkellana you're here. If either one of us makes it through this alive, we'll be back."

Benna squeezed her tightly. "You've been like my own child. You and your sisters, both. I will plead with any who will listen to keep you and Mikkellana safe." Benna leaned and kissed her forehead. "Until you return," he said, then he asked her to wait, and he walked inside. He returned a moment later with a bag of fruits. "Take these with you. They may provide much-needed nourishment if you're lost."

"Thank you, Benna." Melissara hugged him again, then Shifted back to the Hall where Rahg and the others waited.

Chapter Thirty-Three

ANCIARA SAILS FOR ARANGAR

Tirzinitzia finished a mug of ale, then handed it to the barkeep. "I've had enough for the night." She then turned to Anciara. "Should we search Pomanda and Sykor now? Or do you want to wait?"

"I want to get this voyage moving. I'm convinced they sailed somewhere to the south of Entiria, so that's where we're going."

Tirzinitzia nodded. "Good. We'll leave in the morning."

"And don't forget," Anciara said. "We'll be taking a ship with a full crew and Shifting to that island. There will be no sailing through rough waters this time."

"We'll leave at dawn," Tirzinitzia said.

Aenaila waited for ten days, estimating the time it might take for them to sail from Entiria to Arangar. She assumed correctly that they would Shift to Entiria and sail from there. She just wanted to engage them before they landed in Arangar.

Mikkellana approached as Aenaila finished her morning khaffe. "What do you have in mind, Aenaila?"

"I'm going to Shift to the vessel they used and destroy it. It will grant us a lot more time."

"It sounds good, Aenaila, but be careful. I know Tirzinitzia is a clever one, and I can only imagine Anciara is more so. *This* attack might work, but I'm certain they'll be planning a trap, eventually."

Aenaila nodded. "I agree. This will give us at least twenty days of peace. After that, we may have to think of something else."

"Do you know other places to hide in this land?" Mikkellana asked.

"In fact, I do. My own land is quite far from here and borders on another sea—the Endless Sea, we call it. I think we should go there. If nothing else, it would take them days longer to reach us even if they manage to find Arangar."

"Good," Mikkellana said. "I'll have everyone make preparations while you're gone."

Aenaila waited for dark, then she Shifted to the spot on the ship she had previously marked. The Shift point was a narrow passage covered by shadows and protected on two sides.

She reappeared and quickly checked to ensure her privacy. Once that was done, she focused on spreading the ambergis all over the deck, then used one of several strikers she'd brought to light it, setting the ship ablaze. Afterward, she Shifted off the ship and back to Arangar where Mikkellana awaited.

"Were they there? Any trouble?" Mikkellana asked.

Aenaila shook her head. "I don't know the exact location, but from what I saw of the stars, the ship was in our part of the seas, so it's a good thing we got to them when we did. But no, there was no trouble. No one saw me."

"Sit here," Mikkellana said as she led Aenaila to a seat by the fire. "Get something to eat and drink, then we can discuss going to your homeland."

Aenaila took a cup of khaffe from Tobias and warmed her hands. "Thank you, Tobias. I needed this."

"Don't you worry about it, lass. I know what a person needs. If we weren't in the middle of nowhere, I'd have Mollie here bake you a pie. A real pie, the likes of which you ain't tasted before."

Aenaila glanced toward Mikkellana and smiled. "I'd love that, Tobias. I think we should do that when we get to my home."

"Can't be soon enough for me," Tobias said. "I'm gettin' tired of traipsing all over lands I don't even know about and talkin' to people I never heard about. And I'm sure I'm not the only one. I'd bet a wagger's tail that every one of the others are wishin' the same thing as me."

Mikkellana smiled this time. "I bet they are, Tobias. And with any luck, we'll make that happen soon enough."

The smell of burning wood and the crackling of fire forced Tirzinitzia to leap from her bed. She rushed out the cabin door into a wall of flames. The ship was on fire from both ends.

Anciara stood beside her in the passageway. "Shift back to Genda," she said. "This ship is lost."

"What about the crew?" Tirzinitzia asked.

"What about them?" Anciara asked, and then she Shifted.

Tirzinitzia looked around. Men were jumping overboard and lowering lifeboats, but it seemed doubtful if they'd make it considering the raging fire. She thought about trying to save them, but after a mast crashed next to her, she Shifted to Genda and safety.

Anciara stood on the docks looking as if she'd been waiting all day. "About time," she said. "What took you so long?"

"I tried to save a few of them," Tirzinitzia said.

"Foolish girl. Follow me. We'll need a room for the next day or so."

Anciara found a room at the Gull's Gut, a tavern frequented by many of the locals. "Rooms for two," she told the innkeeper.

"I don't know if we—"

Anciara glared, and the man shriveled. "I said *two*."

The innkeeper nodded and moved to his ledger. "I'll have someone get them ready, My Lady. It'll only be a minute."

"It had better be," Anciara said.

A few moments later, a serving girl showed Anciara and Tirzinitzia to their rooms. "If you want a meal and don't wish to come to the table, just let me know, and I can bring the food to you."

"Don't concern yourself with trivial matters," Anciara said, and opened the door as a signal for the girl to leave.

Tirzinitzia sat on the edge of the bed while Anciara paced the floor, fuming. "We were definitely heading in the right direction. They wouldn't have bothered with us if we weren't."

She shoved a chair out of her way, then turned to face Tirzinitzia. "Get another ship and crew and get it now. We're going to get them if I have to go through every vessel in Genda."

Tirzinitzia got up to leave. "Wait, get two ships. No, get three." Anciara smiled. "There's no way they'd have time to destroy all three without us catching them. You'll be on one ship, I'll be on the other, and the third will be manned by sailors only."

Tirzinitzia nodded. "Yes, that would work. No matter which one they strike, we'll be able to strike back before they get the others."

As Tirzinitzia was leaving, Anciara called to her again. "And get ships that aren't at the main dock. I don't know how they got a Shift Point on our last vessel, but they won't get one this time."

Chapter Thirty-Four

IT'S TIME TO GO HOME

Rahg sighed when they walked through the portal into the Paaren. "I can't believe we got off Nelstar alive. Thank the gods for that."

"I wouldn't be so hasty to thank anyone just yet," Melissara said. "We may have escaped the wrath of the Lights, but we still have to deal with the vagaries of the Forsaken Lands and the threat of the dorgans. And as you are well aware, the dorgans are not to be taken lightly."

"Melissara, while I respect your opinion as well as your concerns, don't forget we have an advantage this time." Darstan gestured behind him. "We have two Light Serpents and, according to the Mother, more than one million Slicers, although I haven't counted them." When Melissara didn't respond, Darstan added, "Not to mention the Book."

She nodded. "I am more than grateful to the Mother for her assistance, and I believe—from what I've seen—that the Slicers and Light Serpents will prove to be invaluable, but that doesn't alleviate the problem we face of finding our way back."

"I understand, but the Mother assured me that the Slicers will show us the way. She also said the dorgans will present no problem."

Melissara shook her head. "I hope you're right about both issues. It would be more than a comfort if that proves true."

Wisp held up the Book while speaking. "Let's not forget we have this in case we need it."

Melissara turned to face Darstan, laughing as she did. "Wisp thinks highly of himself, doesn't he?" She then turned to Wisp. "Darstan already mentioned the Book, Wisp. And to be cautious, I wouldn't count on Rahg's shield protecting you from the Book. I think you should put it down."

Darstan laughed along with Melissara. "He has always thought highly of himself. I'd hate to see him if he had more powers than what he does."

As Darstan spoke to Melissara, one of the Light Serpents slithered up and communicated with him.

A scout reported that we should turn east at the stream ahead. Aside from that, all is clear.

Good, Darstan said, *We'll stop at the stream to eat and rest, then continue the journey eastward.*

"I didn't know we had scouts," Melissara said. "And why is it that I can hear them now when they communicate with you?"

Darstan shook his head. "I don't know, but I think they determine who hears them and who doesn't."

Darstan took a few steps, then said, "As to having scouts, I didn't know either, but I'm happy to hear that we do. I told you the Mother said they'd lead us back safely."

They reached the stream and settled in for a long-anticipated rest accompanied by fresh food—fruits, cheese, and even some meat.

"What else did the Mother tell you? Did she say anything about your powers, Darstan? Anything that will help us when we face Anciara?" Melissara bit into a luscious apple, one of many Benna packed. "Slicers or not, I foresee this being an epic battle."

Darstan reached for one of Melissara's apples, then sat back and bit into it. "I don't know if I understand all she said, mostly because I haven't tried anything, but according to her, the Slicers will be valuable."

"What exactly did she say?" Wisp asked.

"First, she said the Book will be invaluable. She said the Book isn't really a book, but a way to link people with power and allow them to transfer that power to just one person. And she said my new powers have to deal with controlling the Slicers."

"You'll have to explain that," Rahg said. "At least for me, you will."

"The way I understand it, the one who takes hold of the Book first becomes what she called 'the Channeler,' the one who all the power flows through. In other words, if we used the Book, and you took hold of it first, once we all linked, you would have the power of all four of us, but even more so. Much more."

"How is that different than all of us attacking separately?" Rahg asked.

Darstan bit the apple again. "Excuse my poor explanation, but what I neglected to mention is that by linking, the power is magnified by at least two or more, so the power you'd have access to would be twice what the four of us have as individuals. And if there were eight of us, it would be twice that. It could be even more."

"Anything else?" Wisp asked.

Darstan nodded. "She said with each Light that died, my normal powers increased slightly, and when all the Lights died, another power became available."

"What power?" Melissara asked, suddenly more interested in what Darstan had to say.

Darstan took a moment to gather his thoughts, then he looked at Melissara. "She said it's something dealing with control of the Slicers and even the Light Serpents."

"What does it do?" Rahg asked.

"She said it allows complete control of them and no one can block them."

"What can they do?" Wisp asked.

"I'm not sure," Darstan said, "but I got the feeling it is a lot."

"What power do Slicers have?" Rahg asked.

"Apparently, *all* people have some power, even though it may not be enough to give them powers they can use. However, it's enough power so that Slicers can increase their power, and if there are enough people, the increase would be significant."

Melissara stood and paced. "That almost sounds like what the Book does. And if it is, it's more than significant. I can see tremendous benefits already."

Darstan nodded. "That was my understanding, except the power isn't magnified like the Book, but a large number of people would mean a large increase in power."

A smile came to Melissara's face. "This is exciting news. For the first time, I see a glimmer of light. With the four of us, plus Aenaila, Camissa, and my sister, the Book will give us substantial power. And with this other ability you speak of, it will be *much* more."

"You think it will be enough to defeat her?" Wisp asked.

Melissara shrugged. "That's something I don't know, and we won't know until we try."

"Then I guess we better get back as quickly as we can and give it a go," Rahg said.

"I agree," Melissara said. "Rest up, and we'll leave early in the morning." She turned to Darstan. "Do we need to keep watch or are the Slicers able to alert us if anything comes?"

"We can rest comfortably," Darstan said. "Nothing will get through without them letting us know. At least that's what the Light Serpents said, and I think I trust them since they kept your father's manor safe all those years."

"Not that I doubt you," Rahg said, "But why do you say we'll be safe?"

"First, because the Light Serpents said so—as I mentioned—but also because I can position the Slicers almost as Sensors, actually better than Sensors," Darstan said. "They'll let us know if anything approaches."

Melissara looked sideways and stared. "You can do that?"

"They listen to me," Darstan said.

Rahg woke to the smell of cooking, something he hadn't expected. He sat on the ground beside Melissara and filled a plate with food, then got a cup of khaffe. "How long do you think it will take to get back with the Slicers guiding us?"

She shook her head. "I have no idea. I've never had this luxury."

"You must have an idea," Rahg said. "Will it be a few days, a few weeks—"

"If I knew I'd tell you, Rahg, but I don't know. From what I can tell, you've been in the Forsaken Lands more times than I have. Perhaps I should be asking you."

Wisp startled Rahg with his arrival. "I didn't know you were up," Rahg said.

"I've been listening to you ask questions that can't be answered. Be patient, Rahg. We'll get there when we do; besides, I'm in no hurry to do battle with Anciara again. We didn't fare well the last time."

"And we may not fare well the next time," Melissara said. "But we won't know until it happens."

Darstan stumbled to the fire and warmed himself. "If we encounter any dorgans, I say we use the Book to see how that helps."

Melissara shook her head. "I don't know, Darstan. We don't know what effects—"

"And we won't know until we try. I'd hate to try it out with Anciara without knowing what it does."

Ragh took another biscuit from the pan and set it on his plate. "It would be nice to try out the Book, Darstan, but I don't know if I want to run into the dorgans again."

"It won't be a matter of planning it out, Rahg. We'll either run into them or we won't. It's a simple strategy. If they find us, we use the Book, and if we get by without running into them, we don't."

Melissara got up and looked at Darstan. "All that is well and good, but I don't suggest we use the Book once we join the others. We don't know if using it can be detected by Anciara, and if she detects its use, she'll know where we are."

"I've thought of that," Darstan said. "We could Shift to someplace she knows about, like Khatara or Pomanda, use the Book, then Shift back to Entiria."

Wisp nodded. "You're right, Darstan. I hadn't thought of that."

A Slicer flew into camp and entered Darstan's head, then flew back out. "I guess we won't have to debate the topic of whether to use the Book anymore," Darstan said. "Two large groups of dorgans are on their way, and they're moving fast."

Melissara's head turned east and west, panic setting in. "Get to that small enclave," she said. "We may be able to hide there."

"I say we stand our ground and try the Book," Darstan said.

"I'm fine with either," Rahg said, "But we need to make up our mind because they're here." The ground rumbled as he pointed ahead.

Wisp stepped up between them. "I've got the Book," he said, and held it out.

"Wait till I say so," Darstan said, as he stared at the rapidly advancing onslaught.

The ground shook as the dorgans moved closer, and the noise grew deafening. "Move closer," Darstan shouted.

Melissara shouted above the roar. "Darstan, touch the Book first so the power flows through you."

He nodded. "Get ready."

When the dorgans got to within fifteen or twenty span, Darstan gave the order. "Now!" he said, and reached for the Book. Once he touched it, Wisp, Rahg, and Melissara placed their hands on the Book as did Therrim and his followers. The

Book made the link with him, allowing him to channel the power.

A surge of power flooded Darstan, raging through his body, infusing him with energy until he felt as if he would burst. When it got to be almost too much, a column of ColdFire shot out of his left arm and raced toward the dorgans.

It hit the first dorgan, slamming into it with an unbridled force. At first, nothing happened, but a moment later, the dorgan shattered as if it had been smashed with a large boulder. After it fell, others shattered, splitting into shards of ice and disappearing from the landscape. Before long, there were only nine or ten dorgans remaining. They split into two groups, moving in different directions.

Melissara braced herself to use BlackLightning on them, but before she could, they had gone too far, fading into the bleak desert behind them.

Rahg struck first, firing a host of Spirals at the ones fleeing north. The Spirals hit with devastation, tunneling holes right through the dorgans as if they weren't there. In an instant, they were gone.

The other group didn't get far before hordes of Slicers attacked them, penetrating every part of their bodies—eyes, nose, mouth, and ears. The dorgans didn't last long, dropping like deer to a long bow.

"Did you see that?" Wisp asked.

"Are you talking about what happened with the Book or the Slicers?" Darstan asked.

"The Slicers," Wisp said. "I've already seen the Book work, but I had no idea they could do what they did."

"I didn't either, Wisp, but I'm excited to see it," Darstan said.

"It's a good thing the dorgans left when they did," Melissara said. "I'm so exhausted from using the Book I can barely move. How about you, Rahg? And you, Wisp?"

Rahg tried forming a shield and failed, and the same happened to Wisp. "I can't Cloak," Wisp said.

Therrim and the ones who came with him lay on the ground. He staggered to his feet. "I feel as if I haven't slept in days," he said.

A wall of BlackFire shot from Darstan's arm and raced into the emptiness. "I'm fine," Darstan said.

"You don't feel tired?" Melissara asked.

He shook his head. "Not the least. Maybe because I'm the one who used the Book, not one of the ones providing power as a source."

"I don't know. It would be nice to have more information, but one thing stands out. The Book worked. Did you see what your ColdFire did to them?"

"But will it do anything to her?"

"As we said, we won't know until we try."

Chapter Thirty-Five

BACK IN ENTIRIA

For five days, the Slicers led them through the Paaren, and they did it without any encounters with the dorgans. Shortly before noon on day six, Rahg called to the others. "I see the portal up ahead, and it's not far."

"Are you sure it's the same one we came through?" Melissara asked.

"I'm sure," Rahg said. "I know the portals change locations, but for some reason, this one stays the same, and so does that rocky creek over there." He pointed south to a swift-flowing stream lined with lush fruit trees.

"He's right," Darstan said. "I'd recognize it anywhere."

"Assuming they're right, I guess that means we're home," Wisp said.

They exited the portal onto the rock ledge, then slowly made their way to the wooded mountainside next to it. "Be careful, Therrim. This is a thin ledge and a steep drop."

They waited for Therrim and the others to join them, then waited some more for the Light Serpents and the Slicers. Once everyone was together, they linked for Shifting. "Get ready," Darstan said. "We'll go to see the others."

"What about the Slicers?" Rahg asked.

"They'll find us," Darstan said. "The Mother said they have an imprint of my mind—like a picture of it—so they know where I am at all times. I told her I didn't know if I liked the idea, but I guess I do."

Darstan formed an image of the temple in Entiria, then he Shifted to the steps in front of it.

Once they appeared, Melissara used her Sensing ability—weak as it was—but she couldn't find Mikkellana. "Darstan, send a few Slicers to look for the others. I can't locate them."

Close to a million Slicers trailed Darstan, awaiting his command. He formed images in his mind of Mikkellana, Rhaven, Aenaila, and the others, then said, "*Find them.*"

More than one thousand Slicers dispatched in all directions, searching the temple and the living quarters attached to it. From there, they scoured the rest of the island, leaving no stone unturned. Within moments, they returned and reported to Darstan that no one was found.

"No one's here," Darstan said to Melissara.

"Where are they? And what about the Entirians? I haven't seen any of them either."

"When I said 'no one' was here, I meant 'no one.' The Entirians are gone. There is no one on the island but us."

"Do you think she got them?" Rahg asked.

"Definitely not," Melissara said. "If she got to them, there would be bodies strewn about everywhere. They must have gone somewhere, but where? And where could the Entirians go that Anciara wouldn't know about?"

"Arangar," Wisp said. "Aenaila may have convinced them to go there. Anciara wouldn't know about it, and the Entirians do."

"And Mikkellana and Aenaila know a lot of places to use as Shift points," Darstan said. "It's perfect."

"How do we find them?" Rahg asked. "It's a big place."

"We Shift to the pass in the mountains, the one separating Arangar and Cergala," Darstan said. "From there, we use Slicers to locate them. It will only take the Slicers a few minutes."

"I like the idea," Melissara said. "Let's do it."

They linked together and Shifted, reappearing at the pass between Cergala and Arangar. Once situated, Darstan sent the Slicers in all directions, searching for the others.

"How did the Slicers get here?" Rahg asked. "They weren't linked to us when we Shifted."

"They don't need to be," Darstan said. "Remember, I told you they know where I am. The instant I got here, they knew and followed. That's how fast they are."

"But how did they know where we were going?"

"They didn't know where we were going," Darstan said. "They know what I'm thinking."

Before Darstan finished speaking with Rahg, the first of the Slicers returned and, within moments, the rest came back.

"They're by the capital city," Darstan said. "Let's go."

A moment later, Darstan and the rest of them stood outside Chingua, and after a few sight Shifts, they found Mikkellana and the others.

Aenaila raced to Wisp and threw her arms around him. A moment later, Adju rushed up and hugged him. "Master Kender, it's so good to see you."

Mikkellana approached her sister and whispered, "How did you find us? And what happened on Nelstar?"

"Perhaps we should sit at the fire. I know I'm hungry, and I'm sure the others are too. I'll tell my story there."

Mikkellana looked around. "We were preparing to leave, but I suppose we can wait a while."

They sat around an enlarged campfire while Tobias cooked. "No need for me to hear," he said, then continued mumbling. "Someone can tell me what happened later. Same thing anyway. Go here. Go there. I'm gettin' tired of goin' places. I want to get something done."

"First things first," Melissara said. "The Lights are dead, and we have the Book."

Mikkellana sat as straight as she was able. "Dead? How?"

Melissara gestured to Darstan. "Mostly him, but with no small effort from the thief and Rahg. I participated, but I don't know if I was really needed."

Mikkellana leaned in close. "And what about those?" she asked, pointing to the Light Serpents. "Are they what I think they are?"

Laughter from Wisp and Darstan ensued. "Don't worry, I heard you, but I doubt the others did. Anyway, those are Light Serpents. According to Melissara, you must have heard legends of them. Now, you see them."

"Light Serpents? But I thought—"

"Yes," Melissara said, "I thought they were only legend as well, but they're real."

Mikkellana shook her head. "I never imagined."

"Not only that, but they helped us defeat the Lights. In fact, they killed two of the Lights themselves."

"What?" Mikkellana asked. "By themselves?"

Melissara smiled. "Another thing you'll be happy to hear. Benna is alive and taking care of the manor. Plus, he has a manor of his own."

Mikkellana smiled. "Benna alive? You're right, sister. That *does* give me pleasure. I had not imagined he still lived."

"It was so good to see him. He was as much a parent to us as mother and father were," Melissara said.

"What about the Book? Did you learn anything?" Mikkellana asked.

"More than that," Melissara said. "We tried it out on the journey home. We ran into a large group of dorgans—actually two *large* groups."

"What happened?"

"We didn't have a choice of whether to run or not, so we used the Book. Darstan focused the power, and with one shot of Cold-Fire, he killed almost all of them. The few he didn't kill ran off."

Mikkellana almost fell over, but Rhaven supported her. "How many did he kill?"

Melissara shook her head. "Fifty. Maybe more."

"Did the Book do anything to him? Have any effect?"

"None that I could tell. It made the rest of us exhausted, but it didn't seem to affect him."

Mikkellana appeared concerned. "My question is, what would have happened if you had to go longer? What would that have done?"

"I don't know," Melissara said, "but what is being tired compared to the consequences?"

Mikkellana held Melissara's hands in hers. "I haven't talked about this to anyone else, but I suspect Aentarra did something similar with the Slicers when she placed them into the heads of the other Council members. I know she grew stronger, but I can't swear that was the reason. But the members she had the Slicers in: Mesan, Xanthes, and the others, were useless. They were alive, but barely."

"Then we need to ask Darstan," Melissara said. "He can communicate with them."

"With the Slicers?"

Melissara nodded. "With the Light Serpents too. It's how we returned so quickly; they guided us."

Mikkellana glanced to both sides of her, then looked behind her. "I noticed he has a lot of Slicers with him, but how many?"

"Most of them are hiding or staying out of sight," Melissara said.

"And it gives me pause just to say it, but the Mother Slicer said there are more than a million."

"A million!" Mikkellana shook her head. "Can we trust him?"

"I don't think we have a choice, sister. I've never seen power like his. As I said, when he attacked the dorgans, they simply exploded, shattered into thousands of pieces. And there were perhaps fifty of them. Do you remember when Lukaan attacked the dorgans; his powers barely an effect."

Mikkellana appeared shocked. "He was that strong? Really?"

Melissara nodded. "It was frightening. The few dorgans who remained fled without a fight though the Slicers caught them and took them down."

"I've never seen dorgans flee."

"Until then, I hadn't either. And you should have seen the way he killed the Lights. It was as if they weren't even there."

"I thought you said the Light Serpents killed the Lights?"

"The Light Serpents killed two of them. Darstan and Rahg killed five, and they did it all at once."

"Rahg? He helped?"

"I can see I have more to tell you than I realized. On the way to Nelstar, Rahg stopped to see the gods, and they granted him more power. One of the things they gave him was the ability to use Spirals. He—"

"Spirals! I've never seen anyone with that ability. I've never even *heard* of anyone with that ability."

Melissara nodded. "Neither had I, but they were devastating. When he used the Spirals, they went right through several of the Lights, and then they continued to go through the outside wall of the Hall."

Mikkellana looked at Rahg and Darstan, then she swept crumbs from her lap and glanced at them again, staring.

Afterward, she turned back to Melissara. "It's frightening to consider joining with such power; it's reminiscent of fighting with

Lukaan, but I don't know if we have a choice, sister. It's join with Darstan and Rahg to fight Anciara or do nothing."

Melissara nodded. "I agree. All we need now is a plan. And it will have to be one that works this time."

"Indeed," Mikkellana said. "Otherwise we'll all be dead."

Chapter Thirty-Six

A MELDING OF MINDS

"We need to Shift to Cartena before we finish this discussion," Aenaila said. "We'll be safer there, and besides, I should warn my family of what may come."

Everyone linked together, then Aenaila Shifted, appearing outside her father's house in Cartena. Once situated and greeted by her parents, they all went inside.

Mikkellana moved toward the table and poured a drink which the servants had brought.

"You seem to be walking better," Darstan said.

She smiled. "Thanks to you, yes. I have no doubts I'd still be lying flat on my back in bed if you hadn't healed me. Either that or dead."

"You can't die yet," Darstan said. "We need you if we're going to kill Anciara."

"Speaking of which, how *are* we going to kill her? Do you have any plans? Learn anything on Nelstar?"

Darstan sat in the chair next to the sofa where Mikkellana was. The others were gathered around him. "I have numerous suggestions, but it will take us all to refine the plan."

"Before we begin," Aenaila said, "who are the people who returned with you?"

Melissara didn't stand, but she did speak. "After we killed the Lights, and before leaving, I planned on asking for volunteers to help slay Anciara, but I didn't get a chance to. Therrim and the others in the room volunteered on their own, and they all have powers to some degree. Most were guards for the Lights, which means they've been vetted for strength."

Rhaven tapped his sword on the floor. "If they came to help, they should be in here to provide input. They're risking their lives the same as the rest of us."

Darstan nodded. "I agree with Rhaven. They've already risked it all fighting the dorgans; in fact, one of them was almost killed fighting the dorgans."

Melissara opened the door and welcomed them inside. After introductions, they all took a seat or a position leaning against the wall. "We were just discussing a strategy for fighting Anciara," she said. "All input is welcome."

"What have you tried so far?" Therrim asked.

"Everything we could," Mikkellana said. "Nothing worked. In fact, we barely escaped with our lives. We used Fire, Lightning, ColdFire, and even a few Slicers."

Therrim pointed to Darstan. "He tried?"

Mikkellana nodded. "Darstan was with the rest of us. We all attacked at once."

Therrim raised his brow and shook his head. "I've seen his power. He killed the Lights with little effort, or at least some of them. If the goddess is that strong, it doesn't bode well"

"We've got an edge this time," Darstan said. "In fact, we have several edges."

"Maybe you should explain," Aenaila said. "It would be nice to have our confidence boosted."

Darstan gestured to Wisp, who held up the Book. "To begin with, we have the Book," Darstan said. "This is the fabled book the

Lights used to kill Antar—the one they used to maintain control over the people of Nelstar. Therrim and the others can attest to how strong it is based on what happened in the Forsaken Lands."

"What can a book do?" Rhaven asked.

"It magnifies the power of everyone touching it, and it concentrates all power into one or two people." Darstan looked to his side. "If we use Therrim and the ones who came with him, we'll have twenty times the power we had before. Maybe more."

"But will that be enough?" Mikkellana asked.

"There's more," Darstan said. "Rahg has new powers, and one of them is significant."

Although Melissara had shared this with her sister, Mikkellana wanted to hear it from him, so she looked questioningly at Rahg. "You want to share with us?"

"It may be better to show you," he said, then he spun a shield and formed a Spiral, which he issued into the floor. The Spiral dug into the floor, then twisted through the tiles and disappeared, leaving a deep hole in the ground.

Rhaven stepped to the edge and looked down. "Darstan, light that up with Fire."

Darstan dropped several balls of fire into the hole, lighting it up, but it extended as far as the eye could see.

Rhaven looked at Rahg and nodded. "Impressive."

Mikkellana stared at her sister. "Is this a trick? Or are the Spirals truly that effective?"

"On the way back here, he dropped several dorgans with one shot, though it did contain half a dozen Spirals; that's what they're called—Spirals."

"All right, we have Darstan and the Book, and we have Rahg's new power. Anything else?"

Darstan nodded. "I have new powers too. I have a power that allows me full control of the Slicers. I got it after killing the Lights, and, according to the Mother, it's one of the most significant powers."

"What does it do?" Mikkellana asked.

"I know what it's supposed to do," Darstan said, "but I haven't used it."

"Tell us what it's supposed to do then."

Darstan paced. "According to legend, this was meant to control how the Slicers and even the Light Serpents worked. Supposedly, they'll listen to anything I say."

"Anything?" Mikkellana asked. "Suppose you asked them to attack another person? Would they do it?"

"Apparently, they will," Darstan said. "Even more so, they will convince people to help. All people have power, no matter how little. Persuasion, the power Camissa has—if it's strong enough—can convince people to do things. If we get Camissa to persuade people to go to Sykor, the Slicers can take over from there and persuade them to attack Anciara."

"Is that all the Slicers can do?" Mikkellana asked.

"I got the distinct feeling there was more. A lot more. But I don't know the details. The Mother hinted at it being significant though."

"I guess we'll have to wait and see," Mikkellana said.

Darstan nodded. "I say we plan the attack on Anciara, assuming they'll be no help, but we incorporate them into the attack plan in case they are. If they turn out to be a big help, great, but if not, we'll have to rely on what we have."

"I won't do it," Camissa said. "I don't intend on luring people to Sykor just to have them butchered."

"If we plan on defeating Anciara, you're going to have to do it," Darstan said. "In fact, my plan is to get you started right now."

Camissa jumped up. "What? Started doing what?"

"We're going to need everything we can muster to defeat Anciara. To do that, we need even more people than there are in Sykor. I say we recruit people from other cities: Pomanda, Genda, Khatara, and elsewhere. We'll get them started on the road to

Sykor. If we time it right, they'll get to Sykor around the time we need them. Then, we'll have an ample supply of people."

"I don't think I can make Persuasion work that far."

"Which is why we're going to use the Book," Darstan said, then he looked at Camissa. "I'll hold the Book—just me, so it's not too much power—and you *suggest* to people in the cities I mentioned that they go to Sykor. Reinforce the fact that they'll have to do battle with Anciara as well. When we're ready to go to Sykor and do battle, we'll have hundreds of thousands of people to draw power from."

Mikkellana stood and paced alongside Darstan. "So we'll have the Book along with an ample number of people to provide power, and we'll have this new power allowing the Slicers to make use of all those people."

"And don't forget we have the Light Serpents and a lot more Slicers."

Melissara smiled. "More than a million."

Mikkellana nodded. "A million! And we all saw what Aentarra did with only a few. Perhaps the odds are shifting in our favor."

"I like the positivity I'm hearing," Aenaila said. "Perhaps we should spend the night here and reconvene in the morning."

Mikkellana moved next to Rhaven. "I agree, Aenaila. Let's plan on it."

"We've got a lot to work with," Darstan said, "but we need to plan it right. We can't go against her unprepared. If we do, we die."

"What's the plan then?" Tobias asked. "I've been through a lot of nonsense these last few years. It's about time we put an end to it."

Darstan walked over and patted Tobias on the back. "We're going to put an end to it, Tobias. And with Mikkellana's brilliant strategic mind, we'll come up with a good plan."

"We may as well work on that plan now," Mikkellana said.

"We could," Darstan said. "Or we could let Camissa get the people moving and work on the plan afterward."

Camissa shook her head. "Then get the Book," she said. "We might as well get it over with."

"Not here," Darstan said. "We don't know if Anciara or even Tirzinitzia can detect the Book being used. I think we should Shift to someplace like Khatara, use the Book to send out Persuasion, then Shift back here before they can find us."

Aenaila stepped forward. "Instead of Khatara, let's use Jattan Kir. It's close enough, but I'm guessing neither of them has a Shift Point, which means it will take them time to get there."

"But I don't have a Shift Point either," Darstan said.

"But I do," Aenaila said. "I could take both of you if you allow me the use of some of your power, Darstan. After we arrive, I'll wait while you use the Book, then bring you back."

"Let's do it," Camissa said. "I'd rather get it over with."

Chapter Thirty-Seven

A PLAN LIKE NO OTHER

Tobias got up early as usual and cooked breakfast for everyone with Mollie by his side—all the while he fought off the servants at Marro's house. He dished out portions of food accompanied by mugs of khaffe and gave them to those who were awake, and as he did, he called to the others. "Get up and eat. Ya can't beat anyone in a fight while you're sleeping. Can't do it hungry either, and I'm not cookin' anything else, so ya better get up now."

People slowly roused and walked to the kitchen, grumbling, but happy to eat a hot and hearty meal after so long on the road and eating what only campfires allowed.

Therrim sat next to Rahg and Wisp. "This is my brother Sujan," he said. "He's the youngest of four. I tried to make him stay in Nelstar, but he'd have nothing of it."

"You have two more back on Nelstar?" Wisp asked.

Therrim shook his head. "Just one. I think you met him—Yettl—the one Melissara left in charge. The other brother was Therram, who died in the same incident that killed Antar."

"So why are you fighting with Melissara?" Rahg asked.

"It wasn't Melissara or her father who did that to him. It was the Lights. When I saw you kill the Lights, I decided then I'd be with you."

Aenaila walked up and took a chair beside Wisp. She leaned in and kissed his cheek. "Good morning, my love. How goes the morning?"

Wisp smiled. "It was bad, but now you've brightened it." Wisp patted her back. "Are we going into Cartena today or staying here?"

Aenaila nodded. "As soon as we finish eating, I plan on going to the city. Darstan already sent a Slicer to alert Jago and to have him let the soldiers know, not to mention the commanders."

Wisp laughed. "I imagine that would be good."

"What would be good, Master Kender?" Adju plopped down on the floor next to Wisp, his smile and good nature adding light to the day.

Wisp tousled his hair. "Hasn't someone captured you yet?"

"Master Kender, you're too funny. You know you would miss me if they did. Besides, you need me for good luck. What would you and Master Darstan do without my luck?"

Wisp looked with horror at Adju's mangled hands, but instead of pitying him, he poured Adju another mug of khaffe. "Don't dare let Aenaila know I let you have two cups."

"Never, Master Kender. Never. You know my lips are sealed. Even the laughing wolves couldn't make me talk."

Aenaila looked down at Adju from the seat right next to him. "You know I'm right here, Adju. Did you think I'd gone deaf?"

Adju laughed. "You always start my day so good, Mistress Aenaila. You're funny."

It took thirty more minutes to finish eating, then those who were joining Aenaila linked together in preparation to Shift.

"Do you need help?" Mikkellana asked.

Aenaila shook her head. "It's not far, Mikkellana. I'll be fine."

Aenaila met with Refugio's son and several other commanders and explained the situation to them. "This is not a mandatory assignment. This is for volunteers only, but I'd like for as many of you as possible to come with me."

"Will BlackWolf be there?" Refugio's son asked.

Aenaila nodded. "He will, as will others you know, including Jago."

"Then count us in," the commander said. "You'll have at least a full column."

Aenaila smiled. It was more than she hoped for. "Go to my father's house in seven days to begin training. We'll leave soon afterward." She then Shifted back to Marro's kitchen.

"All set," she said to Darstan. "Refugio said we can count on his men."

Darstan's smile was broad. "Excellent," he said. "Now for Camissa's part of the plan." He looked to Aenaila again. "When will you be ready to go to Jattan Kir?"

"Shortly," she said. "By the time we finish the midday meal."

Darstan tended to trivial things while he waited for Camissa. He wasn't eating, so he worked while others partook of the midday feast.

K ing Marro embraced Aenaila, as did the queen and Aenaila's brother, Jago, while the meal was served.

"It's good to see you again, my dear," her mother said.

Aenaila stepped back and bowed. "And you, My Queen."

"Cut out the queen nonsense. You're my daughter; besides, pretty soon you'll be queen."

Aenaila turned to Jago. "Brother, did you get the message from the soldiers?"

Jago gestured toward the city. "They make ready as we speak. And being led by no other than Refugio's son, but I'm sure you already knew that."

Darstan had just entered the room when he heard mention of Refugio's son. "Refugio's son? He's leading the troops?"

"He is," Aenaila said, "And proud of it. When I announced to the troops what was needed, and when he heard BlackWolf would be leading them, he couldn't be stopped."

Darstan lost his smile. "But his father—"

Refugio's son—also named Refugio—entered the room. "My father died a hero," Refugio said, stepping forward. "He was proud to serve with you, BlackWolf, and nothing would make him more proud than to have me do the same."

Darstan bowed his head. "Your father was a brave and smart man. I was honored to have him serve with me."

"Will you accept me to lead the troops you need?" Refugio asked.

Darstan shook his hand. "I would be more than honored, Refugio. Although you must know it will be a dangerous mission."

Refugio smiled. "I would have it no other way, BlackWolf."

"Good. Tell the men of the danger, and tell them if any don't want to go, they can stay; it will be no shame. Those that decide to follow you, need to prepare with daily drills. They'll need to be in top shape for this mission. We'll leave in thirty days or less."

Refugio snapped a salute. "Yes, sir, BlackWolf. We'll be ready." With that, he turned, walked outside and ordered the men with him to follow.

Darstan leaned to Aenaila and whispered. "How many men does he command?"

"A full column," she said. "And most of them were hardened in battle alongside you."

Darstan nodded. "Things are looking better all the time."

Aenaila grabbed Darstan's arm and led him back toward her parent's kitchen. "I agree, Darstan. For the first time in ages, I feel better about what lies ahead."

Chapter Thirty-Eight

INITIAL PLANS

Aenaila led the way back to the eating room in her father's house, and when they entered it was as if a feast had been prepared. Several of the larger rooms adjoining it had been rearranged to accommodate long tables and an ample supply of chairs. And foods of all kinds filled plates that spread the length and width of the tables.

"Come in," Marro said. "Sit and eat your fill. All guests must eat."

Aenaila tried explaining to her father that many of them had just eaten, but based on Tobias and Rahg's appetite, he wasn't believing a word of what she said. "Look at that lad," he said, gesturing to Rahg. "He looks as if he hasn't eaten in days."

Darstan laughed and leaned toward Marro. "King Marro, that's my brother, and he *always* looks that way."

Mikkellana waited for everyone to finish, then she cleared her throat to draw attention. "I don't mean to interrupt, but if we're going to plan this battle, we may as well get on with it. We won't have a second chance. I believe this is going to be a true do-or-die situation; in other words, we kill Anciara or she kills us. I have no doubt of that."

Melissara stepped forward. "I don't like to be the one to spoil an enjoyable time, but my sister is right. Not all of us were here for the first attack."

She looked to those who came with them from Nelstar. "We fought her once, and as I told you on Nelstar, it was a disaster. If we hadn't had a safe place to Shift to, it would have been our demise. Nothing we did affected her. Not Lightning, Fire, Shields, not even ColdFire."

"What makes you think this time will be different?" Therrim asked.

"This time will be different because we have the Book. And you," Darstan said. "With your power added to the Book, it will increase our power by ten at the least."

"But will that be enough?" Therrim asked.

"That's not all we have," Melissara said. She placed her hand on Darstan's shoulder. "Darstan's powers have also increased, and as most of you know, he now has command of one million Slicers. Not an insignificant number even when facing Anciara."

Melissara moved to Rahg. "And I'd be remiss if I didn't mention that Rahg has been blessed with new powers, the kind of which none of us have ever seen. We don't know the effect—if any—it will have on Anciara, but if what it did to the Lights and dorgans is any example, it could be significant."

She gestured to Sujan. "You and Therrim saw those powers at work when we fought the Lights. Have you seen anything like it?"

Sujan shook his head. "Not in my lifetime."

"None of those powers will be worth anything if we don't get a chance to use them," Therrim said. "From what you've told me, Anciara may simply kill us all before we know it."

Mikkellana walked to the middle of the room and wagged her finger. "We have plans for that too. We have among us someone who can Cloak." A gasp came from the men who accompanied Melissara from Nelstar.

"Yes," Mikkellana said. "And it's not just Cloaking, but complete Stealth, which means Anciara won't be able to see, hear, or sense us. And, if we use the Book to let him be the focus of the power along with Rahg and Darstan, he'll be strong enough to conceal all of us. We can attack Anciara, and she won't know where it's coming from."

"I didn't see any signs of Cloaking in Nelstar," Costar said.

Melissara stepped in front of Darstan and addressed Costar. "Were you there for the entire battle?"

When he nodded, she said, "Did you see us arrive?"

Costar seemed to give it thought, then said, "No, I didn't."

Melissara smiled. "That's because we were already there. We had been there for hours under the aegis of Wisp's Cloak. Once the Lights arrived, we switched to let him be a source of the Book's power while Darstan used it to strike."

Therrim and his brother Sujan looked at each other and nodded. The rest of the Nelstar group joined in. "This may not be the suicide mission I presumed," Sujan said.

"None of us plan on forsaking our lives," Mikkellana said. "That some of us will, is a possibility that we've all come to terms with, but no one plans on it."

Sujan sat in a chair next to Rahg. "Then I think it's time to discuss the specifics. It sounds like something we dare not get wrong."

Darstan called attention to Camissa. "Before we work out details, I suggest we use the Book to let Camissa put out a summons to all people in the cities close enough to Sykor so they can make it on their own. When we leave to do battle, we can take a handful of soldiers, battle-hardened soldiers, with us."

"What are a handful of soldiers going to do?" Therrim asked.

Aenaila's laughter rolled from the back of the room. "I think what Darstan means by a 'handful' is really a full column—ten thousand soldiers. And when he says battle-hardened, he means it. These men have fought in a war where people used powers against each other. In fact, they've fought in several wars, including one against Lukaan."

Sujan nodded. "If they've fought against Lukaan and are still with us, that's good enough for me."

"Tell us your plan, Mikkellana," Therrim said.

"I'll mention the defensive part since Shields are my specialty, but I'll let Darstan tell you about offense, since that's obviously his." She sat on the sofa again next to Rhaven. "First, though, as Darstan said, we should allow Camissa to begin the process as it may take as long as a full cycle for some of the people to reach Sykor."

Darstan motioned to Wisp, who brought the Book to the center of the room. "Camissa, we're going to need you for this."

She moved slowly—very slowly—to a position alongside Darstan. "I don't want to do this," she whispered. "People will die. It's no different than killing them myself."

Darstan held her by the shoulders. He was tempted to use Voice, but he didn't. He didn't know if it would even work against someone with Persuasion. "Yes, Camissa, people will die, but you know who we're dealing with. Anciara will kill far more people if she isn't stopped, including all of *us*. It's not something any of us want to do, but it has to be done."

Camissa looked into Darstan's eyes. "How many do you think will die?"

Somber as can be, Darstan said, "Not as many as if you don't do it."

Camissa thought for a moment, then nodded. "All right, let's get it done."

Darstan looked at Wisp, then searched for Aenaila. "Aenaila, it's time we went to Jattan Kir."

She stepped forward and linked with Camissa and Darstan, then she Shifted.

They appeared in the desert not far from the gates of the city. "Here's as good a place as any," Aenaila said. "It will be close enough to let them know where someone used powers—assuming they Sense it."

"I'm sure they will," Darstan said, then held out the Book. "Take hold of it first, Camissa. Then be quick about using it. Call all people from the cities I mentioned, and you better include Jattan Kir. She may not treat the inhabitants well after this."

"Do you want me to touch the Book?" Aenaila asked.

"Not unless I say so," Darstan said. "Camissa's never used the Book, so I'm leery of her getting too much power at once. I'll try it out with just me to see how much she can handle. We'll add more if necessary."

Darstan took hold of Camissa's hand. "It's time. Just place your hand on the center of the Book. I'll open it and link when ready."

Camissa reached for the Book and put her hand in the center, then braced herself. She nodded to Darstan, who then placed his hand on the Book and took hold of her. He then opened the Book, unleashing a torrent of Lightning, Fire, and Storm.

The infusion of power forced Camissa to stiffen, but after a moment, she nodded again.

Darstan looked to Aenaila, who then placed her hand on the Book. Once again, power surged into Camissa, hitting her like a jolt from a Lightning bolt.

She closed her eyes and focused, thinking of that place in her mind where Persuasion dwelled. Once she found it, she commanded it forward and sent it to the images in her mind: Genda, all through the steep rolling streets; Pomanda, around the curvy lanes and wide avenues and into the plazas; and Khatara, squeezing into alleys so narrow two people abreast couldn't fit down them.

"To all the people nearby: go to Sykor. Join me in fighting the evil one, the Goddess of Death. Come now. Don't delay. The world needs you."

When she finished, she stumbled, falling to the desert floor and collapsing. Sweat rolled down her cheeks.

Darstan picked her up and grabbed hold of Aenaila. "We should leave now. Anciara will have surely sensed that power, which means she won't be long in getting here."

Aenaila Shifted to her father's house, and Darstan set Camissa on the sofa.

Rahg rushed to her and held her in his arms. "Are you all right, Camissa? What can I do? Camissa, are you all right?"

She shook her head. "Nothing you can do, Rahg. I'll be fine. Let's just hope the rest of us will be fine."

"On to the strategy," Darstan said. "The first part is done."

On the other side of the Endless Sea, Tirzinitzia approached Anciara. "Did you feel that?"

Anciara nodded. "It was a surge of powers. It's them, and they're planning something; otherwise, why use so much power?"

"I couldn't place where the power came from," Tirzinitzia said.

"I didn't either, but I've issued numerous sensors to see if we can locate them."

"I don't think they were close," Tirzinitzia said. "I would have known if they were. I'd send the sensors toward the isle where we were. Have them spread out from there."

Anciara smiled. "You contribute enough to keep you alive, Tirzinitzia. Just make sure your contributions make your value high enough to warrant my good grace."

"If we can locate the power surge, we'll have them," Tirzinitzia said.

"Yes," Anciara said. "Yes, we will."

A few moments later, the sensors returned, reporting nothing. "Send some the other way," Anciara said. "Scour the east, then the north, but find them."

It only took ten minutes for the sensors to report back. "Jattan Kir," Tirzinitzia said. "It's the far eastern border of Khatara. I would have never thought to look there."

"Which is obviously why they chose it," Anciara said. "Give me a Shift Point."

A nciara and Tirzinitzia reappeared on the outskirts of Jattan Kir, not far from the city gates. "This is a desert," Anciara said.

Tirzinitzia glanced around. "Just like her to think of this," she said. "But what were they doing here? I don't recognize the power."

"Do I need to find someone with more talent?" Anciara asked. "Perhaps I was too hasty in choosing you to help me."

"I'm expressing my concerns, My Lady, nothing else. I'll find the answers."

"Then I suggest you do so now," Anciara said.

"As you will, My Lady," Tirzinitzia said, and she made her way into the city while Anciara waited.

She returned moments later with three of the city's leaders. "These are the rulers of Jattan Kir," Tirzinitzia said. "If anyone knows what goes on, it's them."

Anciara smiled and drew close to them. "Tell me, good citizens. Who was just here using powers, and what did they use them for?"

The three men looked at each other and then shook their

heads. "We have no idea," the tall man said. "We didn't even know powers were used."

Anciara looked to Tirzinitzia. "Who is he?"

"The one who rules the city," Tirzinitzia said. "He is called the annir."

"Such a shame," Anciara said. "You should pay more attention to what transpires in your city."

"But I don't know of anything that transpired," the annir said.

"Such a shame," Anciara said, then she focused on him, and he dropped dead.

She turned to the others. "Do either of you have any idea what happened?"

A long silence followed, but when pressed, both admitted they knew nothing.

"I'm appalled at the lack of monitoring," Anciara said, then she repeated what happened to the annir.

"Where shall we go now?" Tirzinitzia asked.

Anciara looked at her with amazement. "Ask the people of the city what they know."

Tirzinitzia stared. Dumbfounded. "But, My Lady, I doubt if they'd know anything."

"I guess we'll find out," Anciara said. "Now go, and hope I don't mete out punishment before you return."

Tirzinitzia returned within moments, breathing heavily. "Nothing, My Lady. No one heard or saw anything. And I might add, I believe them. I think we should move on."

Anciara laughed. "And I think we shouldn't."

She faced the city of Jattan Kir and extended her hands. She focused her power, then emitted a ForceBolt that rolled toward the city's gates.

It struck the fortifications, consisting of brick walls and metal gates, shattering them at the first touch, then the ForceBolt rolled toward the main part of the city, razing houses and small businesses in its way.

It grew wider and taller as it moved, tearing down larger and taller buildings as it moved further into the city. The largest buildings stayed aloft longer, but after a few moments of shaking, they toppled to the ground, crushing other buildings and people alike.

By the time the ForceBolt had made its way through town, everything was gone—everything. Not a building stood, and not a person breathed.

Tirzinitzia looked on in amazement. "That was one million people!"

"Was," Anciara said.

Chapter Thirty-Nine

PLANNING THE DETAILS

It took Camissa two days to recover from using the Book, but on the third day, she seemed fine.

"I don't understand why it did that," Darstan said to Mikkellana. "I used it twice now, and I haven't felt any effects."

Mikkellana laughed. "Darstan, some day, presuming you live long enough, you'll realize how strong you are. People are going to react differently to using the Book, just as they will to using powers. Remember when you first used ColdFire? You lost consciousness the first few times."

Darstan tilted his head back and thought. "I guess you're right. I'd forgotten that."

"Having powers is a wonderful thing, but you need to remember what it's like to be a person who doesn't have them, or one whose powers are much less developed than your own."

Mikkellana struggled to stand, falling back twice before Rhaven helped her. She put a hand to her back and pressed.

"Are you all right?" Darstan asked.

"It's getting worse," she said. "I just need to suffer through until we finish with Anciara."

"I can fix that," Rahg said as he moved toward them. "I've learned how."

Mikkellana looked at him with a skewed eye. "The back is a sensitive area."

Rahg nodded. "Lie down on your stomach. It won't take long."

"Are you certain, Rahg? When did you learn to heal?"

∽

"On the way to Nelstar. The gods granted me the power to heal when they gave me the power to use Spirals, though they want me to set them free when we're done."

Melissara shook her head. "We're not doing that, Rahg. It would be as bad as facing Anciara, perhaps worse."

"But I almost promised them—"

Melissara continued shaking her head. "Some promises are meant to be broken, Rahg, and this is one of them."

Rahg opted not to argue any more, then he helped Mikkellana lie on the bed. When she seemed somewhat comfortable, he placed his hands on the lower part of her back and focused.

At first, he saw nothing, then he concentrated on where his hands were. Long, thin tendrils of Shield extended from his fingers and crawled along her lower back. He felt the ridges in her skin and saw through the pores dotting every space. He looked under her skin and into her bones. It was there he noted a crack in one of the bones. "Found it," he said.

A strand of Shield even thinner than the others oozed forth from his fingertips and entered her body, entering through the pores of her skin and weaving around her lower bones. The shield filled the crack and closed it, making it one with the rest of the bone. When the healing was done, Rahg encapsulated the bone by wrapping another layer of Shield around the outside, offering protection against shock or impact.

When he finished, he stood over Mikkellana and grinned. "It's done, Mikkellana. It worked."

Mikkellana appeared skeptical, but eventually she rolled over, and for a moment, sat still. Then she stood and took a hesitant step. Then another. A smile appeared and grew into a laugh. "I can't believe it. I'm healed. I can't feel a thing."

"The bone was cracked," Rahg said. "It's fine now though."

Mikkellana turned to him, astounded. "You could see it?"

Rahg nodded. "Once I concentrated on it, yes. After that, it was easy."

"That's remarkable," Mikkellana said. "I've never seen its like."

"Master Rahg, can you do that to me?" Adju asked, holding out his hands.

Rahg looked at Adju, then at Wisp. "Tell me again what happened."

"The guards in Khatara smashed his hands with a hammer," Wisp said. "I doubt you can do any more than what Aenaila has."

Rahg gently held Adju's hands and examined them. Once again, he focused on seeing the internals, taking note of the cracks in the bones. After a few moments, he let go of Adju's hands and asked him to sit, then he turned to Wisp. "I think I can help. There are a lot of bones in the hand, and many of his have been shattered or cracked, but I think I can do it."

Adju's face lit up. "Can you, Master Rahg? Can you really?"

Wisp tugged on Rahg's sleeve. "Rahg, if you can't do it, don't try. I don't want to get his hopes up."

Rahg nodded. "I'll do it, Wisp. Don't worry."

Rahg asked Adju to lie down on the sofa, then he went to work on Adju's hands. Within moments, he found the problems and started to fix them. Thirty minutes later, he asked Adju to sit up. "How do they feel?" he asked.

Adju stretched a few fingers, then he made a fist, then he laughed hard. "Master Kender, it works. He fixed them." Adju jumped from the sofa and ran over and hugged Aenaila, then he punched Wisp. "See. I can even punch you."

Wisp laughed along with him. "I see," he said. "And I can't believe it."

He walked to Rahg and hugged him. "Thank you, Rahg. Thank you so much."

Mikkellana sat in a chair next to Rhaven and smiled while nodding. "Impressive," she said. "Impressive indeed."

"Now that we've taken care of that," Rahg said, "let's move on to devising a strategy we can use to defeat Anciara."

With her newfound confidence, Mikkellana almost danced through the room. "The first thing we need to address is the shielding."

"Meaning what?" Therrim asked.

"When we first attacked her, she seemed invincible, as if the assaults had no effect. Initially, I thought it may have been simply because she was so strong, but Darstan mentioned that his Cold-Fire had no effect—none. And of all the power we used against her, that's the one that should have."

"I don't understand what that tells you," Sujan said.

"It tells me she had a Shield that stretched beneath the surface. One that not only stopped the ColdFire from reaching her up top, but it prevented it from creeping underneath her shield."

"All well and good," Rahg said, "but what can we do about it? I don't see any way of preventing her from weaving a shield."

Mikkellana turned to Rahg. "You're right, Rahg. We can't stop her from weaving a Shield, but if we pick the spot of the attack, we can prepare so that her Shield can't go underground. If *we* weave a Shield beforehand that penetrates the surface—actually uses the ground's energy and strength as part of the Shield—then she won't be able to break through it. At least not easily. Given enough time, she could, but not in the short amount of time the battle will allow."

"So we'd have to lure her to the spot we choose?" Rahg asked.

Mikkellana nodded. "Exactly. And I don't think that will be too difficult."

"Once we get her where we want, then what?" Wisp asked.

Mikkellana sat back down. "I'll let Darstan handle that. He's more skilled at offense."

Darstan went to the center of the room. "I think there are three keys to the attack, none of which can afford to fail. The first one is the Book, and this is a big one."

"We already know how the Book works," Therrim said.

"And therein lies one of the problems," Darstan said. "Knowing how the Book works in general and knowing how it should be used specifically are different."

Therrim acknowledged his misinformation. "Forgive our ignorance, Darstan, but for those of us who don't know, the details may be significant. Please explain."

Darstan sighed. "The Book allows the one who touches it first to increase their power by magnitudes—depending on who else has hold of it when linked. But be warned, the Book drains the people who use it, and it takes a long time for those people to recharge, so to speak."

Aenaila smiled. "I know you think that was an explanation, Darstan, but it wasn't."

Darstan grinned back at her. "Let's try explaining it by what I have in mind. If Rahg, Camissa, Wisp, and myself want to have our powers increased by the Book, we will have to touch it first *and* at the same time. After we touch it, everyone else with powers needs to touch it to link with us. When they do that, our power will be magnified ten- to twenty-fold—perhaps more."

Darstan looked around the room. "What that means is that Camissa's Persuasion, Rahg's Shielding, Wisp's Stealth, and my ColdFire will be twenty times stronger—or more."

Darstan paced for a moment, then began again. "When we know Anciara is coming, we will activate the Book.

"Once we do that, Wisp will Cloak us so that Anciara won't

know where we are. At the same time, Camissa will use Persuasion to convince everyone who has come from all the lands to allow themselves to be used to attack Anciara. Once that happens, and everyone has been persuaded, Mikkellana and Camissa will switch places, allowing Mikkellana to weave a Shield in front of us because Anciara will surely discover where we are, eventually. Keep in mind, Mikkellana will have already woven a shield underneath the spot where Anciara is and bonded it to the ground."

Darstan grabbed a sip of water from Aenaila. "At that point, Rahg and I will attack with everything we have—primarily ColdFire and Spirals. In addition, we'll have the Slicers and Light Serpents attack. And don't discount the effectiveness of them; remember, there are more than one million Slicers."

"This sounds good," Sujan said. "But will it be enough?"

"We have no way of knowing, but it's not all we have. While this is going on, the ten thousand soldiers from Cergala, plus thousands from Sykor, will attack her. Many will die, I'm sure, but they will distract her from us, and they will weaken her power. At that time, I'll also use Slicers to access the tens of thousands that Camissa used Persuasion on."

Melissara patted Darstan on the back. "That sounds so good, you have me convinced we have a chance."

"I'm convinced," Sujan said. "I almost think we might live to see Nelstar again."

Sujan spoke to clarify things. "So the ones providing power to the Book will be myself, Mikkellana, Melissara, and the others who came from Nelstar?"

Darstan nodded. "Until Camissa is done, then she'll switch with Mikkellana so that Mikkellana can erect a barrier."

"And what will I be doing?" Rhaven asked. "I don't intend on sitting this out."

"Neither do I," Tobias said.

Darstan smiled. "I felt certain that would be the case. I thought the two of you could lead the soldiers. Rhaven taking charge of

Takar and his Sykoran soldiers, not to mention the Lorns who we hope will arrive in time, and Tobias taking charge of the Cergalan soldiers, but only to provide the necessary information for Refugio, since he doesn't know Sykor."

"I'll need to speak to Takar before the attack so we can prepare," Rhaven said.

"Likewise for me," Tobias said, "but I guess I can talk to Refugio while we're here."

"I don't see how we can lose," Rahg said.

Mikkellana laughed. "Rahg, I love the enthusiasm and optimism of youth, though at the same time it frightens me."

Rahg appeared confused. "How so?"

Mikkellana paused to give it thought. "Just because we have a large number of people—even talented, powerful people—it doesn't mean we'll be successful. We have to have the right people, and it has to be the right time."

"I think it *is* the right time," Rahg said. "I don't see how we can lose with what we have."

"I hope you're right," Mikkellana said.

"Something we need to be aware of," Melissara said, "is that those who are connected to the Book will likely be drained of their energy as Darstan mentioned." Melissara looked at Therrim and his men. "We know it takes a long time to recover after use, but what we don't know is what happens if they use the Book for too long. It's possible it may kill them. So if you're one of the ones providing power, and you feel too weak to go on, let go and recharge."

"I believe the most important thing is to coordinate the attacks so they all happen at once. I understand we don't know the extent of her power, but it's hard to imagine anyone being able to withstand this kind of onslaught," Darstan said.

Wisp moved next to Darstan and sat, then leaned down and whispered. "You never mentioned that thing you did when we were fighting the soldiers of Arangar, when so many thousands died."

Darstan nodded. "I thought about it, Wisp, but I don't know

how to use it without it affecting all the innocent people. I realize a number of them will die anyway, but I don't want to be the butcher of so many."

"I'd ask Mikkellana," Wisp said. "I bet she could think up something to do with her Shielding that could be used. I'd talk to her if I were you. We've got nothing to lose by talking."

Darstan smiled. "As usual, my wise friend, you're right. I'll talk to her when we're alone."

For several weeks everyone practiced honing their skills. Camissa used Persuasion at every opportunity, and Darstan worked with her when she did. Rahg focused on the use of Spirals, and he soon got good enough to weave them as small as the thickness of a person's finger and as large as a small tree. Wisp practiced with Stealth, cloaking more and more people simultaneously and extending the time he could maintain it.

The following day, Mikkellana called a meeting. "It's time," she said. "I Shifted to a spot outside of Sykor last night, and the Pomandans and Gendans were already there. The Khatarans were less than a day away."

"Should we wait until they're inside the city?" Aenaila asked.

"I don't see a reason to. We can Shift to Talanvar's manor and use the time we have to instruct him on what to expect and what to do. Meanwhile, Rhaven can seek Takar out and inform him."

"What about the soldiers?" Aenaila asked. "The ones we are supposed to take from Cartena."

"I think it would be too risky to take them before we launch the attack. It would be safer if my sister joined the two of us and Shifted back here the morning of the attack, then took them to Sykor."

Aenaila nodded. "I like that idea. Anciara will know when we

Shift that many people to Sykor, so we better be ready once we do."

"Exactly," Mikkellana said. "I thought we'd Shift to the plaza before the sun rises. The soldiers can position themselves in every hiding place available while I weave a Shield under the ground to block Anciara from bracing a shield of her own."

"In that case," Aenaila said, "I'll remain here and make sure the soldiers are ready before dawn. In the meantime, you can go to Talanvar's and get the rest set up."

"I'll have it done," Mikkellana said. "Now I must speak to Darstan."

Mikkellana stopped Darstan before he poured his khaffe. "You mentioned the possibility of using the FearMist the other day. I've given it thought, but I don't see how to make it work without bringing a lot of harm. I suggest we go with what we have, but if it's not working, we can try the FearMist."

Darstan nodded. "I agree," Mikkellana. "That makes me feel better."

Anciara summoned Tirzinitzia to stand before her. "There are thousands of people coming to Sykor from both directions. Why are they all coming here? What are they up to?"

Tirzinitzia bit her lip and stared into Anciara's eyes. "I wish I knew what they were up to, but I don't. I'm sure Melissara and her sister are behind this, but I don't know what they're planning, and I have to admit I'm puzzled. What can ordinary people do? Even in numbers like this?"

"I don't know what the people can do or what the others are up to, but I expect you to find out. Be alert for any sign of powers in the city. For your friends to accomplish anything, they have to be here."

"I think I should interrogate a few of these people so we can see why they're here."

"I believe you to be right, Tirzinitzia. See that it's done, and quickly."

Tirzinitzia bowed. "Your will, My Lady." She then left the room and walked through the city. She thought of taking a few of the recent visitors, but opted to take a few of the ones just arriving from Khatara. She Shifted to a spot outside the city where tens of thousands walked along the road from Khatara. She picked a few near the front of the line and took them with her to a house in Sykor. Once inside, she began questioning them.

"Why are you coming here?" she asked. "It would be wise to tell me."

"I don't know."

"What do you mean, 'you don't know'? How is that possible?"

"I just don't know. I was fixing a meal for my son when I got the urge to come here. It was like someone was in my head telling me to come here, and I couldn't say no."

Tirzinitzia talked to the other two people but got the same answers. "Stay here," she told them. "I'll be back."

She went to see Anciara. "I spoke to three of them, and, by the way they answered, it seems like they've been subjected to Persuasion of some kind, but I never heard of it being so powerful."

"Even if it was that powerful, what good would it do? What can a bunch of ordinary people do to us, no matter how many there are? I could kill them all with a few walls of Fire."

"What could it be then?" Tirzinitzia asked. "They're here for *some* reason."

"And we'll find out why soon enough," Anciara said. "We'll be ready for whatever they have planned."

~

Mikkellana appeared in Talanvar's library along with all those helping her. Talanvar greeted her with a hug. "So good to see you again, My Lady." He then made the rounds with all those he knew, staying to talk with Wisp for a long time. "We're going to have to share a bottle or two of wine and tell each other stories, my friend, though I'm sure your tales will dwarf mine."

Wisp patted Talanvar on the back. "We'll do that soon. As soon as we finish with Anciara—the one holding the people of Sykor prisoner. And before I forget, how is little Dirk?"

Talanvar laughed. "Dirk is fine. He's become near a master gate-keeper, and he's learned to do almost everything, even without his thumbs. He dresses himself, and he cuts his own food. He's made significant improvements."

Wisp and Talanvar spoke about old times, and about the Trader's Inn, and about the thieves' guild. The conversation lasted long into the night. They were still talking when Rhaven walked in. "I talked to Takar. His men will be ready before dawn."

Talanvar stood and yawned. "Since that isn't far from now, I'm going to get a short nap. It looks as if it will be a long day."

"And a difficult one," Mikkellana said as she stepped into the library, followed by Melissara.

"What are you doing up?" Rhaven asked.

"Going to Cergala to get the soldiers, or did you forget?" She leaned in and kissed him. "I won't be long. Try to sleep a little before you get Takar. As Talanvar said, it will be a long day."

Mikkellana and her sister Shifted to Cartena and came back moments later with Aenaila and her support troops—ten thousand Cergalan soldiers. They reappeared in the Sykoran plaza, where Mikkellana told them to seek any shelter they could find until they heard the signal. She then went to work constructing a shield under the ground to prevent Anciara from weaving one using the ground as a brace.

While Mikkellana tended to the shield, Aenaila Shifted to Talanvar's house, taking Adju with her so he could stay at the manor with Dirk. Wisp would die if anything happened to that boy.

"Why do I need to stay here?" Adju asked.

"Be thankful I brought you this far," Aenaila said. "I should have left you with my brother in Cartena. How I let you convince me to bring you here, I don't know."

Aenaila turned to leave, then spun around and faced Adju and Dirk. "Stay here! I mean it. If we survive, we'll return. If not, take anything you can and get out of the city. Go to Genda and hide."

"How about Khatara?" Adju asked. "I know it better."

Aenaila nodded. "Khatara will be fine, Adju. Just make sure to watch out for Dirk."

Adju smiled. "You can count on me for that, Mistress Aenaila. You know you can."

Aenaila smiled, then leaned over and kissed both of them on the forehead. "I know I can, Adju. Now watch the windows while we're gone so you can be forewarned if anything happens."

Wisp handed a small pouch of gold to Adju. "Take this to live on in case we don't return. And do like Aenaila said and take care of Dirk."

Adju wiped tears from his eyes. "You'll be safe, Master Kender. I know you will."

Wisp ensured the lads were safe, then nodded to Aenaila, indicating he was ready. She took hold of everyone, then returned to the plaza with Wisp, Talanvar, Rhaven, and Tobias. Mollie insisted on coming too, and since Aenaila had no time to argue, she allowed it.

Melissara Shifted to Genda, where Malakai waited with several thousand men, according to a prearranged plan. All were armed with curved swords and spears.

Chapter Forty

PRELUDE TO DEATH

Darstan, Rahg, and the others gathered in the plaza while waiting for Anciara. "I expected her by now," Darstan said. "It doesn't matter though, as soon as Camissa uses the Book, she'll definitely come."

He nodded to Camissa, and she placed her hand on the Book, joined by Darstan, Wisp, and Rahg. A few heartbeats later, Darstan turned to Camissa and said, "Do it now."

~

Camissa used Persuasion on everyone that had been packed into the city from all the lands. All those from Genda, Pomanda, Khatara, and elsewhere. When she finished, she removed her hand from the Book. "It's done," she said.

Darstan nodded. "That will bring Anciara here for sure, and once she's here, we can begin."

Anciara awoke, calling to Tirzinitzia immediately. "Did you feel it? They're here. In the plaza."

"I didn't feel it, but I'll dress quickly, and we'll be on our way." Tirzinitzia rushed from the room returning moments later decked out for battle, including the victory ring she earned at the Battle of Katsintal. "Ready," she said.

"You look like a woman prepared to die," Anciara said.

"If need be, yes."

"I don't intend for that to happen," Anciara said. "When we get to the plaza, stand to one side. You may keep watch, but only join the fray if you feel the need. I can manage whatever these puny ones throw at me."

Tirzinitzia bowed. "Yes, My Lady. Your will."

Anciara stretched her hand to Tirzinitzia. "Link. We go now."

Anciara Shifted to the plaza, prepared for a battle, but nothing greeted her. Nothing.

She glanced to all sides, as did Tirzinitzia, but neither of them detected anyone.

"Did they leave?" Anciara asked. "If so, where did they go, and why come here to begin with?"

Tirzinitzia walked to the center of the plaza to stand beside Anciara. "Worry not, My Lady. No matter where they went, we'll find them."

Wisp, using the energy infused in him by the Book, kept everyone fully cloaked so that Anciara couldn't tell where they were. It also allowed them to communicate without her hearing them.

Darstan, Rahg, and Mikkellana were also among the beneficiaries of the Book's power, while Camissa, Aenaila, Melissara, Therrim, and the others from Nelstar provided the power.

Mikkellana had woven a partial shield secured to the ground earlier. Now she worked on closing it in. "Help me out with this, Rahg. Watch what I do, then use your own Shielding to reinforce it. With both of us using the Book, it will likely be enough to hold her. At least for a while, it will."

Mikkellana wove a convex-shaped shield from the ground up and over Anciara's head. The curve of the shield gave it a natural strength, but she further strengthened it by bracing it against the ground with support pillars as wide as a man is tall. "Weave one just like it, Rahg. With both of ours blocking her, she shouldn't be able to strike at us."

"But how long can we hold this?" Rahg asked. "Even with the Book, we'll tire eventually."

Mikkellana shook her head. "Once you weave the shield, you can move on. When it's braced in this fashion, using the ground, it doesn't need continual power to maintain it. Once we're done weaving, you can go back to using your power to make Spirals. I'll need to continue here to allow openings for attack, which you'll have to do as well when Darstan gives the order."

Rahg nodded and allowed the power from the Book to build inside him. He prepared for a strike.

Anciara noticed a contingent of soldiers on a street to the south. She reached out to strike them but was stopped by a shield. Frustrated, she hammered against the shield with Lightning and Fire, but it was all in vain. Nothing worked.

"It's like the Sethian Shield," Tirzinitzia said. "The more power you use on it, the stronger it gets. How did she build this so quickly?"

"They must be using the Book," Anciara said. "But where are they? I see nothing."

Anciara tried Shifting, but the shield wouldn't allow her to move. "Relax for now, Tirzinitzia. We may not be able to get at them, but the reverse is true as well; they can't get us. And if there is anything I learned during aeons of imprisonment, it was patience."

❧

"Rahg, Mikkellana, open the shield on the whole east, that's Anciara's left side," Darstan said. "Open the entire left side and make it wide enough for a full strike. And as soon as you see the ColdFire enter, close it back up. But you'll have to tell me when to issue the strike because I can't see the shield."

A moment later, Mikkellana called out, "Open the shield now, Rahg." She waited a second, then said to Darstan, "Now!"

Darstan had already focused his power, now he let loose with a blistering wall of ColdFire aimed to fit the opening in the shield. Once it shot through, Mikkellana and Rahg closed the shield again.

The ColdFire struck Anciara full force, sending her reeling into the wall of the building behind her. Her head struck the stone, and though it didn't do any damage to her physically, it infuriated her. Once again she lashed out with all her powers only to be stopped by the shield.

The Coldfire didn't stop with Anciara, though. It continued on and struck Tirzinitzia, and though not quite full force, it was enough to immobilize her, then destroy her. She shattered into a thousand pieces, as had the others before her.

"Prepare to open the shield again in a few moments," Darstan said. "This time, we'll go straight at her."

"I await your directive," Mikkellana said.

"Mikkellana, do you think you can hold the shield yourself while Rahg uses his Spirals?" Darstan asked.

"My brother Sujan is strong in Shielding," Therrim said. "If you need support, let him provide it while Rahg attacks."

Darstan turned and addressed Therrim. "How strong is he?"

"He once held off two Lights for more than several moments. And that was by himself and with no Book."

"That's the best news I've heard today," Darstan said, and turned to address Sujan. "Sujan, take hold of the Book when we release, and then we'll re-establish contact with the Book. Your Shielding strength will be more valuable that way than it would be as a source of power. But we'll have to move because once Wisp lets go, we'll be visible."

Sujan nodded. "I'll watch for the sign."

"Good, and make sure to listen for my signals on when to open your shield to allow our attacks. And watch Mikkellana. Mimic her shield for design. It will be constructed for strength."

Darstan yelled for Tobias, but he was too far away and behind a shield; instead, he sent a Slicer, then he sent one each to Rhaven, Talanvar, and Malakai. It was time to distract Anciara, which would allow he and Rahg to absorb more power from the Book.

The Slicer carried the message, and it arrived to all men at almost the same time.

"Death to Anciara!" Rhaven called, and he and the Sykoran Guard—several thousand of them—charged Anciara from the northwest side.

Simultaneously, Malakai and a few thousand Gendans attacked from the eastern side of the plaza, all wielding cutlasses, knives, and even harpoons.

While they were advancing, Tobias issued his command to attack, and ten thousand soldiers from Cartena charged from the southeast and southwest sides of the plaza.

Finally, Talanvar moved in from the northeast with several hundred thieves and even a few bounty-men.

At the last moment, a hundred or more Lorns appeared, and all were armed with bows as well as arrows dipped in poison.

Anciara tried striking at all of them several times, but the shield prevented her, then Darstan issued the order to open the shield.

Mikkellana and Sujan waited until the soldiers were almost upon her, then they opened the shield on all sides, allowing the soldiers to attack.

From all sides, soldiers fired arrows, threw spears, and attacked with swords, knives, and more. None of the assaults did much damage singly, but together the massive assault had an effect. Twice, she faltered.

The poison arrows didn't have the hoped for effect, but they did do *some* damage. As each one struck, Anciara winced. When a dozen or more hit her at once, she fell back.

❧

Anciara shielded her eyes, then erected her own barrier to stop the projectiles from reaching her. Then, she lashed out once again, sending a gigantic wall of BlackFire against the soldiers.

❧

"Close the shield," Mikkellana ordered. "Don't let the Fire reach the masses."

Within heartbeats, Mikkellana and Sujan closed the shield, and although a few thousand soldiers were trapped inside, the rest of the people in the plaza survived.

"It's almost time," Darstan said. "When I give the order, drop the shield, and then provide power to the Book. Rahg and I will do the attacking."

Moments later, Darstan gave the signal for Mikkellana to open the shield. Once she did, Darstan and Rahg attacked with everything they had.

The Spirals struck first, the larger ones not being able to penetrate Anciara, but they forced her to maintain shields in those areas to protect herself. Some of the smaller Spirals got through, striking like small daggers into her legs and arms—all the places she wasn't fully protected. A few managed to go through her legs, causing her to stumble. When a Spiral hit one of her knees, it dropped her to the ground.

The Spirals may have struck first, but Darstan's ColdFire proved to be more devastating, roaring in behind them, propelled by all the power from the Book.

The ColdFire hit Anciara with such force it knocked her down, and while it damaged her ego more than it did her physically, it *did* do damage. When she stood, it was with noticeable effort.

Anciara fumed. She attacked with BlackFire and BlackLightning. Sujarn had not finished closing his part of the shield, and it allowed Anciara's attacks to reach the soldiers in the plaza. Columns of Fire hit the group led by Malakai, and it rolled over them as if they weren't there, sending many of them to their graves. Malakai stood among them brandishing a cutlass and issuing orders, his red locks catching the first rays of light. The BlackFire engulfed him and took him down.

Rhaven and the Sykoran Guard had been anxiously waiting to join the fray again. With the shield opened, they attacked from the north, with several patrols of archers positioned to the east firing constant barrages of arrows. Anciara turned to attack, but when she did, Tobias and the Cergalan soldiers swarmed her from the south and west and they were ten thousand strong. Not an insignificant number, even for Anciara.

Anciara hurled BlackLightning where the men were crowded together the thickest, and it struck with ferociousness, killing dozens of soldiers with each strike. Then she focused, and use a ForceBolt against them, attacking with a strike that killed thousands at once.

Darstan looked at the men dying—thousands of them—and he pondered what to do. He couldn't use FearMist or it would affect the men, and ColdFire would kill them before reaching Anciara. With no recourse, he let the power of the Book build within him.

As he pondered what to do, Anciara's ForceBolts killed thousands.

Perhaps we need to strike again with everything we have.

Chapter Forty-One

THE LAST BATTLE

Anciara struck several more times with Lightning, then used a ForceBolt again. It killed thousands more and destroyed everything in its path, knocking down buildings and ripping up streets, not to mention horses and oxen that pulled carts. Women and children died alongside the soldiers from Cartena, who had been waiting to attack again.

A peddler walking with his horse and cart was caught in the last strike, and simply disappeared.

Mikkellana got Rahg to help with a shield to stop the ForceBolt, but it didn't hold. Anciara's ForceBolt hit the shield so hard, it jarred Mikkellana's head and knocked her down. Rahg was pushed back a step, almost losing touch with the Book.

Darstan fumed. *This is enough.* He turned to Rahg and shouted over the tumult surrounding them. "Let the power build in you, Rahg. Don't use anything until I say so, then give it everything you've got."

Despite the frenzy of battle, Darstan closed his eyes and concentrated. He sought out the palace in his mind, and he located the door at the top of the stairs. It was time to see if the Mother was right. He opened the door and stared into darkness. Darkness and emptiness.

As he wondered what to do, a strand of mist crept out the door near his feet. It was followed by a few more, then by many much-longer strands—thousands of them, then ten times that many. A smile came to Darstan's face.

He sent a Slicer to Mikkellana to let her know of his plan. *"Mikkellana, open up a channel for the FearMist."*

Then he focused on his power. *"Go. Seek out the one we fight and destroy her."*

The FearMist crept down the stairs of the palace, then out the door. At that moment, Darstan looked down and realized the door represented the stump of his hand as a shaft of mist oozed from it. The mist moved along the ground, diverting to the funnel Mikkellana had created, a long, thin tube of Shield that led directly to Anciara.

Rahg screamed and started to move, but Darstan grabbed hold of him. "You can't let go of the Book."

"It's Tobias! He's been hit."

Darstan looked to the side where Tobias had been. A large empty spot was all that remained.

"I don't even know what it was," Rahg said. "She attacked with something I've never seen. One minute he was there with Mollie, and now he's gone."

Darstan nodded. "There's nothing we can do, Rahg. Focus on having the Book fill you with power, then we'll attack."

Anciara noted that more of the attacks had come from a spot on the southwestern edge of the plaza. Coincidentally, fewer of the soldiers came from that direction. She struck a few more times to the pesky guards on the north side of her using Lightning, then she issued a barrage of strikes using Fire at the place she'd noted. Finally, she used a ForceBolt one more time to those on the east side of her.

The first bolt of Lightning hit dangerously close to Rahg. He was about to weave a shield, when he heard Mikkellana yell that she'd handle it. While Mikkellana worked on protection, a Force-Bolt struck Melissara, dropping her to the ground instantly.

Aenaila rushed to Melissara's side, kneeling next to her to see what could be done. Therrim, while keeping one hand on the Book, reached down and tapped Aenaila on the shoulder.

"Maybe Rahg can help?" he said. "You saw what he did with Mikkellana."

Aenaila stood and touched the Book again. "I doubt if it's any use, but I'll move her out of harm's way, and we'll get Rahg to look at her later. The best we can do now is avenge her."

Aenaila glared at Anciara, wanting nothing more than for everyone to strike her with all they had, but as Darstan had noted earlier, they would be better off letting the power build before attacking. As she watched the carnage, Talanvar rounded the corner to the east of Anciara with several gangs of thieves. They had taken refuge after the last attack, but now wielded knives and swords and charged into the fray as if it were a party.

It didn't take long for Anciara to dispatch them using nothing but BlackFire, and Talanvar was one of the first to fall, flames running over him and taking him down. After Talanvar and a hundred others succumbed, the rest of his men made a hasty retreat.

Pressure built within Darstan to the point where he couldn't take it anymore. He felt as if his skin would burst like it was a dam holding back the Endless Sea. He used Voice to order the remaining soldiers to step away from Anciara and return to safety. Then he turned to Rahg and shouted. "Now!"

Rahg threw everything he could at Anciara, from the tiniest of Spirals to the largest, and he varied the attacks, aiming them at her legs, torso, and head.

Darstan unleashed all his power in the form of ColdFire and FearMist, and all of it directed at her head and heart. With power such as that, not even Anciara should be able to withstand it.

~

Anciara felt the first of the Spirals hit and erected a Shield to stop them. It worked for the larger Spirals, but many of the smaller ones got through, and they did damage, no matter how minor. Each strike produced a grimace.

She concentrated on using the bulk of her Shielding to stop what she knew was coming—the ColdFire. It could be devastating if it hit her head on, but it was proving to be difficult to stop. The Shield buckled and moved back regardless of how she tried. *They must be using the Book.*

As Anciara struggled, Darstan persisted, continually releasing ColdFire in an unremitting barrage. It was then the FearMist emerged from the tube. It encircled Anciara's head and found its way inside her, entering through her nostrils, her mouth, and even her eyes.

She fell to her knees and cowered, having lost the courage to fight.

Darstan noticed her weakness and focused. Just then a blinding flash of light came from the western part of the plaza, causing Darstan to glance in that direction. What he saw chilled him.

The streets were filled from building to building and from curb to rooftop with Slicers—a million of them. They appeared fierce with the sun's rays bouncing from their crystalline forms. Leading the charge were the Light Serpents, looking every bit as fearsome if not more so.

Acting upon an unknown command, they charged forth, striking Anciara with a relentless onslaught. After more than a hundred thousand Slicers must have struck, the Light Serpents joined in, climbing her legs and wrapping around her body, enveloping her.

Darstan held off on further attacks, not knowing if the Slicers would be hurt, but a directive from the Light Serpents convinced him otherwise.

"Continue the attack. Do not let up."

"Keep going," he shouted to Rahg. "Don't let up."

Faced with continual attacks, Anciara could no longer maintain her Shield. She stumbled, falling to one knee. She tried attacking again, but had no energy. Slicers entered her body by the tens of thousands, piercing her skin and attacking her mind. The Light Serpents squeezed life from her while leaving wounds every place they'd been. She was forced to use her Shield against the Spirals, and the ColdFire continued freezing her. She couldn't take much more.

Anciara's face twisted into a scowl, then she roared, and it looked as if she prepared for a massive strike—then, things changed. The features on her face softened. Eyes that had narrowed to slits widened and lost their intensity, and her lips went from tightly pursed to wide apart. Her overall posture relaxed substantially.

Now, thought Darstan, and he focused everything on ColdFire, issuing every bit of power he had. At the same time, the Light Serpents resumed attacking and ordered a million Slicers to attack as well.

The ColdFire that struck Anciara was one hundred times the power that hit the dorgans. At first, it didn't seem to do anything, then as she tried to move against Darstan, she stumbled, then stumbled again.

When she tried to move the third time, a crack formed in her left arm by the elbow. It started small, no thicker than a few strands of hair, then it grew in width *and* length, getting wider as it spread up her arm toward her shoulder.

The Light Serpents ordered all Slicers to infiltrate using the access allowed by the breaches. Bloodcurdling screams erupted from Anciara as the Slicers forced their way inside and spread throughout her body, infecting her as if they were a plague.

Before long, a breach appeared on the right side of her chest, just below her shoulder. It quickly grew and spread. Then a third crack appeared across her stomach.

Her screams grew so loud that those closest to her fell, some succumbing to the deafening noise and dying. As the breaches spread, the ColdFire and Slicers dug deeper.

After a few more moments, Anciara collapsed to the other knee, then, with one final scream, she shattered into pieces and was gone. Gone forever.

Chapter Forty-Two

AFTERMATH

A moment later, all was quiet save the sobbing of those who mourned the loss of their loved ones—and those voices were many.

Darstan walked to where Anciara had made her last stand. He kicked the pieces lying on the ground and used all his Sensing abilities to ensure she was gone. He had the Light Serpents confirm this as well.

Aenaila took hold of his arm and told him about Melissara. He ran to the east side, where Melissara lay on the ground, unable to move. He knelt and placed his hand under her head, lifting her.

She reached toward his face and rubbed his cheek. "I wasn't much of a mother. I'm sorry."

Darstan leaned down and kissed her cheek. "But you *were* a mother. And you helped when it mattered. No one can blame you."

Tears formed in her eyes. "Do you mean that?"

Darstan wiped a tear of his own and nodded. "I do, Mother. I truly do."

Melissara smiled and closed her eyes.

Mikkellana approached from the rear and placed her hand on Darstan's shoulder. "Is she—"

"She's gone," Darstan said. "We need to bury her." He looked up at Mikkellana. "Any suggestions on where?"

Mikkellana closed her eyes as if giving it thought, then nodded. "I don't know how happy she was during her stay in Sethia, but she spent hundreds of years there. I would cast my vote for Sethia. Get things ready, and I'll take you there."

"I'll get Rahg and anyone else who wants to go. It won't take long."

Mikkellana patted his back. "Do what you need, Darstan. While you do that, I'll tend to the others."

~

Darstan gathered Rahg, Wisp, and a few others, then Mikkellana Shifted them to Sethia so they could bury Melissara.

"Why didn't you choose that place above the Great Whites? The one Rahg told me about."

"I presume you mean Vallah, and while it often seemed serene, it was mysterious. We never knew who built it or how they built it. Aentarra knew more than any of us about it, but she kept everything a secret, and her secrets died with her. I still think Sethia is the better choice."

"I won't argue," Darstan said, then he looked around. "Sethia is a big place. Where should we place her?"

"I know just the spot," Mikkellana said. "There is a small pond near the border. I met her there, and she seemed at peace."

It didn't take long to bury Melissara, then they Shifted back to the plaza to continue cleaning up.

~

Rahg walked quickly through the plaza, stepping over the bodies littering it. "Darstan, have you seen Tobias?"

Darstan shook his head, worry now painting his face.

Rahg ran off toward the west side of the plaza. "Tobias!" he yelled and raced to the spot where Tobias had been. Burnt bodies covered the street, most of them unrecognizable. "I can't find him, Dar. I can't find him."

Darstan composed himself and joined Rahg, but neither of them located Tobias, although many of the bodies were burnt beyond recognition. Tears formed in Rahg's eyes. "I saw her hit him with . . . *something*. He was there one minute and gone the next."

Rhaven stepped alongside Rahg and Darstan, then placed a hand on each of their shoulders. "I know how difficult it is. I know what Tobias meant to you. But know that he left us on his own terms. He would never have sat this battle out. He wanted to be part of it. That's the kind of man Tobias was."

Darstan wiped his eyes on his sleeve. "You're right, Rhaven. That *is* who Tobias was. And he taught us to be that way too."

Rhaven laughed. "Indeed he did. I remember meeting you two when you knew nothing but baling hay and tending sheep. You've come a long way. Today, you killed a goddess."

"*We* killed a goddess," Darstan said. "It took all of us, not to mention the Slicers. Without them, I don't think it would have happened."

"I agree," Rhaven said. "I still don't know what they are or how they work, but they did well today, and I was thankful to have them."

Therrim walked across the plaza, blood dripping from his arm where a Lightning strike had opened a wound. "I know this isn't the time, but my men are asking how we'll get back to Nelstar."

Mikkellana stepped forward and said, "I'll take you back. Rhaven and I are going to settle down there."

Rhaven looked puzzled. "We are going to settle down? I thought it was just another adventure."

Mikkellana nodded. "I'm sure there will be a few adventures, Rhaven. Enough to keep us busy, anyway. Besides, without the Lights to guide them, the people of Nelstar will be lost and more likely to get into trouble. I thought we'd return the Book and establish order."

Rhaven moved close to Mikkellana and whispered to her. "You know I want to go with you, but I have to know that Argus can go with us. I could never leave him."

Mikkellana looked upon Rhaven with a face filled with sorrow. "Nelstar doesn't have much use for horses."

"Whether it does or doesn't have use for horses makes no difference. If we go, I need to take Argus. I'll never desert him."

A smile lit Mikkellana's face. "You are a true hero, my love. Of course, we'll take Argus. And if you're worried about getting him over that ledge leading to the Forsaken Lands, don't. I can build a bride out of Shield, one he can cross easily. And you don't have to worry about Nelstar because my father's manor is so big, Argus can have his own room if he wants."

Rhaven laughed. "I don't think we need to go that far, but knowing he'll have a place to roam is enough."

Rhaven grabbed her and kissed her hard. "As the thief would say —I believe you've secured an agreement, My Lady."

Therrim smiled. "Your sister would be pleased," he said. "She left Yettl in charge while we were gone. I'm sure he'll be pleased as well."

Mikkellana turned to Darstan. "Companion, friend, and nephew —can you spare a Slicer or two so they may lead me back to Nelstar?"

"You know it's different there, Mikkellana. You may not like what you find."

"Darstan, things are different here as well, and Nelstar is where I was born. I belong there; besides, Melissara said Benna is alive. He was family."

Darstan hugged Mikkellana, then Rhaven, then he smiled. "How about a million Slicers? Would that do? I'll throw in a couple of Light Serpents as well."

The Light Serpents moved to Darstan's side and wrapped around his legs.

"*We're staying with you,*" the Light Serpents said, then a thousand or more Slicers moved alongside him.

"*As are we.*"

Darstan's eyes went wide. "The Light Serpents and these few Slicers said they're staying."

Mikkellana laughed. "It appears as if I'll have to be satisfied with the Slicers minus those few. Just as well, I'm still not comfortable with the serpents."

Rahg gave Mikkellana and Rhaven a hug and a handshake as well. "I don't think I can call what we've been through fun, but it's been interesting."

Rhaven laughed and clapped Rahg on the back. "That it has." Rhaven then said goodbye to Wisp, Aenaila, and Camissa. "You've taught me a lot, thief. I won't forget it."

"Learning is everything, Rhaven. I just wish we could have taught Gregor before he died."

Rhaven turned to Mikkellana. "Before we leave, I want to gather some more poison for Kyra to use. Can we do that?"

"You can get all you want," Mikkellana said. "Let's go." Then she addressed Therrim. "We won't be long. Wait here and we'll be back to pick you up so we can go home."

W isp held Talanvar's body, or what remained of it, in his arms. He looked up to Aenaila. "I've got to give him a burial."

Aenaila nodded. "We'll make it one to be proud of." She reached out her hand. "Come with me now. We should go to the manor and tell Dirk."

"And don't forget we have to retrieve the little thief."

Aenaila laughed. "How could I forget Adju?"

Wisp grabbed Aenaila's sleeve. "What do you have in mind?"

"I thought we'd go to Cergala and rule as king and queen. Any objections?"

"If it means sleeping in the same bed, no objections."

After saying goodbye to Darstan, Rahg, and Camissa, they Shifted to Talanvar's manor, reappearing in the library where Dirk, Adju, and Barton, swarmed them.

"What happened?" Dirk asked. "We heard a lot of noise."

"I'm so glad you're safe, Master Kender and Mistress Aenaila. Is it over? Is she gone?"

Aenaila hugged Adju, then placed her arms around Dirk and nodded to Wisp.

"Where's Master Talanvar?" Dirk asked.

Wisp knelt beside him. "Dirk, I hate to tell you, but Talanvar didn't make it. It was a long and terrible fight, and he died while bravely fighting her."

Dirk broke free and ran for the stairs, tears running freely before he reached them.

"I'll go to him," Barton said. "Master Talanvar was everything to him."

As Aenaila and Wisp pondered what to do about Dirk, Adju handed an envelope to Wisp. "Master Talanvar said to give this to you in the event he died and you didn't."

With a puzzled expression on his face, Wisp opened the envelope. It contained a letter.

My friend of many years, I am charging you with dispersing my wealth as I wish it. I know you don't need any, not with what you've saved plus what you'll have from that beautiful lass, Aenaila, so here is how I want it to be distributed.

Bartol is to be taken care of for as long as he lives. He is to maintain the same lifestyle and keep his room in the manor. The manor, and all it contains, goes to Dirk. He'll need gold to cover expenses and upkeep, which you'll find plenty of in the place where we always met, buried in the northeast corner.

Do this for me, friend, and may you live forever. Oh, and tell Dirk I loved him like a son.

Aenaila reached over and wiped tears from Wisp's eyes. "You should go see Dirk. Nothing will cheer him up right now, but it may make him less sad."

Wisp nodded. "I'll do this, then we'll go. Tell Adju to get ready."

The plaza never looked so bad. Bodies lay everywhere, torn apart, charred, and burnt to the point where recognition was impossible.

Rahg stood next to Darstan, Camissa at his side. "I can't believe it's over, Dar. Finally over."

Darstan nodded. "At a high cost, Rahg. We lost Talanvar, Malakai, Melissara, thousands of innocents—and Tobias. Somehow I never thought he'd go. I guess I hoped he was immortal and would be around forever, telling lies and spinning tales."

"Me too, Dar. Me too."

Darstan forced a smile on his face and turned to Rahg and Camissa. "Enough of that. We've got a life to live, and apparently it's going to be a long one. What do you two plan to do?"

Rahg looked to Camissa, then back to Darstan. "I'm tired of this hectic pace we've kept, Dar. I think Camissa and I are going back to Twin Forks. We might rebuild the house and settle in like old folks, raising animals and planting crops. I think it will be fun; besides, no one will know us there, and that's just what I want."

"It'll be relaxing if nothing else." Darstan hugged them both and kissed Camissa on the cheek. "I wish you well."

"What about you, Darstan?" Camissa asked. "What are your plans?"

Darstan shrugged. "I don't know yet. I'll figure it out though."

Darstan walked through the plaza alone, kicking at weapons that once belonged to brave soldiers. He pondered what he would do when a rift opened before him. Startled, he lifted his head quickly and seemed as if he prepared to fire.

"Easy going," Wisp said. "I don't want you hitting me with any of that ColdFire."

Darstan embraced him and hugged him hard. "Wisp, I was hoping you'd come back before you left."

"And thanks to my bride, here I am."

Adju wrapped his arms around Darstan's waist. "Master Darstan, I'm so glad you're safe."

Darstan picked him up and hugged him. "Not as glad as me, little one." He squeezed tightly, then said. "I was glad to have known you, Adju. It is an honor to be your friend."

Tears formed in Adju's eyes and rolled down his cheeks. "Master Darstan, the honor is mine. I only have three friends: you, Master Kender, and Mistress Aenaila."

Darstan kissed him on the forehead and set him down. "I'm sure you'll make plenty more friends, Adju. Just try to keep your hands to yourself."

Aenaila kissed Darstan on the cheek. "Come see us often, Darstan. You know where we'll be."

Wisp pulled Darstan aside. "You should find someone to make you happy, Darstan. Don't try to live life alone."

"And who did you have in mind? I know you do since you mentioned it."

Wisp shrugged. "Have you thought of going to Pomanda?"

Darstan looked at him quizzically. "Pomanda? For what?"

"I seem to remember a time when you thought highly of a girl named Nirida. Think on it before deciding."

"Maybe," Darstan said, then he smiled. "Wisp, you may have hit on a good idea. I hadn't thought of that, but I think I will visit her. No reason why I shouldn't."

"None at all," Wisp said. "And there's also no reason why you and she can't visit us in Cergala; it'll only take you a few heartbeats to get there."

Darstan's smile widened, and he slapped Wisp on the back. "Right again. You can count on it. Now get going. I'm going to clean up before I see Nirida."

"Do what you will. In either case, we must be off. I've got to teach Aenaila how to run a kingdom."

Chapter Forty-Three

A LONG TIME HAS PASSED

Before traipsing off to see Nirida or anyone else, Darstan had to find a place to stay. More importantly, a place for the Light Serpents and Slicers to stay. They were far too dangerous on their own. He thought long about a location and finally decided on King Favian's old palace. No one lived there, and there would be plenty of room for the Light Serpents.

The palace wasn't his ideal place to live, if for no other reason than he was too well known in Sykor, and that's something he didn't want. *It will do for now, though.*

Darstan cleaned up the mess at Favian's palace, and he took the gold which had been left behind, leaving most of it in a bottom-floor room for safekeeping. *I know it will be safe here with the Light Serpents.*

He took a few pouches with him for spending, then instructed the Light Serpents to guard the rest. When he felt he was ready, he spoke to the Light Serpents and Slicers a final time. *"I have carved out several large rooms on the level below the ground. Is that suitable for your accommodations?"*

"We have already seen it," the Light Serpents said. *"It is more than acceptable. We will guard your domain when you are not here."*

Darstan nodded. He felt at ease knowing all would be safe with them as protectors. *"I won't be long. Maybe seven or eight days."*

The Light Serpents sunk through the floor and into the level below. They were followed by the Slicers.

Darstan packed a few changes of clothes, then he Shifted to Pomanda. He wanted to get this over with quickly, but mostly so nothing happened to the people of Sykor. He wouldn't want any ambitious thief trying to get into the palace with the Light Serpents there.

We may soon have tales to rival Antar's manor on Nelstar if anyone tries to get into the palace.

Darstan made his way quickly through Pomanda, and it didn't take him long to find who he searched for, even though the hour was late.

A knock on the door had Nirida rushing to put on a robe. *Who can be calling so late?*

She opened the door, and her jaw almost dropped to the floor. "Darstan! What are you doing here? I never expected to see you again."

Darstan held up the arm with the missing hand. "If you remember, I had my share of problems, but they're finished now."

She swung the door open and stepped aside, then sat on a sofa and suggested he do the same. "What does that mean? Why are you here?"

"I'd say it was to ask for a drink of water, but it's a little more than that."

Nirida jumped up. "Forgive my manners. I never—"

Darstan grabbed her arm and pulled her down next to him. "Forget your manners. Forget everything. I've thought a lot about this, and I want to know if you'd like to spend the rest of your life with me."

She stared at him, blinked a few times, then stared more. "What? Are you serious?"

"I wouldn't be here if I weren't."

"But . . . but you barely know me. And you know what I've been. What will people say?"

Darstan laughed. "I know you well enough, and I don't care what you've been or what people might say. The only thing I care about is your answer—do you want to or not?"

Nirida flashed a smile, then broadened it, and finally laughed. "Yes. Yes, of course I would, but—"

Darstan pulled her close and hugged her. "There are no buts. If you want to do it, it's done."

"It's not that easy. I've got a business that needs to be looked after. And how will we live? And—"

Darstan placed his finger on her lips. "Shh. Don't say anything else. Fix some khaffe and we'll talk." He stood and took her hand. "Better yet, show me where things are, and I'll fix khaffe, then we'll talk."

"But the business?"

"We don't need the business," Darstan said. "In fact, we don't need anything. As far as living, we can go anywhere in the world. And I mean *anywhere*. We can go places you never dreamed of."

Nirida shook her head. "I don't understand."

Darstan laughed. "Remember, Wisp?"

Nirida nodded. "He was the tall, thin one, right?"

"He's marrying a queen in a land far away, a land that's bigger than Pomanda, Sykor, and Genda combined."

"What? Where is this land?"

"Never mind that. I'll take you there. And Rhaven? The one who gave you the gold? He is living with the legendary Mikkellana on a world so far away that you can't imagine it."

"What about Camissa, that nice woman who helped me so much?"

"She's with my brother, Rahg. They're living in a small town not far from here."

"All that is good," Nirida said, "But there is still the matter of taking care of ourselves. I don't want to do what I'm doing, and you . . . excuse my saying so, but you only have one hand."

Darstan raised his arm and looked at it as if he were surprised. "I hadn't noticed," he said, then he emptied the contents of one of the pouches on the table. A sizable amount of gold poured out.

Nirida's eyes widened. "What? Where did you get that?"

Darstan pulled the other pouch out and showed her that. "I have much, much more where that came from. We have no need to worry about money."

Nirida squealed, then threw her arms around Darstan. "Yes, yes, yes. I will spend my life with you."

"Then make arrangements to give your business to someone who works for you and pack up so we can be off."

She jumped up and ran for the stairs. "I won't be long, Darstan. Don't dare be gone when I get back."

D arstan and Nirida left Pomanda and traveled the world. He took her to Khatara, Sykor, and eventually to Cartena to visit Wisp and Aenaila—and Adju.

"Why did those people call you Black Wolf?" Nirida asked.

Darstan paused as if giving it thought, then said, "It's a long story, Nirida, and it's one I'm not proud of. I'll tell you about it later if that's okay with you."

After a lengthy visit with Wisp and Aenaila, they returned to Sykor. Darstan liked Sykor, but too many people knew him and worse, knew what happened. While sharing a few mugs of ale at the Trader's Inn, Darstan announced he wanted to visit Rahg. "I haven't seen him in a long time," he said.

"Why haven't you gone before this?"

"Rahg and Camissa wanted to settle down someplace where

they weren't known. It seems odd, but he chose the village we grew up in. I understand why he did. The village was burnt down long ago, and everyone was either dead or gone, so nobody knows him there."

"Where is it?" Nirida asked.

"Not far from here," Darstan said. "We'll surprise them, but make sure not to give their secret away."

Chapter Forty-Four

OLD FRIENDS

Darstan Shifted to a spot not far from Sykor where the road leading north intersected with the old caravan route from Khatara.

Nirida appeared confused as she looked around. "I don't see anything, Darstan. Where's the village?"

"It's difficult to explain, but I need to have been somewhere before to establish a point to Shift to."

"I thought you grew up here?"

Darstan shook his head. "This is the difficult part. I did grow up here, but at that time, I wasn't able to Shift which means I couldn't get a Shift point."

"I don't know if I'll ever understand, so let's just get to the village."

Darstan sight-shifted the rest of the way, stopping at a spot not far from his childhood home. He pointed to a small house nestled in a grove of trees. "That's where I grew up," he said. "Not that house; our house burned down. But that spot, and in a house not unlike that one."

Nirida tugged on his arm. "Let's go, then. Don't you want to see Rahg?"

"I do," Darstan said. "But I want to surprise him."

They waited a few minutes, until Rahg walked out the door and headed to the barn, then they sight-shifted to the porch and sat in the chairs.

A moment later, Rahg returned, carrying a pail in each hand. "About time you did some work around here," Darstan yelled. "You always were one to ignore his chores."

Rahg stopped, then must have recognized who it was. He dropped the pail of milk and ran to the porch, embracing his brother. "Darstan! By the gods, what are you doing here?" He then looked to the side. "And Nirida. I haven't seen you in years. Come in. Come in."

He opened the door, yelling loudly as he walked inside. "Camissa! You'll never guess who's here."

Camissa's voice carried from the other room. "I'll guess it's Darstan and Nirida," she said.

"What? How did you know?" Rahg asked.

Camissa entered the room laughing. She opened her arms to greet Darstan, hugging him, then Nirida. "Rahg forgets who he's married to sometimes, Darstan. After living together for even this long, I can read his mind as if he were talking."

Rahg grabbed a kettle, filled it with water, and was about to heat it up, when he smiled and turned. "Instead of waiting for this to get hot, why don't you help out, brother. Heat it up quickly."

Darstan laughed and placed the kettle on the table, then wrapped his hand around it and produced immense heat. "Done, brother. Now how about you do the rest of the work and make some khaffe—good khaffe."

Camissa sat next to Nirida and chatted. "Tell me how you and

Darstan got together again. And what you've been doing since I last saw you in Genda."

Hours later, Rahg stood from the table. "I know everyone must be hungry, but instead of us cooking supper, suppose we go to Havril's to eat?"

"Havril's?" Darstan asked, seeming surprised.

Rahg laughed. "That's right. I forgot you wouldn't know, but Ella survived the attack on the village and several years later, she returned and had the place rebuilt. She runs it now, just like her parents did. And the food is just as good as it ever was."

"But doesn't she—?"

Rahg nodded. "She knows who I am, but I asked her not to say anything, and she hasn't. Still the same old Ella."

Darstan got up from the table, his grin as wide as Rahg's. "I'm all for it," he said. "I can almost taste that lamb stew they made."

They all went to Havril's and got a table near the back, not far from the fireplace, which looked as if Ella had picked up the old one and moved it there. It was just as big and looked as if the same stone had been used to build it.

Darstan took his time looking around. "Looks the same as when we left, Rahg. I can't believe it."

Rahg nodded. "Ella did a good job of rebuilding it just like it was."

Just then, a young lad opened the door, poked his head inside, and yelled. "Traveler coming. Comin' here."

Darstan looked at Rahg and they both started laughing. "I guess things never change," Darstan said.

Nirida looked puzzled. "What do you mean?"

"We used to sit in this tavern in the old days and wait weeks for a traveler to come telling tales. It was usually the highlight of a boring summer."

Ella brought a few mugs of ale and almost dropped them when she saw Darstan, but somehow she managed to keep composure and not mention his name. She did, however, lean over and give him a big hug. "It's so good to see you, sir."

Darstan smiled and hugged her back. "And you, fine lady." He then gestured to Nirida. "And this is Nirida, my wife."

Ella took her hand and held it. "You are a lucky woman to be with such a fine gentleman."

"Thank you," Nirida said. "I am reminded just how lucky every day."

～

The door to the inn opened and an older man walked in with a woman at his side. Both appeared dusty and worn from travel.

The man brushed dirt from the front of his clothes, then took a seat at an empty table. She sat in the chair next to him. He placed a pipe in his mouth, then took tobacco from a pouch at his side and packed it. The woman at his side lit a striker and then lit the pipe.

He leaned back in the chair and puffed on the pipe, blowing billows of smoke into the air.

"For all of those interested in how things came to be, and how things were before that, I suggest you grab a chair or a stool or just sit on the floor and listen 'cause it's not a tale I'm likely to repeat. I'll say it once and leave it for you to remember."

People moved toward the table, some quickly and some in a meandering way. The traveler waited while people took their seats.

～

Rahg leaned toward Darstan and whispered, "It'll be curious to hear what he has to say."

"I can't make out who's talking. Do you know him?"

"Can't tell from here, but we get our share of storytellers in here. Not much different than the old days."

"I remember them," Darstan said, then he tapped Rahg's arm. "Looks like he's starting up again."

Once the seats were occupied, the traveler puffed his pipe a few times and began telling his tale. "It was about ten years ago or so, when there was a fearsome war in all the lands. It was so bad, I don't know how to describe it."

He reached over and patted the woman's backside. "This sweet old girl was there. She can tell ya. And mind ya, this wasn't no war with swords and arrows and such. No, lads, this was a war to end all wars. People had powers like ya never seen. Fire and Lightning shot from their hands, and they could do other things too. Things your mind can't imagine. Some of them could shake the land under your feet, and others could make a storm appear from a clear sky."

The man stopped to light his pipe again and take a sip of ale. "A few of them could make it so no one could see them. Or even hear them or smell them. And one of them could make you do things you never dreamt of doing."

He shook his head several times, then he leaned in over the table and whispered. "One of them had something called *ColdFire*, and it was so bad even the others were frightened of it."

An older man sitting at the next table scoffed, then stood. "I guess I've heard enough," he said.

The old man looked over at him. "What's the matter, fellow? You think these tales are just for young ones? Why, I could tell you tales that'd make your head spin. Scare the skin right off your bones, they would."

Then he looked around and whispered even lower. "But that's not all. This man could do things that nobody—nobody—dreamed of. He could take your life just by thinking about it."

He sat back and nodded a few times, then said, "And he commanded an army of these things, well . . . I don't even know what to call 'em, but they were so small and thin you couldn't see 'em unless your eyes were wide open and your head clear. And they flew through the air so fast, once they started, they were gone—until they got where they were goin', that is. And once they got there . . ."

He stopped and shook his head two more times. "Let's just say, once they got there, you better pray they weren't lookin' for you 'cause nothin' in this world—nothin' in any world was gonna stop 'em."

A young lad of about fifteen laughed. "C'mon, there's no such thing as that. People can't do those things."

The man looked over at the lad and stared. Just stared. "They can't, huh?"

He stood, brushed a few crumbs off his pants, tapped his pipe on the bowl in the center of the table, then walked toward the door. "C'mon, Old Girl, no sense in stayin' here any longer. Seems like these folks know too much for an old man like me."

Several of the younger men taunted and jeered at him. Others threw trash and bits of leftover food, hitting the man and woman both.

∾

Darstan tapped Rahg on the shoulder. "I might be crazy, but there shouldn't be anybody that knows of the things he's telling."

"What are you saying?" Rahg asked.

"Look closely, Rahg. Really look."

Rahg stared, then he stood and stepped a few paces closer before returning. "By all that's holy, Darstan; it's him! It's really him."

"It is, and I've seen enough of him being taunted, brother. No need for you to do anything that would let people know who you are; leave it to me." Darstan stood and shouted. "Hold it there, old man."

Just before the man hit the door, a strong gust of wind whipped by him and slammed it shut. People ran to the windows staring outside as darkness covered the town long before it should, and bolts of lightning flashed all about.

The room drew deathly quiet as red, white, then blue flames rose from Darstan's hands to the ceiling.

A man had just placed a few logs in the fireplace, and as he stepped back, Darstan shot a thin column of flame to set them ablaze.

He then formed ColdFire into an even thinner stream and directed it to a tray of mugs one of the serving girls carried. When the ColdFire hit, all the mugs shattered, and the girl dropped the tray. Before it hit the ground, Darstan issued another stream of ColdFire and shattered it as well.

All eyes in the inn focused on Darstan. He moved toward the door, put his arm on the man's shoulder, and said, "The next time this man tells you a story, you better listen and listen good. His name is Tobias, and if anyone, I mean *anyone* shows him disrespect, I'll come back here and shatter them like I did those mugs." Darstan glanced around the room. "Understood?"

From all sides, people shouted their understanding. Two of the younger men rushed to the man and apologized, but he brushed them off as he smiled at Darstan.

He threw his arms around Darstan and hugged him, fighting back the urge to shed tears. "I didn't know where you were," he said. "I've been traveling all over to try and find you."

"I've settled down," Darstan said, then he turned to Nirida. "You remember Nirida, from Genda. She and I are married now."

Tobias grasped her hand, and then he hugged her. "Well, I'll be. I sure do remember you, lass. I'm glad to see you."

A somber look overtook Tobias then. He lost his smile, replaced by concern. "And how about Rahg? Have you heard anything from the lad?"

Rahg stepped from behind a column in the room, Camissa standing beside him. He placed a finger to his lips. "I've heard he's doing well. I think he settled down in some little village where no one knows him."

Tobias used a sleeve to wipe tears from his eyes. Three times he tried speaking, but each time he choked up. Finally, he got it out. "Lad, if you ever see him, tell him Old Tobias was asking about his health. Askin' about Camissa too."

Camissa gave a slight nod and a brief smile, then she sent a thought to him. *We live here now, Tobias. And we're grateful that you kept our secret. Stop by Rahg's old house. We've rebuilt it and live there now.*

Tobias smiled and then smiled some more. He reached his hand out to shake with Darstan, then he winked and nodded to Rahg and Camissa. "Time for this old man to get moving. Mollie and I don't stay in one place very long, though that may change now. Now that I don't have to be traipsin' all over these lands lookin' for two lads who didn't know enough to come in out of the cold."

Darstan laughed. "I'll walk you outside, Tobias. I'm thinking my time here will be short but I could extend it a few days; besides, you have to tell us what happened. We thought you were dead." Darstan turned to Rahg. "How about you, good fellow? Would you care to join us?"

Rahg smiled as he and Camissa walked alongside them.

ACKNOWLEDGMENTS

It is with great honor that I give eternal gratitude to my wife and all four of my grandkids. They give me the inspiration to keep going.

ABOUT THE AUTHOR

Giacomo Giammatteo is the author of gritty crime dramas about murder, mystery, and family. He also writes non-fiction books including the No Mistakes Careers series, No Mistakes Publishing, No Mistakes Grammar, and No Mistakes Writing.

When Giacomo isn't writing, he's helping his wife take care of the animals on their sanctuary. At last count, they had forty-five animals—eleven dogs, a horse, six cats, and twenty-six pigs.

Oh, and one crazy—and very large—wild boar, who takes walks with Giacomo every day and also happens to be his best buddy.

nomistakespublishing.com
gg@giacomog.com

ALSO BY GIACOMO GIAMMATTEO

You can see all of my books here.

And you can buy them on the platform of your choice.

This brings up a thought: with more than eighty books out now, it is becoming difficult to try to update the list at the back of all of them. If you want to know what books I have out, use the link above, which takes you to my website, or download the latest copy of my GG recommended reading list, which is free.

Nonfiction

Careers

No Mistakes Resumes, Book I of No Mistakes Careers

No Mistakes Interviews, Book II of No Mistakes Careers

Grammar

Misused Words, No Mistakes Grammar, Volume I

Misused Words for Business, No Mistakes Grammar, Volume II

More Misused Words, No Mistakes Grammar, Volume III

Visual Grammar (this is a compilation of volumes I–III with a bit of new information added. It also includes pictures and is the world's first visual grammar book)

Misused Words and Then Some, No Mistakes Grammar, Volume V

Simply Put: The Plain English Grammar Guide

How to Capitalize Anything

More Grammar

No Mistakes Grammar Bites, Volume I, Lie, Lay, Laid, and It's and Its

No Mistakes Grammar Bites, Volume II, Good and Well, and Then and Than

No Mistakes Grammar Bites, Volume III, That, Which, and Who, and There Is and There Are

No Mistakes Grammar Bites, Volume IV, Affect and Effect, and Accept and Except

No Mistakes Grammar Bites, Volume V, You're and Your, and They're, There, and Their

No Mistakes Grammar Bites, Volume VI, Passed and Past, and Into, In To and In

No Mistakes Grammar Bites, Volume VII, Farther and Further, and Onto, On, and On To

No Mistakes Grammar Bites, Volume VIII, Anxious and Eager, and Different From and Different Than

No Mistakes Grammar Bites, Volume IX, A While and Awhile, and Envy and Jealousy

No Mistakes Grammar Bites, Volume X, Could've and Should've, and Irony and Coincidence

No Mistakes Grammar Bites, Volume XI, "Quotation Marks and How to Punctuate Them" and "Plurals of Compound Nouns"

No Mistakes Grammar Bites, Volume XII, "Latin Abbreviations"

No Mistakes Grammar Bites, Volume XIII, "Redundancies" and "Ax to Grind"

No Mistakes Grammar Bites Volume XIV, "Superlatives and How We Use them Wrong"

No Mistakes Grammar Bites Volume XV, "Shoo-in and Shoe-in" and "Horse Racing Sayings"

No Mistakes Grammar Bites Volume XVI, "Which and What" and "Since and Because"

No Mistakes Grammar Bites Volume XVII, "Hyphens, and When to Use Them" and "Em Dashes and En Dashes"

Uneducated

Whiskers and Bear—Volume I, Sanctuary Tales

A Collection of Animal Stories, Volume II, Sanctuary Tales

More Animal Stories, Volume III, Sanctuary Tales

Surviving a Stroke—Or Two

Life and Then Some

Fiction

Friendship & Honor Series:

Murder Takes Time

Murder Has Consequences

Murder Takes Patience

Murder Is Invisible

Murder Is a Promise

Murder Is Immaculate (coming soon)

Blood Flows South Series

A Bullet for Carlos: A Connie Gianelli Mystery

Finding Family, a Novella

A Bullet from Dominic

The Good Book

The Ranger

Redemption Series

Necessary Decisions: A Gino Cataldi Mystery

Old Wounds

Promises Kept, the Story of Number Two

Premeditated

The Ranger

Rules of Vengeance Series (Fantasy)

Light of Lights (the beginning, a novella)

A Promise of Vengeance

Undeniable Vengeance

Consummate Vengeance

Vengeance Is Mine (2019)

Note: The Light of Lights is a novella. It's about 100 pages long and sets the stage for the series. The other books in the series are between 650 and 850 pages long.

OTHER BOOKS

You can always see the current and coming-soon books on my website.

Fiction

***Memories for Sale* (mystery/sf)**

***The Joshua Citadel* (SF novella)**

Children's Books

No Mistakes Grammar for Kids, Volume I—Much and Many

No Mistakes Grammar for Kids, Volume II—Lie and Lay

No Mistakes Grammar for Kids, Volume III—Bring and Take

No Mistakes Grammar for Kids, Volume IV, "Would've, Should've" and "Your and You're"

No Mistakes Grammar for Kids, Volume V, "There, They're, and Their" and "To, Too, and Two"

Shinobi Goes to School—Life on the Farm for Kids, Volume I

Fiona Gets Caught, Life on the Farm for Kids, Volume II

Coco Gets a Donut, Life on the Farm for Kids, Volume III

Squeak Gets a Home, Life on the Farm for Kids, Volume IV

Biscotti Saves Punch, Life on the Farm for Kids, Volume V

The Adventures of Adalina, Volume I, Adalina and the Five Tiny Bears

Coming Soon

The Adventures of Adalina, Volume II, Adalina and the Underwater Bears

Get on the mailing list and you'll be sure to be notified of release dates and sales.

Mailing list

And don't forget to leave a review!